Tiezzi's Board

Tiezzi's Board

A Novel by

Ham Martin

Black Rose Writing | Texas

ISBN: 978-1-68513-015-2
PUBLISHED BY BLACK ROSE WRITING
www.blackrosewriting.com

Printed in the United States of America
Suggested Retail Price (SRP) $20.95

Tiezzi's Board is printed in EB Garamond

*As a planet-friendly publisher, Black Rose Writing does its best to eliminate unnecessary waste to reduce paper usage and energy costs, while never compromising the reading experience. As a result, the final word count vs. page count may not meet common expectations.

Art direction and photography by James Root
Wood carving by Ham Martin

For her who can never be imitated on the written page.

Prologue

Honduras, 1941

A solitary figure moves along a dusty village street. Male, more boy than man, his white, blousy shirt and too-large white pants, crudely chopped off at the calf, are gray with dust. He drags something by a short length of rope.

About this dragging there is purpose. The barefoot boy pulls the thing the distance of several long strides, stops, looks down at it, and looks all around for other children.

The thing is a slice of a tree, a disc perhaps four inches thick and twelve or fifteen inches across. At one edge there is a hole large enough for the rope to pass through where a knot on the underside holds it fast.

The boy hears voices; he brightens and bounds in their direction.

He reaches a group of children—five of them—comes to a stop—and nimbly hops onto the wooden disc. "El Gordo?" he asks with a laugh in his voice. His eyes are pinched shut—tight, tight as to persuade the others that he truly cannot see anything.

This is Miguel, asking the village children to play his game again today. Miguel is not so much their friend—more a fixture of the village life. He seems their age, eleven and twelve, but they know that their older brothers and sisters played Miguel's game before them and have outgrown it.

Dirty and disheveled as he is, he is beautiful. He has a long and very broad nose that hooks over slightly. Crudely cropped hair sprouts off in every direction. In his eyes there is a wildness, but Miguel does not frighten anyone. The grown-ups think they know why he looks this way, but no one speaks of it anymore.

"El Gordo?" He pirouettes elegantly on the little disc, eyes shut, this spinning, this twirling of the tattered white garments, a final imploring that, out of kindness, the other children cannot refuse. They make a circle around him.

Eyes still tight shut, Miguel spins on the balls of his feet, stops, and trustingly falls backwards into the arms of one of the children. They do it twice more, each time laughing at the game they have played a thousand times; it is Miguel's imitation of a falling mahogany tree.

The eyes of the children are drawn to unusual noise and motion in the near distance. In the treetops there is a soft, broad rustling. From the crown of the biggest tree in the village, a flock of small, green parrots suddenly takes flight. "Es El Gordo," a girl shouts to her companions.

Miguel thinks she is speaking of his game and he smiles, left standing by himself on his little stump as the others run to the edge of the lush hillside.

From a distance, they can see that men from a logging company have built a six-foot high platform at the base of El Gordo and that a crew has been sawing at the giant tree. Now the men are hopping off the platform and scampering to safety.

The big tree creaks and leans.

Miguel, eyes scrunched closed, starts another spinning dance, stops, smiles, and begins his backward lean, his warning to the kids that he is about to fall. But they are not there.

There is a horrendous, earth-shaking crash. Miguel's head hits the ground hard. He lifts himself just enough to look in the direction of El Gordo, but his head hurts so very much; he lets himself back onto the earth.

There has always been plenty of mahogany. No one has ever spoken of cutting down the big tree. "Es para la Gran Guerra," the oldest of the boys says. The children are wide-eyed and nod knowingly.

Miguel thinks he will stay on the ground for a little while. They have always caught him, every time they have caught him, and now his head hurts so very much.

Chapter 1
Leaving the Garden

Today would be an easy day for Joe Carroll. He'd made it to the finish line of a woodworking job he'd dreaded, partly because it was going to be boring, but mostly because of a succession of warnings dropped at the grocery store, at church, in the hardware store, and at the lumberyard about Linda Howe. "Bitch" was the word most often used to describe her. But Joe needed the work and was even piqued by the challenge of winning her over.

Joe approached the scores of hours spent in close company with Linda Howe with a belief that they would grow fond of one another. Joe and Maggie's friends thought Linda Howe unworthy of Joe's artistry—unworthy even of his company, but Joe knew he got along with people. And he needed the work. From the first day, Linda found opportunities to press the point that Joe was working for her, but Joe felt pretty secure in a different paradigm. He told himself that he had outsmarted the guys with straight jobs by not having to punch a time clock. As a doctor, Linda's husband, Lou, made lots more money to be sure, but a wood carver didn't have to file endless paperwork with insurance companies, didn't have to release hemorrhaging, tubed-up, barely conscious people from the hospital prematurely, just to take care of his family. Joe Carroll's concept was simple: money for wood carving. One third down, the balance C.O.D. for honest work that sometimes even rose to the level of art.

This job for Linda Howe was not art; it was more like good craft. Joe had agreed to remodel most of the Howes' kitchen for the privilege of executing fifteen cupboard doors. Joe made that crystal clear when he took the job. "I'm a wood carver, Linda, not a kitchen guy," he'd told her. He'd make the boring boxes and the face frames for the fun of doing the pretty doors. He'd told that to Linda—it wasn't about the money—it was for the fun of carving the doors.

Each paneled door was decorated with a relief-carved and delicately painted herb. Linda loved herbs. She told that to Joe at their first interview about The Garden—that's what she was already calling the new kitchen. During the weeks he labored for Lou and Linda, she had never cooked a meal at home, even though Joe had been explicitly instructed that part of the deal was that he must keep the kitchen "fully functioning for Linda"' because "she loves to cook."

Today he will hang the herbed-up doors, wipe some paste wax on the finished work, and, his job complete, schlep his tools out to the truck. He looked at the carved door in his arms, DILL, and past it through the big window over the sink to Linda's Lexus pulling in the drive. Linda, dressed (camouflaged, was how Joe thought of it) in a celadon designer sweat suit, was back from Starbucks with her coffee. What is the point of a two hundred dollar sweat outfit? Joe wondered. He had never seen Linda do any physical labor, much less perspire.

Joe's mind wandered to his wife Maggie who in a burlap bag was prettier than Linda Howe. All that jewelry and makeup and hairdo and clothes marshaled to present to the world the Linda she wanted it to see. Joe thought he saw through all of it, that the anatomy courses he took twenty years ago, and the life drawing classes, and his artist sensibilities revealed Linda Howe stark naked under the celadon folds. Joe could see everyone naked, or as he liked to say, metaphorically, depending on the company, in their nakedness.

Dave and Annie are Maggie and Joe's oldest friends. Dave knows that his old college buddy who majored in Dissipation now goes to church and reads books on spirituality. And Joe understands that Dave is a little sad that his great friend has gone off on this spiritual thing without him. At every opportunity, Dave tells a joke from his small comedy repertoire: "Brother Joe has discovered that he has a remarkable spiritual gift; he sees people with their clothes off."

Sometimes Joe responds in a serious way. "Well, Dave, so does God." Joe likes that idea a lot—counts on it really, that God knows all about the real us, warts and all.

Joe was up on a stool holding the first door, DILL, in place over its assigned opening. With a bradawl, he marked the locations in the doorframes for the brass screws that would go through hinges already attached to the doors. With a small cordless drill, he counter bored the screw holes and fastened the first door in place. Repeating the process for the ROSEMARY, he thought that it didn't look quite level. He hopped down from the stool to look at the two companion doors from the ground. A level confirmed a downward sag in ROSEMARY. He took it down, removed the hinge, and took a sharp chisel from its denim roll.

A canvas bag held a short board with a scrap of leather glued flat to it. Against the leather, he made several quick stropping motions with the shiny chisel, first the back, then the front—a final polishing step. Carefully, he brought the sharp edge to the back of his left hand. Just the right angle and a slow forward push and quarter-inch blond hairs gathered on the bevel edge of the tool. Razor sharp. Returning to ROSEMARY, he relieved a thin wafer of cherry wood from the hinge mortise.

Linda Howe's only evident work was the care and feeding of a 10-year-old male child, who was now set up with his cereal in the midst of Joe's power tools. The kid fed out ten feet of a metal tape measure in the direction of the Howes' very expensive and rare Abyssinian cat that was circling a shallow tray of mint green pellets. Joe was amused by the aloofness of the exquisite, sleek creature. All the same, he wondered what makes educated people introduce cat shit and cat litter into the environment where they keep their food and cook their meals.

Joe put the hinge back on, and mounted the stool for another try. Better this time.

The kid hit the tape measure's yellow button. The steel tape whipped back at him out of control. Orange juice went flying all over the new center island.

"Do you absolutely need to eat in here today? I'm putting the finishing touches on your mom's kitchen," Joe asked the boy.

"Mom says the workmen can function around me," the kid answered, deadpan.

Joe grabbed a roll of paper towels and began to wipe up the spill.

Even this child speaks to me this way, Joe thought. It's not the kid's fault that he's an obnoxious brat. Joe knew that. He could take him home to his house—sort of a tough love summer camp—and nurture him into a sweet, polite kid. And the boy would be better off for it, and probably happier too. "What's your name, son? You know, your given name?" Joe knew it already.

"Zander," and he looked back into his cereal.

"I know that's what people call you, but what's your real name?" No answer.

"I'll bet that's short for Alexander." Zander was smart as hell and for many days had quietly observed the family dynamics with the hired kitchen guy. Zander knew that his mom had called him both names in front of the kitchen guy lots of times and he'd adopted his family's mild contempt for this workman who was behind schedule on The Garden.

Joe worked to quiet himself. "Alexander, that's a good strong name. Well, Alexander, there are no workmen. There's only me—Joe Carroll. Joe, that's short for Joseph, and what I'm doing today is a little tricky and I really need to concentrate, you know, to not screw it up. It's important to me that my customers are happy with my work." Joe looked directly at Zander hoping for a faint acknowledgment of understanding. No such luck. "I'm sorry you didn't get to see me doing the cool part, Zander—the carving. I had to do that back in my shop. When you get just a little taller—you're already strong enough, but a little height gives you some leverage over the carving at the bench, I could show you how to do it. It's not that hard. Does that interest you?"

The pudgy kid slid off his stool and hit the ON button on Joe's radial arm saw. A loud whirr rose in the room and Joe let out a startled "Ahhhhh!" as the kid calmly opened the fridge and reached for the Tropicana.

Linda and her ubiquitous stainless-steel travel mug were there pronto. "My God, what has Zander so worked up?"

"Actually, it was me who screamed. Alexander is remarkably calm. He turned on a highly dangerous power tool and I damn near fell off this stool," Joe answered.

She didn't even hear him. "I hope you've got insurance. Oh, the island, Joe, I've been thinking about where you've put the island. I'm afraid with it there, Lou's going to back into it going into the fridge. Can we move it back this way—maybe a few inches—however much you think."

"Right here's where I think. Do you remember we blocked it all out before I started?" Joe began.

"And these three cabinets maybe could swing the other way, you know, with whatever you call the little hingey things," Linda said.

The herb carvings were truly beautiful. Mere craft though they were, Joe had said to Maggie and to himself, "No one in town has anything nicer in their kitchen." Two carvings were in place now and Joe had looked forward to Linda's reaction to the finished effect. But Zander's stunt had co-opted the moment.

"The hinges, that would be an awful lot of work and—"

"Oh, and Joe, over here, Joe—" and he began to shut down, his defense against the disappointment that was probably inevitable. "I'm rushed this morning, Joe. This SAVORY, you'll fix these things for us, won't you? This savory is looking kind of sage-ish, do you know what I mean?"

He'd try to stay with her, make a joke and keep his patience. "Um, you mean not so much spicy, more wise and all-knowing."

Linda's extended arm and coffee mug stretched to reach one of the doors over the sink. "This leaf, and maybe this little bunch, do you think they're right?"

"Are you serious?" Joe asked. Joe's prized carving tools and big round mallet were laid out on their canvas roll on the island. Those are the tools of my trade, he thought to himself as Zander flopped the canvas a little further open.

Everyone did what Linda wanted. Probably long ago she thought through the fact that it was their money and power that got everybody to snap to, but now she said, "You'll work with us, won't you, Joe?" with a breeziness that scarcely gave Joe a chance to respond. "I'm just concerned that these leaves—"

Joe had been cheated by customers a few times, years back. Maggie worked in a law office, so Joe, who said that he was a 19th century guy, knew something about modern business practices. "These are the leaves from the drawings you and Lou approved." Looking past Linda, he saw that Alexander had picked up one of his gouges. "Put that down, kid!"

Linda shot Joe a stare that said, "Watch it!" and then turned to her son. "You've got that big collaborative history unit today, sweetie. Are you going to be all right?" She turned back toward Joe and said, "I don't think you need to speak to Zander like that."

"Yeah, yeah I do, because he's messing with the tools that I support my family with, and if he even puts a nick in one of them, it will take me two hours to get it perfect again, unless I have to grind past the hard tempered part of the steel to remove the nick, and then it's ruined and I'll have to drive half a day to Woburn, Massachusetts to replace it." Joe moved toward the kid who feigned fear and dropped the gouge on the floor.

"I think he's just confused," Linda said.

Zander said, "I'm so confused, Mom."

"You're in his home and he doesn't understand."

"Not for much longer." Joe picked up the gouge from the floor, examined it, and rolled it up with the other wooden-handled implements. "It's undamaged, but yes, I can certainly see that Zander needs his space."

Linda's concern for Alexander shifted seamlessly back to the kitchen cupboards. "The herbs, Joe, when will you fix the herbs—and the island, Lou wants—" She'd dropped the trump card—the physician husband. Poor bastard.

Joe said, "Lou wants—Lou and his whole a-hole family can find someone else to jerk around. I'm leaving."

"He swore, mom. The workman, he swore. He called us a-holes," Alexander whooped with delight.

"Quick, phone Daddy," Linda responded. Zander pulled from his pants pocket his own cell phone and got his dad on the phone. Linda took her son's phone and walked onto her pretty little wisteria-bejeweled side porch. Joe squeezed past her headed for his truck and sagging under the weight of his radial arm saw. "Joe Carroll's here, we're in the kitchen and he's gone crazy."

Joe understood that this was just hyperbole employed to get Lou's attention. But just the same—crazy—her using that word so casually to describe him, so effortlessly was she able to dismiss his response to their insults. She knows damn well that this is not mental illness. His walking out of the kitchen just does not compute in her reality. I'm crazy to mess with Lou and Linda Howe; that's what she really means. I'm crazy to walk out on a big payday.

Joe returned from the truck for more gear and Linda said into the phone, "This is serious, Lou. I know you have patients. He's refusing to finish the job," she explained as Zander shouted from right behind her.

"He called Mom an a-hole."

"We've got that party here a week from Sunday." Joe knew that Linda had looked forward to dropping The Garden on her rich neighbors, so his loading up his tools and threatening her plans had jumped ahead of the trauma to poor Zander.

Joe had black and yellow plastic cases of drills and saws in both hands and passed her again on the porch as she said, "Lou's getting Ari Pappas on a conference call."

Zander said, "Tell Dad I'm missing school."

Joe said, "I can drop him off, I'm going right by there."

Ari Pappas was the attorney that Joe's wife, Maggie, worked for and was the lawyer that all the smart, connected people in Lyme and Old Lyme used. Oh great, Joe thought. These guys stick together. Joe looked at his watch. He knew Ari's routine and that he was probably just back from his fancy Monday breakfast up in Essex and would find this intrusion annoying.

Joe had not at first thought about how his quarrel would so quickly ripple into Maggie's workplace, and it was, at the moment, the regret foremost in his mind. Everybody loved Maggie at her work, especially the nice old secretary, Cecile, who was probably at this moment beckoning Ari to the phone.

Joe went back to the kitchen to load some more of his stuff.

The law offices and the doctor's office and Linda were now all hooked up on a conference call, and Linda pierced the air of her sweet porch, shouting toward the kitchen the verdict that she knew she could extract, "Our attorney says not a red cent more and we keep everything."

Linda followed Joe back into her kitchen, not the least bit afraid of the madman. "Our lawyers say we won't owe you a penny."

"Makes sense," Joe answered. On this morning, hanging the doors decorated with the carved herbs, the last day of a long job, the anticipation of the big check—none of it excited Joe Carroll—not like it would have years back. But this skirmish with these people that he had, against his wishes, grown to dislike intensely, made him feel alive. "Is that Lou, great. Let me speak to him." Joe took the phone from Linda and she just smirked. Joe was very calm. "You'd better come home right away, Doc."

"I'm busy here, Joe. Hey, thanks, Ari. We're all set. I'll call you later," and the lawyer clicked off. Lou continued, "What the hell's going on? Just finish the goddamn job and get out of there." No mention of the a-hole remark. "Is Linda there, is she alright?"

"She's fine, well, safe anyway, Lou. It's the kid I'm worried about."

"Shouldn't he be at school? What about him?"

"He's awful, Doc," Joe said calmly.

"Yeah?" Lou said, and Zander was leaning hard against his mom now. They were craned in close to Joe, not wishing to be left out of the play.

Joe went on. "Save your money on the lawyer stuff, Lou. I'm powerless to fight you, but at least I'm free to go home. I think that's true, isn't it, that I can choose to leave, and that's what I'm doing. I'm leaving The Garden. I'm going home," and Joe handed the phone to Zander.

Zander didn't like it that his family seemed to have lost the upper hand, that the temperature had dropped, and he shouted, "Daddy, he called us a bunch of assholes."

Chapter 2
Rich in All the Important Things

The Connecticut River rises from big lakes in northern New Hampshire near the Canadian border. From there it heads due south, separating New Hampshire from Vermont, in many places little more than a large stream. By the time the Connecticut reaches western Massachusetts it is a full-fledged river, and as it runs to Hartford, bisecting the state that shares its name, it is wide and majestic.

Not far upstream from where the Connecticut meets Long Island Sound, there is, on the eastern side of the river, a quiet cove. Eighty years ago, this broad pool, mostly safe from the tidal eddies and currents that make some spots unsafe for swimming, had been the humble inspiration for a neighborhood of little seasonal cottages. Here Joe and Maggie were able to buy a cheap place. That was eighteen years ago.

It was a hot afternoon in the middle of September. Dozens of small sailboats were on the river that glistened with little white-capped waves worked up by warm wind. Beyond the boats to the west, on the Saybrook side of the river, the maple trees planted by humans along the narrow village streets had begun to yellow—not because it was cold, but because they were dry and tired from living too long where pavement and sidewalk sneak up around their trunks.

This is not the seaside of dramatic, open ocean breaking on wide sandy beaches. It is a place whose subtle and complex beauty is in the blood of the people who live there, old and wealthy year-round communities populating ocean and river and land. Joe and Maggie believed that they were blessed to live in so beautiful a place.

Joe thought that the guys in town who worked at jobs they didn't enjoy grew to despise these little towns along Interstate 95 between New York and Boston. And when their joy had been robbed, they spent fortunes to get their families to Martha's Vineyard and Cape Cod because they had fouled their own nest. Maybe it was to reassure himself in his choices, but when he frequently told Will what a great life they had, Joe really wanted his son to know that his father was grateful to God for His blessings.

Two days had passed since Joe walked out of Linda Howe's kitchen without a thank you—or a compliment—or a check. At this last gasp of summer, his family, seeking normalcy in routine, was having a row and a swim within sight of their little house. Joe stood in the prow of a lovely, large rowboat in his favorite red swimming suit. His trunks were covered with lots of little sailboats. Will, content in his own world, played in the river at a distance. When Joe looked down at his mostly naked self, the person he saw from his tanned tummy down was a young Joe Carroll—strong and equipped to engage a mostly benevolent world. That view of the world—that it was essentially good—Joe thought was shaped more by one thing than by any other, that God had given him Maggie for a friend and mate.

His imagination had permanently captured the September morning when he saw his wife for the first time. In a boy's white oxford cloth shirt and a denim skirt, Maggie glided across the campus where he and Maggie and Annie and Dave on long winter evenings would decide who they were and what they would do with their lives. Lots of other boys spied Maggie on those same early September days, before the darkness and cold and alcohol-assisted introspection of the school year began. They'd all noticed her. How he had ever leapt to the idea that he could spend a whole life with her, he could not remember. He didn't really want to think about it— about how Maggie had fallen in love with his idealism and his devotion to his art. His adolescent college-boy self had let Maggie adore him. The more evolved, self-aware Joe was less comfortable with any such devotion. Joe thought that other married people must be burdened in the same way— having a wife or a husband who thinks you are better than you really are.

On this day, the disappointment over the Howe kitchen still had a grip on him. He wound a threadbare white towel around his eyes, ready for the firing squad. Maggie leaned slightly backward in her seat at the stern. She was wet from swimming and had pulled on a shirt over a teal tank suit. When the mail order catalogues came in the spring, Joe had occasionally bludgeoned Maggie into buying herself something, but she never cared. "I have a perfectly good bathing suit," she automatically answered, not remembering which sun-damaged, elastic-shot costume was currently at the front of the rotation in her bottom drawer.

"No, you don't," Joe said because he knew that it had been three years, at least, since she'd bought her last one. But the swimsuits in the catalogue were only forty dollars and Maggie was the reason that they make these plain little suits—so that on a day like this one, Maggie Carroll could dangle her tanned wrist over a gunwale and twirl an elegant finger in the brackish Connecticut River. Joe thought that women at forty were more beautiful than girls at twenty. Maggie said that he had to think that because a tired, mature woman was what he had, and something in his psychology made him need to affirm the goodness of everything in his world. Maggie accepted with amused gratitude that her husband thought she was beautiful. It was not how she thought about herself.

Straining for balance and standing blindfolded on the forward-most thwart, Joe snuck a peak at his feet. "Go ahead, Maggie. Shoot me, for your own sake and for the good of the boy. Finish me off."

"Come down from there. You're going to fall and hit your head and I'm not strong enough to get you back into the boat. It's not the end of the world. It'll work itself out. We've got it made." She liked her life. And out here on the river today in the glorious sunshine, she was able to enjoy the moment. Her friends spoke of Maggie's grace. She won't take any credit for it. She knew that her personality just was what it was and that she had not had to work very hard at being patient or modest or grateful.

"I don't think I've got it made. I think I live right up the street from the river and have to borrow a neighbor's boat to take my family on a weekend row. I think I'm carving herbs on cupboards for rich ladies."

"Not any more, actually," Maggie said, not able to resist the cheap joke. Joe let the terry cloth blindfold fall onto his shoulders.

"What a bargain you got—a carver of inane trivialities who doesn't even get paid for his labors. I'm like a double loser. Shoot me and get another man. Maybe a lawyer next time." Joe shouted, "Will," turning his head in the direction where he last saw his son floating quietly on his back, "would you like a wealthy father who could get you a big new speedboat?"

Will flipped onto his front and started breaststroking toward the boat. "I thought you said we were rich in all the important things," Will replied flippantly. Joe heard himself in his son's words and, miserable as he was, he could still enjoy Maggie's calm and his teaching manifest in the boy. "Dad, can I swim to the point and back?" They'd done it together lots of times and it wasn't as far as it looked.

"Sure, yell really loud if you think the current is doing anything scary and we'll row right after you."

Maggie understood this was male stuff she had to let Joe decide. First of all, he might say to her, nothing is going to happen to him because I'm going to watch him like a hawk and I can row over there in about a minute if he cramps up or something, and we've got to let him do stuff like this if he's going to grow into a strong man. And Joe might gratuitously compare Will to some Zander Howe-type kid as an added deterrent to Maggie's impulse to protect her only child. Maggie liked the way their parenting collaboration worked.

Their bony and brown boy quickly was halfway to the muddy promontory. Joe was not through needing Maggie's attention. "You'll be free."

"Why don't you come down from there?"

"I'm sorry about the money, Mags. This isn't what I wanted for us." Joe sat down in the boat. "I thought that I would do something important, make lovely things, things that people would admire and that would make the world more beautiful."

"Beautiful things like that brave little man who's swimming toward us? You have, Joe, and you can."

Joe wasn't so sure. He was weary. It had been nearly twenty years since they landed in this place. "Oh, come on, Mags, how am I? Anyway, the job for the Howes—you're right, that'll work itself out. I'll just have to grovel a little and we'll get the money. I can grovel."

"We're fine, you know," she said. "Don't owe anybody. Borrowed boat, yeah, but we're okay. And as for the making great things thing, you will, if it's what you really want; you just will. Nothing will stop you."

Will returned, pooped from the long swim, and pulled himself up to where his chin was hooked just over the gunwale. "Aren't you going to do it, Dad?" Joe always did it. It was his trick that told them all he was still young and athletic and fearless. He climbed back up into the stern of the boat, rewound the condemned man's towel around his eyes, and did a high, arching backflip into the river.

Chapter 3
They Were Pounding on Me

The deal with the Howes worked out pretty much the way Joe expected it would, but not because Joe had brilliantly sized up everybody's priorities on the fly that morning in the kitchen. Actually, it had seemed so right, so exciting really, the jousting with Linda and the kid and the walking out. At the time, Joe truly had chucked the whole thing. But Lou Howe knew that Zander *was* awful. And as different as were their worlds, some primal core of Dr. Louis Samuel Howe admired the free spirit of the wood carver that had been caged in his kitchen for weeks. Lou Howe could not afford too serious an examination of his life. He was in deep with bills and responsibilities; Lou Howe knew that if he thought very hard about it, he would have to say that the daily procession of frightened patients and body fluids and blood tests was in its way preferable to days in that kitchen with Linda and Zander.

Linda Howe had contrived an exhausting scheme whereby the adult son of a woman in her book club would come down from Essex and finish The Garden under a financial scheme buttressed by Ari Pappas' legal muscle. But Lou, practiced as he was at smoothing over Linda's quarrels, and having accepted an apology from Joe Carroll for the obscenity in front of his son, steeled his courage and took his family on a long weekend to New York, ostensibly so that Linda could expose Zander to modern art with the idea that he might like a career as a curator or an art historian. After all, Linda had agreed, college was not that far off.

Joe got the whole thing done in those three days and didn't even have to move the center island back from the refrigerator. "Oh, shit, forget that,"

Lou told Joe on the phone, "I'll bang my tailbone on it once and that'll be the end of it."

It was Tuesday now, Maggie at work, Will at school, as Joe came into Maggie's bright kitchen from his shop for more coffee. They had made do with the blurry reddish-brown stain and varnish on the maple cupboard doors that were there when they moved in. The sparkly white Formica countertops were slightly chipped in places, but serviceable. Maggie's friend, Annie, said the dated kitchen was a shoemaker's children thing, but Maggie would never throw it up at Joe that he could update things for them. It never even crossed her mind. They had added one big double-glazed bow window on the southern exposure and the sun had bleached out several sets of pretty curtains.

Everywhere in their house there were plants and books. All year-round, Maggie foraged for pretty things to put in big vases. Their house was cheery—anybody would say so—but mostly it was a happy place because of who Maggie was.

Joe had never asked her where she got all her books; he was just vaguely aware of her network of smart women friends who shared titles and favorite authors. In the mail Maggie got catalogues from companies that sold remaindered novels at good prices. Piles of books were on the floor at Maggie's side of the bed. Maggie said it was a good thing their double bed was right on the floor, college crash pad-style, since no bedside table could hold all her books. Maggie only rarely urged one of her novels on Joe. She knew that he liked nonfiction, but more than that, she liked having a little world separate from Joe's—a world that she had cultivated more or less by herself.

Joe discovered that Will had left his bagged lunch on the counter by the back door. Oh, good, Joe thought. His day was taking on shape and meaning. Joe made a list on a yellow legal pad and now TAKE WILL HIS LUNCH jumped ahead of BOARDS FOR MURPHYS' PORCH and MAIL and BANK.

Joe presented his physical self to the world in uniform. He thought that by driving the most common pickup truck, an older Ford F-150, and by wearing khaki pants and a blue chambray shirt, a Carhartt jacket, and

Dunham work boots, he was not trying to look cool, he was actually trying to say nothing. This way, he reasoned, his actions and his work would speak of who he really was. To the contrary, Joe's longish light-brown hair, streaked with summer highlights, betrayed what looked more like vanity.

As he approached the back door of the school, the entrance that parents were supposed to use, Joe bounded up the short flight of pre-cast stairs. At the door, he met the eyes of two moms and they brightened at the sight of Will Carroll's dad. Why am I here? Joe thought. Will's bagged lunch. Back to the old truck for the brown bag he had left on the slippery bench seat. He popped it in his jacket pocket.

Classes were changing and in the hallway outside the school office a whole fourth grade class filed by. Joe loved kids and his gaze went to these little ones. He was searching for familiar faces. "Mr. Carroll—Joe," as one little boy weaved from the tight queue to give him a high five. A teacher scowled.

Quickly, two middle school boys surrounded him. "Ricky, I see you are attending eighth grade again this year," Joe said.

"Hold him, Timmy." Timmy was big for his age and grabbed Joe right around the waist and arms as another boy, Jason, approached.

"Jason, I hear you actually passed the ball to someone in the soccer game Sunday," Joe said.

Another kid was there now. "It was an accident," the kid said.

There was a whole group around Joe and they were sort of mock pounding on him and everyone was laughing except a grim-faced teacher. "Have you checked in at the office, sir?"

Sir, oh, that must be me, Joe realized. "Of course, yes, I just got here, I will, thanks." The kids took off.

Joe tucked his shirt in his trousers and hurried toward the office.

At the counter a pleasant lady said, "Can I help?"

"Yes, thank you, good morning, I need Will Carroll. I'm his dad," and Joe crafted the smile and the tone of a grown-up. "I'm getting him for his orthodontist appointment. He's getting braces and he is not very happy about it." The fib came to him easily.

Joe thought that the power the school had over people's children was ridiculous—that everybody yielded too easily to the entrusting of thousands of hours of care and nurture of their kids to other people. It was not that they were bad places—they were just uninspiring. Homogenizing was what Joe sometimes said of the school—that the curricula was teaching boys in Indiana all the exact same facts, and what's worse, the same ideas, that Will was getting in Connecticut. And Joe thought that the whole setup wasn't very tolerant of boys who couldn't sit still in their seats all day. But these people won't own Will Carroll, Joe had said to Maggie. He will be his own man, even though that will make things hard for him sometimes, like it had for his dad.

The nice office secretary played it straight. "What grade is Will in this year, Mr. Carroll?"

Joe never knew stuff like that—birthdays and anniversaries, what year it was, how long it had been since he mailed the last mortgage payment. He leaned in closer and whispered, "Which grade has the really big and mean lady English teacher?"

Right away deft fingers flicked toggles and over the intercom went, "Mrs. Scott, please send Will Carroll to the office for his orthodontist appointment."

In the time it took Joe to fill in the lines on a form on a clipboard Will appeared at his side. Joe said to him quietly, "I'll tell you all about it outside." Joe quickly made his way toward the truck coaxing Will to hurry along behind him.

"The orthodontist, dad? Where are we really going?"

"Hopefully we'll get by with just the braces and you won't need that whole headgear thing. How do they sleep with that damn thing?" Joe saw his son's annoyed expression. "Can you go with me to the lumberyard for a while?"

"I'm missing a math test," Will said.

Joe pulled the brown bag from his jacket pocket. "Ricky and another kid smashed your lunch, so I thought—"

"Ricky smashed my lunch?" That his father had somehow engaged Ricky or any of forty or fifty other kids in his circle of classmates, church youth group friends, Pinewood Derby racers, soccer teammates, or kids from the last school play, did not surprise Will. He knew that his dad knew all their names and had even pretty accurately sized up the character of all these kids. After all, they were father and son and Will had come to accept the fact that his father even liked the same kids he liked. And Will knew too, but did not understand fully, that his father loved all these kids—that his unusual effort to know all their names, to treat them all individually, even if in a smart-ass way, was part of his caring for them. But mostly, the daily stream of love that flowed to him from his father made it all right that today something, something ridiculously inappropriate, had happened at his school.

"Yeah, they were pounding on me. I'll get you back quick. I promise." When Joe made a promise to Will or Maggie it was rock solid and Will knew that, so he just made a perfect-teeth smile and looked away in amused resignation.

Chapter 4
A Little Lesson in Lumber

A good feeling always came over Joe when he pulled into the big gates at Davis Lumber. Things there hardly ever changed: the stack of half inch CDX plywood against the big steel barn on the left, and the bundles of 2 x 4 and 2 x 6 studs against the older wood barn on the right, a green flatbed truck with Vermont plates unloading fresh pine boards and congesting the traffic flow.

This was a place to which he belonged—the locus of an unspoken membership in a club of homebuilders and remodelers and farmers and do-it-yourselfers and craftsmen. Joe had learned the rules and customs of the club and knew precisely where he fit into its hierarchy. If, today, he and Will were to find Harry Carlson limping toward the big cardboard tubes of crown moldings, the chameleon Joe would adopt some of the calm cheer that he admired in Harry and his dying breed of old carpenters. Harry and a few others were at the top of the pecking order that they would surely eschew, were they not so humble as to be completely unaware of it. Joe had no delusions that he would ever approach them in authentic goodness. But he did hope that, like Harry Carlson, he would leave behind a body of work with an integrity of design and craftsmanship that would say something about his life. At least that was within his control; even a flawed man can make a choice about what to do with his gifts.

Harry's wife was dying and he was all but retired. Joe pictured Harry limping toward him with that one built up boot and the big open, forgiving smile.

Maybe fifteen years ago Harry had invited Joe to a monthly breakfast held in a greasy spoon across the river in Saybrook. It was nice to be with Harry and the other men, and Joe wasn't surprised when an old insurance guy from East Lyme was asked to read from the Bible. These men were all serious about religion, but not in a way that made Joe uncomfortable. Joe had his antenna up for anyone telling him what to think, but Harry Carlson and his friends acted as though they liked Joe and wanted to be with him, wanted to be with him at 6:30 in the morning in the dead of winter for two eggs over easy, white toast with grape jelly, and squiggly bacon. There were a few young guys there the times Joe went—some with earrings and tattoos. That had surprised Joe a little. He knew from exchanges at the lumberyard that these young guys knew and liked Harry, and Joe had even noticed that these masons and drywall hangers had some of Harry's sweet aura. Joe never figured out if the whole roomful of men were Christians or if they just came because they couldn't turn Harry down. Joe wished he were more faithful in attending. It had been years. The breakfast was on the second Monday of every month, or it used to be, and he'd intended to stay with it, but finally decided that the early hour just worked better for the older men like Harry than for men with young families.

It wasn't in Harry Carlson's nature to show any disappointment in Joe, or anyone else for that matter. He did occasionally say, "We'd love to see you at the breakfast." He never said, "We miss you at the breakfast," to lay a guilt trip.

Lately Joe had read a spiritual book that a carpenter buddy who'd been through a rough stretch had loaned him. It was about a God who understood men and men's passions and fears and Joe found it interesting. Maggie was excited when Joe told her about the book.

Joe goes to church probably half the time. It's no secret that he doesn't like it very much. "But we can't just do what we want all the time, son," he has said to Will. The structure and discipline of the thing is good for their family life. Joe had heard some preachers that inspired him to go deeper, but the current minister at Maggie's church, Joe thinks, is not one of them. He's just mailing it in. Joe once whispered to Will that the pastor was getting his sermons through the mail in a plain brown wrapper. In the pecking order at Davis Lumber, there was a big jump from Harry and the old guys who walk on water down to a large pool of professional guys with long histories of quality workmanship. These guys were just trying to make a living the only way they knew how. You could do worse than build nice houses and additions. They were mostly into making money and Joe thought that was okay. It was just that you have to keep an eye on them because they weren't exactly self-policing. Hard-working guys that might forget a 1 x 10 Select and Better pine board when they recited their purchases at the checkout counter. Nowadays there were lots of hot shots in big, new pickups with their freshly dreamed-up company names professionally painted on the doors: Ed Beausoleil Decks and Garage Doors Quality Installation since 1991. Joe guessed that lots of them were in deep hock for the trucks and tools. Joe wished them well, as long as they respected the little universe of the lumberyard as understood by the veterans.

And there was an entertaining assortment of rough characters, young and old, more sketchy and dangerous in groups than operating by themselves. They were the reason for the new sign Davis's son put up last month. Joe knew that he would have fun initiating Will to all these things in due course, but he'd promised a quick visit—McDonalds for a Big Mac—then back to school, hopefully in time for the math test.

He and Will parked over close to the steel barn. Most of the material they'll grab today was in there.

BOARDS FOR MURPHY'S PORCH was on his list and Joe contrived a little lesson in lumber selection. Joe and Will were standing at racks of the 1 x 6 and 1 x 8 and 1 x 10 pine boards that were mostly sold for house trim. "Okay, son, we're replacing some rotten columns on Mrs. Murphy's front porch and we need 1 x 8 pine boards which are actually only 7¼ inches wide. Don't ask me how these conventions got started. The actual sizes of board lumber are printed on the back of some Stanley tape measures. Board lumber, that's what all this stuff is in here, the two-by-fours and two-by-sixes, and all that framing stuff, we call that dimensional lumber. Anyway, the short course. These on top have been pretty well picked over, so they'll be good for a lesson."

Will's eyes wandered around the big barn. "Pay attention, this is stuff I know about," Joe said. He pulled out the top board on the stack. "Okay, this one's checked. See the big crack running in from the end. If some paint or glue had been applied to this board when the green lumber was first milled, this wouldn't have happened, but that's time-consuming and expensive, and the check doesn't always happen this bad, so the mill just didn't do it."

"So, it's no good," Will said.

"It's fine; you just have to saw off the bad part." Joe pulled out another board and upon quick examination shouted across the room to Gary who worked there. "Gary, I remember this board from when I started coming here 19 years ago." Joe loved Gary. To his son he said, "Will, look at it from the end and tell me what you see."

He tugged at the fourteen-foot-long board, got it out of the dark rack and onto a stack of plywood in the middle of the floor where he could see it better. Will's nose was right at the end of the board and he saw that it bent over one way, then back over the other way. "It's all crazy and twisty."

The lesson was going well. "Right! We would say that board is twisted. Now look at the end of this one." Will made a bowl-shaped motion with his hand. "Exactly, it's cupped," Joe said, "and it won't go back flat ever, so it's junk unless you plane it down a lot thinner. Get us six good ones with no loose knots, fourteen footers, and tie them on the truck. I'll go inside and pay."

Inside Joe strode to the counter where Jimmy, a huge double-knit guy, brightened at the sight of Joe Carroll. Silently he brought Joe's charge account up on the computer terminal and said, "What have you got, Joe Carroll?"

"Premium pine, 1 x 8's, six fourteens; that's it today, Jimmy." Immediately a printer began to spit out a slip in triplicate—one for the lumberyard, one for the customer, and one for a man in the yard to check against your load. Waiting for the printer Jimmy remembered, "Hey, Joe. Did you ever look into that big mahogany board I told you about?"

Jimmy was a sweetheart. You just wouldn't take a tip on anything from Jimmy as authoritative, but this was why Joe liked it here, that these men cared about one another, that Jimmy really would like him to possess a huge mahogany board that someone had told Jimmy about. That the board probably didn't even exist doesn't matter. So, if the big board was real, it would be sold by now. It had been a year and a half, at least, since the Saturday morning when Jimmy scribbled the board's vital statistics on a Post-it note. If Jimmy told tall tales to attract attention to himself, so what? I can't bear to hurt Jimmy Newhouse—not for anything, Joe thought. Jimmy put the receipt on the counter for Joe's signature. "No, I didn't have the spare cash, Jimmy. Someone else has got it by now."

Gary had heard Joe's whole lumber lesson with the kid and sidled over near Will as soon as his father was out of sight. "Let's have some fun with your old man, who thinks he's so freaking smart." Gary dug through the pile of 1 x 8's for one with brown pine bark on round edges along the last ten or twelve inches of the board. "See this shit, it's just bark. The tree it came from wasn't very big. This board is really nice though. Not a knot in it, it's just a little waney. Got it kid, WANEY, the bark shit?"

When Joe came out of the office Will was still climbing around on the back of the pick-up and Joe said, "Everything tied down good?"

"I don't know, you better check," Will said.

"If you think you've done the best you can, let's go." Joe's truck in first gear, they slowly approached a huge plywood sign near the exit gate: Loads Must be Checked in Yard before Leaving.

"They have to check our load," Will said.

Joe just smiled at him. "We're all set, son. They trust your dad. Let's get a hamburger and a shake and get back to school."

Once underway on the state highway, Will said, "I think I picked some good boards; one's a little waney, but I figured that's okay because otherwise it's completely clear."

Waney, huh. That's pretty funny. Gary's handiwork. There is nothing better than this, Joe thought. My beautiful son has no idea how I love him.

All the way to the restaurant, and then on the last leg to the school, Joe kept a discreet eye on the lumber with all three mirrors, just in case a poorly tied knot should put their load on the road. Even that teachable moment would be his joy. Why, Joe wondered, does every kid in every town in America go to school in September? They need their dads more than they need the math tests. Crazy, really.

Chapter 5
They Needed the Jaws of Life

Maggie said that her job was fine, but Joe thought that it must be boring and that the lawyers at her office didn't deserve her. Joe respected that it was for Maggie to say whether or not she liked her work, but just the same, it ate at him. Joe probably remembered better than she how it all started. Three or four winters ago, there had been a slow stretch in Joe's shop and there were missed mortgage payments and even a foreclosure threat from the bank. It wasn't that they were in real trouble, more like the unevenness of income that self-employed craftsmen like Joe dealt with all the time. Joe usually dismissed these events as "cash flow problems." It made him crazy sometimes, that the world didn't respect the entrepreneurs struggling to support families with nothing but their skills and hard work.

How many drawings had Joe made of hand-carved toy boxes and firewood boxes and jewelry boxes and candle boxes, gold leafed quarter board signs, tavern signs, bakery signs, optometrist signs, orthodontist signs, free-standing carved and painted geese and pigs and facsimiles of beloved, departed house cats. How many nights had Joe sat at the kitchen table with a horrible mug of herb tea, putting watercolors or felt markers to his proposals: gorgeous, careful representations of eyeglasses and human teeth and fat tabby cats, and then had to make up some price that would not scare off the client, because, after all, the mortgage was past due.

Then he'd buy the materials, grin and bear it, bite his tongue, and carve the smiley teeth for the orthodontist. Okay, I'll make the post for it, too, even though that isn't the business I'm in; oh man, dig the hole, okay, run to the lumberyard for a couple bags of Sakrete. No, I can't do the landscaping, even though Dr. Krahulick is much busier than me and his time is worth so much more, too; everybody knows that.

"Try adding up all those separate jobs I do for umpteen separate clients in twelve months," Joe had said to Dave and Annie, "and get it to add up to even forty or fifty thousand dollars." Never mind the toll of humiliation.

Their intention was that Maggie would work just for a while until they got on top of things again and Joe had more of the fine jobs that his education and training had prepared him for: carvings that could stand on their own as works of art, custom relief-carved doors for institutions and the homes of wealthy people, church decoration, carved oak and mahogany fireplace surrounds, one-of-a-kind furniture pieces of Joe's own design decorated with intricate carving. They both believed in Joe's talent; it was just a matter of getting the jobs, getting some recognition and some forward momentum.

They both said they would be patient; and after all, they had a home full of love. God had always given them everything they needed. Life was good. That was four years ago.

Aristotle Pappas says he can't run the place without his Margaret, that she's worth her weight in gold, which Joe imagines is why Ari pays her about $30,000 a year plus health benefits. Maggie does all of the work to get him ready for his real estate closings so that on most days he can do three or four and charge over a thousand bucks each, depending on the financing complexities. There's not much to them, Joe said, it's just stuff the lawyers have rigged so you can't do it without them.

If he were doing better with his woodworking business, Maggie could stay home and work on her children's stories and maybe get back the part-time job at the little neighborhood library. She had always come home so happy from that. Maggie says that she doesn't care at all and that at least she is out and with people, that Joe, all alone in the shop trying to create beautiful art, has the hard job. He guessed that was true, but it seemed awfully weak when he was in his workshop with Jackson Browne and Van Morrison while Maggie was on the phone with Principal Financial Mortgage, getting the very exciting payoff numbers as of a closing date of

September 20th on the D'Agostinos' first mortgage on property at 1402 Jason Terrace.

And not only that, but as he sat in his pretty old truck in his pretty little town on the Connecticut shore, he had to say that he just plain missed her. That is a good thing; I love my wife to death, he thought to himself as he propped his legal pad on his lap against the steering wheel.

Most days Maggie made a run for lunch for the whole gang, or joined a group for a bite in a neighborhood inn at just past noon. From where Joe was parked in his truck, there was a good chance that any minute his girl would come out of the gorgeous colonial house where Ari has had his offices for twenty-five years. Joe would have a chance to say hi, to tell her that he loved her before getting on with his day.

Joe looked up from the legal pad and saw a laughing Maggie, Teddy Pappas, and two young women come through Ari's white gate. As they approached an oncoming group on the sidewalk, they narrowed to single-file. Teddy, the boss's nephew, put both hands on Maggie's waist as though they were in a Conga line. Joe's arms on the steering wheel stiffened. Maggie was a strong woman and Joe had never doubted her faithfulness to him. Surely, she could handle this Teddy Pappas whom she has said she doesn't particularly like. One time she even called him smarmy. Joe said to himself that he won't say anything because it's none of his business, but something in him wanted to jump out of the truck and toss this punk into the hedges. Joe liked this part of his nature and was not sure it was such a good thing that it had been mostly civilized out of him.

He was thinking about that, about what would happen if he roughed up Teddy Pappas for putting his mitts on another man's wife. He might actually get arrested, but the charges would be dropped, even though the recent events in Doctor Howe's kitchen, where Mrs. Howe was frightened half to death, would argue for a pattern of erratic acting out. Among another whole group in town such a story would take on folkloric proportions. Joe had told Will about the Happy Days episode when Fonzie told Richie Cunningham that if, just once, he would punch somebody in the nose, he'd be all set for the rest of his school days. Teddy Pappas all tangled up in the privet hedge till the cops extricated him and his ruined, blue double-breasted Brooks Brothers suit. "They needed the Jaws of Life to get him out of that hedge," the story would go. It would probably be worth it.

"Hey!" It was Maggie poking her face in the passenger side window jarring Joe out of his reverie. "What are you doing in town? I was just going back to the office to phone you to see if you could deposit my check. We need to pay the mortgage today."

In his dream he was accepting beer-lubricated slaps on the back from some lumberyard friends for his assault on white collar, predatory pretty boys everywhere. "Yeah, okay, I'll write it down, Mags," and he straightened up the legal pad that had tipped over sideways in his lap.

"Can you have lunch with me?" Maggie asked.

Of course, he could, if he wanted. He had controlled his emotions and now Teddy was clear out of sight. "I had to drive Will's lunch to school; he forgot it again." No mention of the McDonalds. "I can't really, Mags. I need to get some things started in the shop. But I can't wait to see you at 5:17. We can take a walk down to the river." Maggie handed Joe her sealed pay envelope from her cloth bag and gave him a kiss through the truck window.

Chapter 6
How Big Is It

Joe went home and upstairs to put the invoices in the box that kept all his business expenses. He spotted his bed. He would like to just fall asleep, but he knew that the items checked off the yellow legal pad list had not earned him an afternoon nap. He thought about Will and how he carried off that waney board joke. Gary was definitely in on that. What a bunch of characters old Davis has assembled at the lumberyard. It's a paradox: Davis hired really nice people, even knew that they were nice, and then treated them lousy.

Joe knew a lot about all the boys at Davis Lumber: who has a little problem with his beer, whose wife left him last year, who would give him a cigarette because Joe bought him a whole pack of Marlboros last spring, who's running out of steam and especially hates the winter work and is dreaming about Florida, who's getting jerked around by the boss. In Joe's whole world, this is the "guy place" that has most revealed the essence of men.

Davis is going to fire Jimmy Newhouse. Joe was sure of it. Jimmy has put so much work into learning all the arcane terminology about joist hangers and plywood grades and anchor bolts and hot box galvanized nails which was all new to him because he had never even driven a nail. But Jimmy's a little slow moving and sometimes he phones in late with fibs about car trouble. Gary says that it's something about Jimmy's wife and that Jimmy can't help it. Davis was an outwardly affable and friendly man, but he's going to fire Jimmy Newhouse like he has lots of other guys. Joe has thought about whether he should tell Jimmy what he has seen over twenty years, about the long list of chipper new men he has met around the yard. Joe remembers all their names. What a shame, Joe thinks, that people aren't nice to each other, nice like Jimmy Newhouse when he told me about the big mahogany board.

Joe went to his bureau with its two small top drawers. First the left where he excitedly spotted a flat, rumpled Marlboro package concealed under athletic socks. Oh, wow. There was one in there. Stale, but so what. Jimmy's Post-it note—Joe thought it was yellow—maybe the right drawer where my dark socks live, Joe thought. Why do I think that I saved it at all? Is it possible that Jimmy Newhouse told me something important this morning, mentioning the big board again?

Joe rummaged harder and some of his balled-up dress socks bounced on the bedroom floor. He was excited about the cigarette and couldn't wait any longer, didn't want to, and threw a window open wide, and lit up. Maggie would probably smell traces of the cigarette in their bedroom tonight. She knows that he sometimes sneaks a smoke and definitely won't cuddle a stinky smoker. And, of course, Joe admitted to himself, she shouldn't. That is the strongest deterrent to smoking—that it's gross—and that the people who think it's awful are on the right side of the issue. About this smoking thing there is always an argument, even in Joe's solitude. He thinks that the hot button is probably in the shame of the thing, and this morning he easily gives in to familiar ruminations. People can't picture so easily that they will get sick and die, he thought, but they can understand that they smell bad. When everyone smoked, the stinky people were cuddling one another and could be forgiven for not knowing what they smelled like. Looking back on it, Joe thought, as he lit the dried-up Marlboro, it is ridiculous that cigarette smoking was ever the default condition; the smokers predominated and they had power. Why else could the smokers possibly rule in public places, in confined airplane cabins? All that smoking was something from a long time ago. But he still smoked. Stupid, stupid really. Everyone talked about how powerful an addiction nicotine is, but he thought his will power should be stronger than that.

The smoke balanced on the windowsill as Joe burrowed around in the drawer. Credit cards tucked away from temptation because they were still active, but with high interest rates because of late payments, grocery store cards that had engorged his wallet, shoe laces, a tiny skein of yarn that came with a new sweater, foreign coins, a deck of Bicycle playing cards kept safe for bridge with Annie and Dave—and, there it was, stuck to the side of the drawer, a yellow Post-it. Carini Tiezzi North Main Street Saybrook Mahogany 1 ¼ x 6 feet x 14 feet. Joe's memory was that Jimmy had written it all down, but, no, this was in his own neat printing. And he had saved it.

Something had brought the search this far, he considered, and besides, the afternoon was wide open. He picked up the cordless phone from Maggie's bureau and walked to the cigarette on the windowsill.

"Yes, operator, thanks. In Saybrook, last name Tiezzi, T-I-E-Z-Z-I, Carini, on North Main Street." He grabbed a pen from the top of his chest of drawers.

"I'm sorry; there is no listing for Karen Tiezzi in Saybrook."

"It's Carini, C-A-R-I-N-I."

"I'm sorry, she's not listed, sir."

"That's okay," Joe said. "Do you have any Tiezzi on North Main Street?"

"No, there's just one Tiezzi listed in Saybrook."

Joe had been on wild goose chases on the phone before. Not long after college he had phoned a high school friend with help from directory assistance and had chatted up the groggy buddy for a while. It was eleven at night and the old friend was already in bed. "Are you in bed alone? You usually aren't," Joe had joked.

"No, my wife's here, but she's asleep."

But the high school friend wasn't married. Maggie and I would have been invited to the wedding, Joe realized. He processed the thing on the fly. Oh, crap. This was the wrong guy. "I'm sorry to bother you, sir, I have the wrong number."

"Which Tiezzi is that?" Joe asked.

"Giordano Tiezzi on East Main Street."

"Great, yeah, that's it, operator, thank you." Joe wrote the number down as the cigarette in his mouth filled the little room with smoke.

After the wild goose, two rings, three rings, and a frail, foreign-sounding hello at the end of the line. "Hello, I'm sorry to trouble you. My name is Joe Carroll and I am calling from Lyme, Connecticut, and I'm trying to find Carini Tiezzi."

"Is it about the board?" an old man answered.

"Yes, my name is Joe Carroll and I'm down in Lyme and I'm trying to reach Carini Tiezzi."

"Is it about the board?"

Whoa, this is too easy, Joe thought. It's like a joke that everyone's in on but me. Can we slow down? After all, haven't I waited a year and a half to call? This isn't even Carini Tiezzi's phone number.

Joe answered that yes, it is about the board, and the man continued in an Italian accent. "We have the board. Are you going to buy our board?"

"Yes, I am very interested. I would like to see it in person. Are you Carini?"

"No, I am Giordano Tiezzi. Are you going to do something wonderful with the big board?"

"I'm sorry. I don't mean to be rude, but who owns the board, you or Carini Tiezzi? I was given Carini's name by a friend."

"Carini is my brother. He has been dead two-and one-half years. We have the board. Do you want to buy our board? It is very large."

"How big is it, Mr. Tiezzi?" Joe asked holding the yellow note in his own hand.

"It is five quarters thick and as wide as a man is tall, and fourteen feet long," the charming voice said. Just like Jimmy told me, Joe thought.

Joe wrote down instructions to a place in Saybrook next to a brake shop, a place he had driven past many times, and made a date to meet the old man on Saturday morning.

Chapter 7
A Fresh Beginning

It was a cool Saturday morning in September, and Will could go on this errand with his dad because soccer practice wasn't till eleven. They got into the pickup truck all happy, Joe because Jimmy Newhouse and the Tiezzis had him on a treasure hunt that had lifted him from the routine, and Will because going anywhere with Dad was fun—even exciting.

In only minutes, they were high up over the Connecticut River on the I-95 bridge that separated their town from Saybrook to the west. "I don't like it up here, Daddy." Joe didn't like heights either and didn't tell Will that a bridge on this same highway a little farther west, but still in Connecticut, collapsed a few years back. "Where are we really going? You told Mom the lumberyard."

"We sort of are. We're going to see a man about a dog—about a board actually— that's an old expression. I don't even know what it means—sort of that you don't want to tell where you're really going, but you're with me, so the secret's out, right?" Joe told Will the whole story. They had this chunk of time together, so Joe included all the lumber yard stuff about Jimmy Newhouse and Mr. Davis, so that Will would also enjoy the imperative before them.

They slowed down in a neighborhood of modest two-story bungalows now interspersed with a Meineke brake shop, a Dunkin' Donuts and a quick lube. In front of one house there was a sign: Tiezzi and Sons, Millwork. They pulled into a pitted drive and wound around behind the house to what could be the shop.

Joe knocked on a windowed wooden door, peered through the glass at a cluttered workbench, wooden barrels, and tools. He let himself and Will inside. "Hello, Mr. Tiezzi, hello." The overwhelming impression of the place was of wood—warm, white and amber, sensual wood. Joe was thrilled. He looked around this space that in another era he might just as well have created himself. He knew almost instinctively where and what everything was. There was a woodstove, large bench power tools with huge old-fashioned motors and leather drive belts, benches stacked with bundled short lengths of moldings and small furniture parts, short lengths of hardwood lumber stored in homemade racks. The walls were covered with antique hand tools, not for display, but for ready use by men who knew how to use them. And there were out-of-date calendars with pastoral Italian scenes, a picture of the Blessed Virgin, and a crucifix.

Joe took a small maple molding plane from the wall and examined its cutting profile.

"Dad," Will whispered, and motioned his father to come look at something. It was a photograph, a picture of a group of men. The handsome, shirtless, black-haired one in the middle was laughing. And he had one leg.

Joe and Will heard the door shut behind them and a voice, "Carini, with the other men from his PT boat just after the war." This was Giordano from the telephone call and he was small and frail and probably eighty years old. He wore overalls and looked ready for work, but a film of dust and time had covered everything in the room and Joe knew that this was a shop that had gone quiet. Even so, Joe could easily picture this place alive with people and activity. It was wonderful. Giordano approached his guests. "Mr. Carroll, welcome, and who is this?"

"Mr. Tiezzi, this is my son, Will."

"And your papa will buy our big board," Giordano said smiling.

They all shook hands and Joe said politely, "We'd love to see it, Mr. Tiezzi."

Giordano moved slowly as he led them toward a back door. Joe's eyes scanned the workshop. It was a treasure trove of sturdy old tools that probably had been well cared for by these old-timey gentlemen, Carini and

Giordano, and it was all just sitting here. Maybe I can buy some of this great stuff, Joe thought, but he suppressed the idea that he knew was not very nice. We're here about the big board and this man is so lovely, so forget about buying all his cool stuff.

Only twenty or thirty feet from the workshop was another small building that had once been barn red, but which now was mostly gray and weathered with sumac trees growing close up to its sills. At its wide batten door, the three stood close together as the old man maneuvered rusty hardware that he knew by heart. Things had sagged and some lifting and tugging was required to get the latch free. When the door opened only a crack, a startled chipmunk or mouse scurried and rustled in a dark corner of the littered floor. With some effort the big door swung open wide and light flooded the small shed.

It was right there, right in front of them, with one end facing the doorway and the length of the thing running directly toward the back of the shed. A couple bent and dirty sheets of plywood were leaning against it, but Joe could see instantly that about this one thing, Jimmy Newhouse had not been the repeater of lumber apocrypha. Here the damn thing was, up off the uneven floor of the shed on short lengths of thick timber, and from Joe's first, quick appraisal, flat as can be.

Joe helped Giordano move the plywood to a dark opposite wall and looked back at the mahogany. He guessed that it may have been months or years since a shaft of light had illumined it through the crooked doorway. "Will, look at this thing." Joe couldn't pretend that it was not amazing. As if by habit, the thought came to him that he should restrain his enthusiasm, not let on how much he wanted it, but it was no use. What was this monster piece of wood doing out in this shed? He had an impulse to look behind them into the yard where some other buyer might appear at any moment to outbid them. It's ridiculous that I have this chance to have it, Joe thought.

With a short scrap of board, Giordano swept at decades of windblown leaves that had found their way into the shed. "Where did you get this?" Joe asked. There was no answer. Giordano's head was down as he kicked a little pile of dusty leaves toward the open doorway. It's possible that the old man can't hear me, Joe thought, or that it's none of my business. That's okay.

Giordano gathered himself and turned to Joe. "During the war there was mahogany in our town for the PT boats that the Navy was building and one big piece came to us, to Carini and me."

Giordano and Joe had fun marking Will's height against the width of the great board. Giordano said, "Let me see if I have grown taller these forty years," and he took his turn putting his back to the board. "Yes, our board is still wider than the height of a grown man." Joe looked at the board carefully and slid a fingernail in one of the little cracks that came in on the end sixty years back when the board first dried out. The board was still rough and fuzzy from its sawing, and Joe understood that unplaned he couldn't know much about the grain or the figure of the wood. It doesn't matter, he thought. It is huge, flat and rare, and Joe wanted very much to have it.

Back in the workshop, Joe broached what he expected would be a negotiation. "What were you thinking would be a fair price, Mr. Tiezzi?"

"Carini said that we should ask one thousand dollars for the board. Our papa said that Carini was good at business and I was better with the tools and making things, so that is the way we have always managed. I leave the pricing of the board to my brother." Joe had no impulse to haggle. Haggle with whom, with the brother who set the price and is long dead, Joe thought. This was so fun; surely this is meant to be. It must be right and the one thousand dollars was exactly what he had withdrawn from his and Maggie's overdraft account. Joe placed crisp one hundred-dollar bills on a bench before Giordano who put them in a breast pocket without counting.

"Wait right here. I have something for a special occasion." They were in no hurry and now, alone in the shop, Joe pointed out to his boy all the wonderful old tools: a drill press, a mortising machine, a jointer, a planer, a shaper, and a monstrous table saw. Joe pictured himself working in this place. It was a rickety fire trap really. He knew that, but he associated it with a simpler time, a time which he had never himself known, but which he craved terribly. And today he had bought this board, a blank piece of

Giordano Tiezzi's simpler world. At this moment, it felt to Joe like a fresh beginning.

Giordano tottered in from his house with a silver tray carrying three delicate stemmed glasses and a bottle of blue liquid that looked sweet and alcoholic. The little old fellow was excited too and was exerting himself to make the most of a rare occasion. "We must drink a toast," and he poured out three portions of liquid lapis lazuli.

Oh, wonderful, Joe thought, a European man who understands that there are times when a boy should have a drink with his dad and his dad's friends and not worry about the drinking age, or what a boy's mother would say.

"To your work, Mr. Carroll, and to Will," and they raised their glasses and drank.

Joe held his glass high. "Mr. Tiezzi, Giordano. I am an artist, and, well, you have just met me, so you wouldn't know this, but I believe I have the talent to make beautiful things. I give you my word. I will make something beautiful from your board." Joe took another sip of the liqueur and all excited said, "I want to look at it again. Is that all right, Mr. Tiezzi? I'll be right back, okay?" and was out the back door.

Giordano poured a little more in his and Will's glasses. "Will, you and I must have another toast."

"To Mr. Tiezzi's giant board," Will suggested, raising his new half glass of liqueur.

"As you wish, to Tiezzi's board," and they raised their glasses again. "What do you think your papa will make from it, Will?"

"Dad's made lots of furniture for people—mostly from maple and cherry. He's made reproductions of antique things. You have a great shop, Mr. Tiezzi. Do you make furniture, too?"

"Not so much. We had a sash and door business. Sash is the wooden part of a window, before you put the glass in. Little shops like ours used to make sash for houses, but that is all factory work these days. People said we were pretty good at it, and fast, too. But that is all in the past."

Joe came back from outside, practically floating off the ground with excitement.

"Should we move it now, Mr. Tiezzi?" Joe said, avoiding saying take it or load it up, guessing that this may be a hard moment for the old man—seeing his precious board go out the door.

The three of them, hitching the board along only in short bites, because Will was small, and Giordano old and frail, took forever to drag the board over lawn and asphalt to Joe's truck. Joe was afraid the old man might have a heart attack, so orchestrated a deliberate loading process at the tailgate end of the truck, using ramps of sawhorses and scrap lumber, and enlisting Will as an impediment to any gravitational backsliding. It was a safe, if incremental, struggle that took about twenty minutes. No one got hurt—not even Mr. Tiezzi's board.

Chapter 8
Everything Washed Clean

Giordano had not really done much physical work in loading the board. Even so, all the visiting and toasting exhausted the old man. He was leaning on a sawhorse at the door to his shop, waving goodbye to the nice young man and his son, but the truck that he saw was not Joe Carroll's, but a black 1937 Ford with big round fenders.

How can it be, Giordano wondered, that a memory sixty years old can have such power in an old man's mind. It was like it was yesterday. Carini and his school friend, Domezio, were laughing in the truck's tiny bed. He turned away, then back to the scene again, and Will Carroll was there too, sitting in the back of the truck among Giordano's childhood friends. Above them like a roof was the gigantic mahogany board.

Most of the time, because of the shame, Giordano fought against this memory. Maybe, he thought, maybe now everything will be washed clean. That handsome young Joe Carroll was not even born at the time of the Great War. Now he is going to make something beautiful from the board. He promised me that he would, and I believe him. Will and I even drank a toast. I wish that God had given me such a son. Another small surge of shame; has He not given me enough?

The board is going down the road now. I will let myself remember it one more time, the story of only one day of a long life. Maybe this will be the last time. At last, the big board is gone. I am glad that it is finally gone, so this time I will not fight off the story that vividly replays—the same every time.

All our gang from the neighborhood were going to have a drink to see Carini off to the war. It was 1942. Except for me, Carini was the oldest of our gang. He had quit his job at the boatyard and was keen to fight the Japanese and was going off for his training in the American Navy the very next day. We went to the little corner bar that is gone now. We didn't need a special occasion; we went there all the time. And if Carini was there, you could be sure the next day there would be stories about the fantastic events of the previous night. For the sake of the excitement, I did not need to be there, but on this night, I was there; I was part of it—my brother's farewell.

Carini and I arrived after the others. My brother would always shave his dark beard a second time in one day to go to the bar. And he wore cologne. He kept himself clean and polished, for the girls, he said, but there were not so many girls in this little place, and if there were girls, they were not the nice ones that our mama wanted for us.

Domezio was there and he was smoking a long cigarette. The Camel and Chesterfield posters on the knotty pine walls showed army officers offering cigarettes to one another. The posters said that we should ship cartons of Camels overseas to our friends and that the Chesterfields were good for you. Everyone was helping to fight the war, so Domezio was never without a cig. Picia, the great friend of my life, was standing away from the group, taking it all in. In his dapper pants and French-cuffed shirt he was drinking with us, but we knew that he was preparing himself for something else, something that he thought was better. We loved Picia and it was okay that he had his own plans.

Mazzarelli was short and full of vinegar. He would mimic Carini, not in a bad way, but because Carini was Mazz's hero. My brother was everyone's hero. Our father said that Carini should be in the movies, but it was just talk. We didn't know anyone in the movies, only the people here in Connecticut, and a few relatives of Mama's in Brooklyn.

When Carini and I joined our friends in the barroom, Mazz was standing in the booth, had rolled Domezio's cigarettes up in his sleeve, and was pretending to be looking through a periscope.

Carini, without warning, grabbed Mazz by the belt and pulled him backwards over the booth into his arms. Holding him like a baby he said,

"Very funny, Mazz, but the submarine is not for me. I don't like to be stuck all the time in tight places." We crowded into the small booth, the five good friends, and Mazz said, "Then you will fly on top of the water." It was as though wherever Carini would go, he was going there for all of us, and we knew that, in some way, he would be a hero; he would soar. We all wanted to picture it.

There was one glimpse of life in the Pacific that we knew something about because of the boatyard where Carini worked. Some rich Yankee men had rushed to start up a little factory down by the river. They were making wooden boats that did not look like anything that you would take to a war.

"When the time is right, I will sign up for PT Boat duty," Carini said.

I remember that I was proud that my brother had decided to take Saybrook with him to Japan or some other place that the Navy might send him. "And you will ride in one of the boats from our own town," I said.

"They'll be making many more boats down at the yard," Carini said. "Today we unloaded big piles of mahogany from Honduras—a country down past Mexico. There are boards six feet wide."

Carini exaggerated all the time, but his stories were so wonderful, no one ever questioned him. "Six feet wide, what a tree!" Domezio said.

"Tomorrow they begin to rip them to narrow strips for the planking of the hulls," Carini said.

I must have wanted to see the big boards because for years after, the others always said that Giordano started it all.

Mazzarelli said, "We should get one of those big boards for Giordano." Next thing, everyone was out the door and piling into our father's truck. I remember that Picia had just gotten a new job at the phone company and he didn't want to go with us.

My brother said, "Mazzarelli is right that one board will not be missed." True enough, but they were talking about stealing it and they thought that it was funny, and it was funny because everyone was laughing. Life with Carini Tiezzi: one minute you are sipping a glass of beer and the next you are in a truck with four fellows going off to steal something.

At that time no one lived down by the river. The river was a place of work, not a place to look at the scenery like it is today, so I didn't think that anyone saw us jumping from the roof of the truck over the boatyard fence. Picia was not so sure it was a good idea. "I'll be finished at the phone company," he said.

With some coaxing we got him to the roof of the cab. "Come on Picia, brother and I will catch you." And Picia jumped over the fence into our arms. Carini could make you do crazy things—crazy.

Quickly he led our little band through the night to the lumber recently stacked down by the river. I remember being up on one big stack with my brother; the others guys were on the ground nearby. Beyond them, the glistening, moonlit river lapped on its bank. My brother stretched his open hands out over the big expanse of the pile as to wordlessly tell the size of the top piece.

"Is it the big board?" Domezio asked from below.

"Yes, it surely is," I whispered.

How I loved all those boys. Little Mazz, he and Domezio dead so many years now. Domezio from cancer from the Chesterfield Kings and Mazz from a lousy heart that he did not even know he had.

"Take it, Giordano, save it from the ripsaw," Mazz urged from below. We managed to slide the board off the stack. It is odd all these years later to think that there might have been lots of other pieces just like the one we took. Surely there were. We have known ours so well, cared for it in Papa's old shed, and the others are not whole anymore; they would have been ripped into narrow pieces. Even the boats that they became are mostly gone now.

Four of us got it on our shoulders and slowly started toward the truck. Picia remembers that Carini jumped onto the middle of it as we were walking through the darkness and that he, Picia, nearly dropped his end from the weight of Carini and the board. I remember that there was a lot of groaning and that we rolled it on barrels for a while to get a rest. At one time a torch shined in our direction and we were sure we had been caught. We lay flat on the ground until Carini said that the coast was clear, and then, the board on our backs, we rose up like a giant tortoise.

To reach the truck we had to cross an open area. Carini said that we ran with the board aloft our outstretched arms, but I think it was on our shoulders. Some of us were not so strong. When we got to the fence, Carini and Mazz and Domezio were at the tail end of the board and Carini said that they should let their end down a little and push the front over the fence. When the front was safely leaning, Picia and I worked our way to the back and helped them let the end all the way to the ground.

First Mazz, and then the rest of us, ran up the great ramp—into the air—and right into the back of Papa's truck. Only Carini was left on the wrong side of the fence. All by himself, he lifted the end of the board and with one loud push shoved it almost halfway over the fence. "Giordano, seesaw!" We had already been working together a long time in Papa's shop, so I understood all his funny shortcut ways of talking.

The four of us in the truck all grabbed the front end of the big board. Carini took a few steps back and tossed himself into the air and onto the teetering lever. We threw all of our weight on our end and Carini tumbled down the ramp toward us and into the truck. Somehow, we wrestled the board off of the fence and made our escape. Picia put his face in his hands. Years later he told me that he was crying all the way to our shop. It was a wild and stupid thing we had done, and it was thrilling.

I can feel that thrill right now. Much of sin is that way. It is attractive and exciting at the moment, but leaves us feeling soiled and ashamed. I wish that I had never asked to see the big pieces of mahogany. I am eighty-two years old and tired and I am glad that Joe Carroll and his nice boy have it on their truck now. It is over.

Chapter 9
Carried Away

Is it an illegal load? Joe wondered. I don't think so; it's just a ridiculous load. Joe and Will sat in near darkness under the shadow of Mr. Tiezzi's board. Joe craned forward awkwardly, peering through the tunnel between the truck hood and the board which extended bumper to bumper. Joe could see the whole road, but it felt weird and dangerous.

They had tied it down with miles of hemp rope, no bungee cord job this. Joe wrestled with the four-mile possibilities. I know all the local cops in Saybrook and back in Old Lyme and Lyme, but if the Staties stop us up on I-95 they can think of something if they want to. "License and registration. Thank you, Mr. Carroll. I see you have Giordano Tiezzi's big piece of mahogany. Have you got a receipt for it, Mr. Carroll? Just a formality." Shit, I don't have a receipt. I guess at the time I didn't have the heart to ask for one. I'll need to expense it on my taxes. I'll get a receipt before the IRS audit, Joe thought. I'll drive over and ask him for one, he'll understand; they had receipts in his time, sure. If he's still alive? Hell, I've never been audited in twenty years. Joe again imagined the police questioning. "We strongly suggest you tell us the truth, Mr. Carroll. Did you really pay that much for one piece of wood? What will your wife say?"

Whenever Will went with his dad for lumber in the truck, he knew his job. He had been waiting for his father's question: "How's it riding, son?"

"Okay." Will thought that this was something different. The material overhead looked the same all over and covered everything, so it was hard for Will to find a reference point to watch to see if it was shifting.

"I'm counting on you."

"When was World War II, Dad? That's what he said—that's where the board came from—they had mahogany in their town during the war."

"It ended in 1945," Joe said, but he was not sure.

"So, Mr. Tiezzi had it from before you were even born?"

"And someday, my son, your son, or your son's son, will sell it to some other sucker." Joe was tired now, too. This driving was hard, and there was the matter of the money. "Actually, I think it was a pretty good buy."

"How much did we give him for it?" Will had seen the hundred-dollar bills, but they were in a tight pile.

"A thousand," Joe said, his eyes fixed forward as they started to climb the curvy ramp onto the interstate.

"That's a lot of money for one piece of wood, isn't it?"

"Only if I sit on it for fifty years like they did." There were small gusts of wind, and Joe had a death grip on the steering wheel. "This thing is like a sail. I feel like if we go too fast, we could get carried away."

"My dad, carried away?"

"Don't laugh, do your job. If you can. How many of those blue drinks did you have with Mr. Tiezzi, anyway? That's what they'll nail us for. You're frigging drunk, drunk on Saturday morning before soccer practice. The father driving the truck was fine, but the kid was shit-faced. You should be kicked off your youth soccer team if nothing else. If for no other reason than the safety of the other kids, they can't have drunk kids on the team. Has it moved at all, I'm serious?"

They were up on the bridge now, high up over the Connecticut River, and moving really slow in the righthand lane. "Want me to run alongside the truck and hold on to it?" Will teased.

"Can you believe they had it for fifty years, just sitting out there in that shed? That's pretty weird, isn't it? What's with that?"

"I don't know," Will said. "It's just great that we got to buy it. Is a thousand dollars too much? You're probably right, Dad, there's probably something really wrong with it or somebody else would have bought it by now."

"I'm just a little nervous about the load and your dark humor's not helping." They were quiet till they were safely over the river. "Don't you think I should have bought it?"

"I was just kidding; you knew that." But Will could tell that his dad was tired, and it was all feeling a little less fun now, but they were on local roads and almost home. Will only had two of those blue drinks. No way I'm going to soccer, Will thought to himself. I don't know about the thousand—what they charge for mahogany. "Does Mom know about it?"

"Not yet."

Chapter 10
A New Canvas

Joe's shop was neater and cleaner than Giordano's. There was a vacuum system to carry away sawdust as it was created, so the bright, machined steel beds of his bench tools were pristine. The white walls were bare and oddly unscratched. Mostly, though, the perimeter was huge windows. Joe had read architecture books and had designed a big overhang at the eaves to knock down the hot, direct rays of the sun in summer. All the time the space was flooded with ambient light. That's what an art studio should have, no direct sun, no shadows on your work.

It is funny, the thousands of days when nothing much happens, and others that are packed with important events, passionate meetings and conversations that become iconic chapters in memory. On the morning of this same day, Joe had been with the old man in his vintage 1930s world; he had loved it and had even envied Giordano.

That was a pretty good world, when your father, who knew you better than anyone, could lovingly establish the rules of your professional life and dictate your partnership in a sash and door business with your brother. Giordano and his people had been new in America and it was understood that if they were going to make it, they would have to work hard. Probably because that was so much the way of things then, it made it easier for a man to produce, not having a wife sharing in the family support, not with credit cards and home equity loans to fall back on if he had a lousy month or two. Perhaps the sink or swim imperatives made it easier—simpler, anyway.

Giordano was so beautiful, Joe thought. It was a privilege to be with him—near the end of his life, in his natural environment surrounded by

49

images from his faith, his tools, and artifacts of decades of Tiezzi and Sons toil. Joe wondered why he'd never heard of him, a woodworker in a neighboring town. What a lovely man. Perhaps he'd been refined by a hard life and shaped by God into this gracious and humble work of art, annealed by life's fire. I like that idea, Joe thought, but all the hard-working guys don't end up like Giordano Tiezzi.

Yesterday Joe's shop was empty, all tidy, no projects underway. Now the big mahogany board was here, this ridiculous fragment of another man's story. The board's very existence here in the middle of Joe's shop was at once exciting and disturbing. It is mine now, ours, he thought. Joe went to it as he had lots of times already on this afternoon, spread both hands flat on its fuzzy face. He wanted to take a plane to a patch of it, smooth one square foot that could be sanded to reveal the grain. There will be a time for that soon enough.

Maggie didn't even know about it yet. She was part of everything that he did and now this piece of wood had moved in with them and she hadn't seen it. Will and he were surprising her with supper out in the shop; Joe can't wait for her to get there and catch up with him, catch up with the emotion and the fun of it. So much had happened very quickly and he needed Maggie to be with him.

Will dashed in from outside with a handful of asters from Maggie's garden. "These are the only thing left out there, but there's lots of them, this reddish-pink one and two kinds of purple. They'll be good, right?"

"Get a nice vase for them, and write the note. Mom will be home from Aunt Annie's any minute."

Joe had put three blue place mats on the board that tonight will be a table. He was putting wine glasses at their places—at all three of them. Will was drinking alcohol with Giordano; he may as well have a glass of wine with his mom. It was a special day.

He thought about the board and if the place mats were too formal or too casual, from the board's point of view. Truly, he didn't think that it had a point of view. In high school a favorite English teacher had taught him about anthropomorphizing, when you attribute human characteristics to an inanimate object. This is not in my theology, Joe thought, that the board has life; it was cut down sixty years ago. Even then, before it was sawn down, Joe knew, because he was a woodworker and had studied all about the life of trees, only the outside layer of the tree was actually alive.

This head knowledge did not settle the issue. Mr. Tiezzi's board surely is traumatized, all in just one day, coming out of the dirt-floored shed in Saybrook to the glistening expanse of Joe's shop in Lyme. Would his bright, elegant space ever feel like a shop again? That was a shop, that dusty, cramped, dark outbuilding across the river behind Giordano's house, with its uneven floors and jury-rigged tools and dangerously exposed belts and pulleys. That was a shop.

Maybe the board had come to a studio and wonders why? Now it spanned sawhorses and was set up as a table in the middle of a big, bright room.

Joe scooched it more nearly parallel with the long row of windows on the eastern exposure. It probably hadn't sat in this orientation in sixty years, not since the Tiezzis brought it home during World War II, and now it will bear doilies and crystal and cut flowers—in a studio.

In the kitchen Will printed a message for his mother on a Post-it note: **Mom, come out to shop for a big surprise.** He unwound a long length of masking tape, fastened the note to one end, climbed on a tall stool, and suspended the dangling note from the ceiling in a flypaper arrangement. She'll see that for sure, Will thought, and he scrambled down from the stool and dashed to the shop with the vase of asters.

Will and Joe heard Maggie's car in the driveway. They hustled to predetermined seats at the big table. They knew where she would set her things down in the kitchen. They could picture her looking up at the flypaper note. They lovingly imagined her as she went along with the game, and they knew almost to the second when she would reach the shop door.

She was at the door and was announced by the sweet bounce of the door harp that years ago Joe got in a swap with a woman at a craft fair.

Maggie, so pretty, their wife and mom. She looked in the direction of the big board. "Wow!" Partly she said things, not just now, but most of the time, that were what Joe expected from her. It was the way she went about loving him.

Joe and Will stood up. Will's eyes darted back and forth from father to mother and back again as he tried to sort out their reactions. He wanted his mom to share in the excitement that he had seen in his dad.

"It's unbelievable, Mags."

"Is it one piece?" she asked. Maggie lightly passed her hand over the board. She knew a lot about wood because Joe included her in everything about wood carving. "Of course, it is," she said. "It's still in the rough, right from the mill."

"Five quarters by six feet by fourteen feet." Joe was hoping for a little more excitement, but it was okay because Maggie looked tired.

"Mahogany? Where on earth did you find it?"

Will brightened because the story was all he can think about and she had given them an opening to the fun part, to a glimpse into their great adventure. "We got it from a really nice old man named Giordano over in Saybrook. He had a brother with one leg and the big board was out in a coop in the backyard for fifty years until today when Dad and me bought it. We think it's the biggest piece of wood in the whole United States."

Joe was glad for the hyperbole, and said, "Which would make it worth a lot of money."

"But Dad won't sit on it for sixty years like Giordano did."

Maggie said, "Well, Giordano and his one-legged brother were very foolish men. That's for sure. Whatever you paid, you guys stole it from them—absolutely."

"What do you really think, Mags?" Joe said.

"I think it's incredible. I'm glad you got it."

"I know that when you look at our whole situation, it seems reckless. I want to help you understand what happened."

"I think it's great," she said.

"Thanks, Mags. Will, pour Mom's wine. Will picked you these flowers. The last flowers of summer. I guess you grew them. Will, careful not to spill, it'll go right into the grain and won't come out."

"He thinks I'm going to spill because I've already been drinking today. Mr. Tiezzi made me drink this sweet, blue Italian whiskey stuff out of a little glass. It was for a toast, but we had a couple extras."

Joe pulled out Maggie's chair and got her settled at the table. "Will, get Mom the blanket off the den couch. It's kind of cold out here." Will dashed.

"I'm okay," Maggie said.

"Last week, I found this note about the board. It had been in my sock drawer for a year. I don't know why I kept it in the first place, or why I called about it now, but I did. When I finally got a phone number and called, a really old voice answered, and when I asked for Carini Tiezzi, the name on the note, the guy said, is it about the board, like he'd been waiting for me to call. The whole thing has been strange like that.

"I gave Mr. Tiezzi a thousand dollars for it. I've never done anything like this, Mags."

Will returned from the house with the skinny throw blanket from the couch, and he wrapped his mom up in it and tucked the ends under her legs, and she gave him a kiss.

"Can we celebrate?" Joe asked, and it was not a rhetorical question. "Do I have your approval, my partner, who knows all about me?"

Maggie raised her wine glass, and her boys followed her lead, and they all smiled now.

Joe said, "Remember in college, when we'd go to the bookstore to get a new canvas, or a new sheet of 400 lb. watercolor paper. The 200 lb. would have been fine, but we'd get the expensive, heavy one. Well, back then, I always imagined a painting more beautiful than anything I had ever done. We had a naïve confidence that we could get onto the blank page an image that was in our heads. We'd fall short, but even so, the next time we'd believe it all over again. It's been a long time since I've had that feeling. A gorgeous tabula rasa, Maggie—an unbelievable piece of mahogany. It feels like an opportunity."

"I understand."

"I'm a vain ass, right?" he said.

"You're an artist, so make something great."

That was the whole idea. They were agreed, and it could be a party.

Chapter 11
Our Story and We're Sticking to It

There was a time when Joe enjoyed going to parties around town. When he and Maggie were younger and everything looked like up for them, his youth and good cheer carried him through every situation. But this year, the idea of going to Maggie's office Christmas party had eaten at him for days. It wasn't that he had considered not going; that he would make a polite and enthusiastic appearance for Maggie's sake was his responsibility. He didn't even tell Maggie that he dreaded it. He thought that she probably didn't want to go either.

Just the idea of Ari Pappas calling this annual self-congratulation fest a Christmas Party had given Joe something to argue about alone in his workshop the previous December. Joe told friends that artists and craftsmen who work alone have to have arguments with phantoms, and that in his case, he wins virtually all of them. Sometimes in a social gathering, Joe will recount an entire such quarrel as an entertainment, but this one he has not repeated. What in God's name, literally, does the power elite of this little piece of the Connecticut shoreline, gathering in some greedy lawyer's tacky office to talk about their investments and their vacations, have to do with Christmas—with the birth of Jesus? Are these guys who are supposed to be smart even conscious of the ridiculousness of it all, Joe wonders.

In the days just before Christmas last year, Joe had been working night and day to finish a carved sign for Sloan's, a local seafood restaurant, to have a chunk of cash for gifts for Maggie and Will. He had kindly tried to suggest to the customer that putting a swordfish on the sign probably wasn't the best idea since swordfish weren't common in the Long Island Sound, but he needed the money. He was tired already when he stopped carving the sign to get ready for Ari Pappas' cocktail party.

At that party, Joe found himself briefly in the company of their host, Maggie's boss, Ari Pappas, who had met Joe at least three times and still didn't know who Joe was. The other guys in the circle weren't helping and Joe decided to allude to his woodworking as a sort of hint, since Ari could probably remember that his paralegal Maggie's husband was a wood carver. "I've been in the shop all day finishing a big new sign for Sloan's."

"Christ," Pappas had said. "Have you ever ordered the swordfish in that goddamn place? It's out of this world." So anyway, Jesus had at least been mentioned at the Christmas party, Joe thought later, alone again in his shop. And what about the way those other guys had acted interested in Ari's menu recommendation. What a bunch of suck-ups. Joe thought that he hadn't been too Christmas-y either. Perhaps they wished they were home watching a football game on television, too. After all, Will and I were only there because of Maggie's job; we had to go, maybe some of them had their reasons, too. He'd tried to give them all the benefit of the doubt, making Ari Pappas the only jerk in this mental essay on the meaning of Christmas parties, which he had constructed as he painted the last iridescent details on the big fish's jagged sword.

. . .

The three of them were off to this year's party at the law offices. It was a frigid December night, clear and starry. The village street was beautiful, lined with antique houses, their edges gently softened with old trees and shrubs and black iron fences and a new dusting of snow that made the whole landscape pure and quiet. It is the Christmas season, Joe thought, and it is pretty nice to be here in this village that is our home. It's okay. It's all okay.

There were other people on the sidewalk coming to the party too, and Maggie whispered to Joe and Will, "We don't need to stay long."

Just inside the big, black paneled door, in what had been the center hall of the place when it was a house, Nick and another guy, uncomfortably stuffed into rented, red holiday neckties and vests, were taking coats.

Joe wished that he could sometimes just go with the flow—that he didn't think about things so hard. But now, here he was, right off the bat, confronted with Ari's man Nick. Joe heard one time that Nick had wanted to be a state cop, but had some incident of hot temper in his past that had kept him from being a trooper, so he did odd jobs for Ari Pappas. Does Nick think that Ari Pappas owns him lock, stock, and barrel? Did Nick chafe at all as he squeezed into this ridiculous waiter outfit, Joe wondered.

Joe was not comfortable letting Nick take his coat like a servant, so he made an extra effort to squeeze Nick's hand and wish him Merry Christmas. I'm just a working stiff like you, Nick, was what he wished he could find a way to say. I am a guest at this party, but I am a man who can hang up his own coat.

"You guys are going to have to fend for yourselves. I need to find Cecile for a minute," Maggie told Will and Joe.

"We'll be fine, Mom. Dad can just tell the story about Mr. Tiezzi's board," Will said.

Having Will with him was like bringing one's own team to an alien gathering. "Yeah, well I know what I'd do with a smart aleck kid if this place wasn't crawling with lawyers."

Joe and Will wriggled their way among the throng to Ari Pappas' private office. It was lush with leather, oriental carpets, a fireplace, and gaudy draperies with giant tassels surrounding a big window which opened on the Connecticut River and the distant Long Island Sound. This must be Ari's symbol to himself of his mastery of the law and of this place that he chose to dominate by charging huge sums for work that was not that hard, that was mostly boring, and where he employed smart people like Maggie to do most of it anyway—and then took all the money as though he had done the work. I am not that impressed, Joe thought. I guess that is unkind, Joe corrected his thoughts on the fly. Maybe if Ari had grown up in a different world, in a different family, he would have known about art and philosophy and finer things and would have made a different life, or he might have been a lawyer like Ben Hackett whom Joe met when Ben was dying. The locals said that Hackett thought his legal education and his place at the bar were meant to help people with problems that they couldn't take care of themselves. He had put his brains to the service of others and died with little wealth. Or maybe something would happen and Ari Pappas would just change; you have to keep believing in people—in what God can do with them, Joe told himself.

Joe resolved to fit in at the party and not embarrass Maggie; I will just roll with it all; it's Christmas.

Ari leaned on his huge mahogany partners desk and a group of men hung on his every word. Joe steered Will in the direction of the great man. Ari looked away from the men in the circle around him—right at Joe and Will. "Look out, it's the crazy wood carver who terrorized Linda Howe." Joe was impressed that Ari's dominion on the Connecticut shoreline permitted him a breach of professional ethics, in referring to a phone conversation with a client. He is interested in me, Joe thought, as a human being. The stunt in Howes' kitchen has at least cemented me in Ari Pappas' busy mind. That's something.

"And what is Maggie's husband carving this year?" Ari asked. Will was right, Joe thought, maybe I should just tell the board story again. It was actually a pretty darn good story, and he slid right into the narrative that was getting better with each telling. The interest of the men was piqued by the strangeness of a six-foot wide board.

From the hallway Maggie glimpsed Joe holding forth and she smiled. Teddy Pappas, Ari's nephew and protégé, was at her shoulder.

"So, a year and a half after writing down the guy's name I decide to call. It's starting to look like a wild goose chase, right? I've got a Tiezzi, but on the wrong street, wrong first name. So, I dial. This ancient guy with a thick Italian accent comes to the phone and I say, my name is Joseph Carroll and I am trying to reach a Carini Tiezzi. And he says, 'Is it about the board?'" The assembled listeners gasp and laugh and are hanging on Joe for more of the tale. Will looked up into his father's face with pride.

In the hallway Teddy and Maggie were still watching and Teddy touched her shoulder. She squirmed a little and turned to Teddy with a semi-scowl.

"So, the old man is acting like it is a foregone conclusion that I'm going to give him a thousand bucks for the board, which, bear in mind, I've not even seen. So, he leads us into his backyard to this incredibly rickety shack—"

"He is an artist," Teddy whispered to Maggie. "I can't remember when anyone held Uncle's attention for this long."

"The board is the only thing in the shed and it's on its edge and, I swear, it's wider than I am tall and fourteen feet long."

"And this is one solid piece of mahogany?" Ari asked.

"Yup. It's an inch and a quarter thick, still in the rough. The upshot is I bought it and hope to do something cool with it."

"So Tiezzi—I've seen the sign at that place by the Meineke shop—he had the damn thing for fifty years?" Ari was mad that such a treasure was there under his nose in Saybrook and he didn't buy it himself. They were all on Ari Pappas' turf, his drinks and his canapés, so the other men let him ask all the questions. But Joe had a charisma that was holding its own, and with the gentle sparring there was even a whiff of testosterone in the air. "Ever seen size like that?" Ari asked in Joe's direction.

"No, I've been asking around, but I wouldn't be surprised if it's the largest piece of mahogany in the country. Anyway, that's our story," and Joe, smiling, looked down and tousled his son's hair, "and we're sticking to it, right, Will?" Ari turned from Joe to speak to another of the men, a signal that Joe's control of the floor was over.

Joe and Will were looking about for Maggie, wondering now how much longer she would need to stay, indentured now as an hors d'oeuvres passer at her office's Christmas party.

A man that Joe thought was a real estate agent came up to them. "Nice fish story, Joe Carroll. And how big did you say it was?" Another fellow held his arms wide apart, laughing.

"Yes, I would say that our fisherman has the hook well set." Joe just smiled. He wasn't fishing, just trying to be fun at a party when he would rather be home watching a ballgame.

Will said, "I think that's the best you ever told it, Dad."

Chapter 12
The Trophy Board

On Monday morning Ari Pappas' secretary, Cecile, phoned Joe to say that "Mr. Pappas is on the line," followed by three minutes of Joe listening to dead silence on the other end.

"What was the name of the old guy who had that mahogany board for fifty years?" Pappas asked. Joe had let himself consider the possibility that his wife's rich boss was interested in the board and was glad that the call had actually come.

"Giordano Tiezzi. Giordano and his brother Carini, who's dead—"

"Work something up for me to look at, Joe. We ought to turn Tiezzi's board into a conference room table. We'll get together next week to knock around some ideas," Ari said. "Set something up with my people when you have something." He didn't say goodbye, just hung up.

During the next several days Joe worked long hours on drawings of tables in several traditional styles—some with elegant Queen Anne legs, some with massive turned legs, others with a plain trestle arrangement underneath; all of them had ideas for relief-carved decoration around the edges—some around the edges and in the middle, too.

The shop floor was covered with discarded drawings on yellowed tracing paper that Joe had had on a shelf for fifteen years. He was excited. Something good was happening for him, for him and Maggie and Will.

· · ·

On the following Monday Joe arrived at 10:00 a.m. for his scheduled appointment with Aristotle Pappas. Cecile looked up from stapling together legal briefs in blue covers and said, "Good morning" in a pleasant tone.

"Hi, I'm Joe, Maggie's husband. Ari is expecting me at 10:00."

"Excellent. Mr. Pappas is having a busy morning. Please make yourself comfortable and he'll be with you shortly, I'm sure. I'll tell Mr. Pappas you're here, and it's nice to see you, Joe." Joe sat next to a young man who was fumbling with a pack of Marlboros.

"Too bad we can't smoke in these places anymore, you know?" Joe said.

"Really." The kid was glad that someone had spoken to him. He was probably in trouble and Joe Carroll was good at talking to strangers, sizing them up quickly, in a caring way, and meeting them where they were. Maggie says that he's a people person and it's too bad he's by himself all the time. Joe would like to know what the kid did to need a lawyer and was about to ask him when Cecile came over and invited Joe to wait for Mr. Pappas in the conference room. Yes, Joe thinks, this is like when the doctor moves you into an examining room to make you feel like you are getting closer to actually seeing him.

Joe unrolled several large drawings on the eight-foot, dark pine table that everywhere was marred by ballpoint pen impressions. Almost immediately, Ari Pappas came into the room and shut the door behind him. He was affable, no question about that, and he gave Joe the Pappas killer handshake and thanked him for coming by. "Sorry to keep you, Maggie's better half. Say, what was the name of that family that sat on that goddamn board for fifty years?" He can't remember my name, Joe surmised. So what. The fish has taken the bait, that's the main thing, even if I hadn't baited the hook in the first place.

"No problem—the waiting for you—not when the nineteen-year-old male population of the community has been subjected to a rash of false accusations and police misconduct." Silence, Ari didn't get it. "Tiezzi, two great old Italian guys, Giordano and Carini Tiezzi. It sat in a shed behind their house next to the brake shop since World War II."

"Well, the goddamn thing is finally going to have its day. I want you to build me a beautiful piece of furniture from it. Give me your best work, Chief, but without the histrionics that Lou Howe's wife got."

Joe was having fun with the male repartee. Ari Pappas has sized him up as a man to be reckoned with; he respects me and wants to pay for my talents, Joe thought. He spread the drawings out on the big table. They try to roll themselves back up and Joe, full of confidence now, pulled four law books off the nearby shelves to hold the corners down. "These are my thoughts, sir. I have a favorite here—of these options—which I will only reveal if you ask, but I think they're all pretty good." Joe showed Ari the details of the different base options, all pretty sturdy to support a table top six feet wide and fourteen feet long, and with even greater pleasure, delicate drawings of indigenous oak leaves and ferns, game birds and squirrels. Meticulous shading and crosshatching simulated the play of light and shadow that the relief carving would exact from the dusty old mahogany board. They were beautiful; anybody would say so.

"Terrific, terrific work. But you know what. I'm an ordinary guy. I'm sure Maggie's told you that. No frills. Don't you think that decorating up that gorgeous piece of wood is just, what's the expression, gilding the flower?"

"The lily. No, in all due respect, sir, I don't think so. The carving, if it is beautiful, and it will be beautiful, Mr. Pappas, the carving can enhance the beauty of the board, the grain, the color, and it will be finished in a way that quietly will make it all work as a unified design. I will make you something you'll be proud of, I'm sure of it, sir."

Ari Pappas knew just where he had placed his checkbook and he pulled it from his breast pocket. "You thought this might run thirty thousand, isn't that what you said?"

"Yes, but that was for a table with all the detail, like a hundred hours of carving, I wouldn't—" and Joe stalled as he saw Ari Pappas write 10,000 on the dollar line of a little blue check and 1/3 down on table from Tiezzi's board on the memo line.

Oh, my God, Joe thought. Thirty thousand. He had a feeling of triumph, of pride really. He was spinning. Ari Pappas knew how men responded to money, big amounts of it, and knew that Joe was off balance now, knew it without looking into Joe's eyes. Ari's seen lots of guys under stress; this was all in a day's work. Men are all pretty much the same.

The check is in my shirt pocket now, Joe thought. I'm sure he handed it to me. No, Pappas stuck it in my pocket. "Yes sir, I understand, just plain, that one, Scheme A, the refectory table plan; that's the one I liked, too. Okay, sure. I'll write up a little contract for you, spelling it all out."

"Don't you worry about the contract. My people will take care of that. You just make the goddamn table beautiful. And anyway, I know where you live, Chief—with my legal secretary, right?—and they sort of laugh.

Chapter 13
Gently Move Him

Joe was pretty sure that he'd done the smart thing in taking the ten-thousand-dollar deposit check from Ari Pappas, even without a contract—without any agreement at all describing the scope and detail of the carving that would go into the project. Anyway, what would be the use of a contract with a guy who was his own lawyer and could tie you up indefinitely? That was the main thing for now; *I got the one-third deposit.* Years ago, Joe and Maggie had had an old neighbor who hammered Joe with cautionary tales of the four-flushers, as Bill Trask called them, people who were out to screw guys like him and Joe at every turn. Joe had given Trask the opening he needed when a drop-in customer had come into Joe's shop with a sad broken rocker separated from its rocking chair. Joe had agreed to make the guy a new oak rocker. The guy would bring in the chair and Joe would make it whole, all for twenty dollars. Desperate for the twenty bucks, Joe spent the rest of that day fabricating the new rocker. Turned out the customer was one of Bill Trask's four-flushers, a person who talks big, but doesn't come through. Joe wondered what it was in Trask's experience that caused him to have so grand and powerful a hatred for the kind of person that Joe thought was just a jerk. But the lesson, nevertheless, was firmly implanted. The rocker guy never came back. The finely sanded white oak rocker took on a prominent place in Joe's workshop, a souvenir of the customer who never returned. The archetypal four-flusher.

In his own way, Bill Trask had been the friend who had really rooted for Joe in those first tough years when Joe and Maggie were struggling and had no family or connections around to back them up.

Trask inevitably found himself in ill health and began to plan for the sale of his and Betty's beloved home that they had scrimped and saved to own free and clear. After they unloaded the place for an exorbitant price on some unsuspecting New Yorker (this was Trask's long-held scheme), they were going to move to a condo nearer doctors and hospitals. In the end they scarcely needed them and they both died within six months of moving.

In all the planning for their departure Trask had told Joe that he wanted him to have his rowboat, a beautiful, handmade 14-foot wooden peapod. It was so named because it came to a lovely point at both ends, so much so that you had to stare at the position of the thwarts and the oarlocks to figure out which was the bow and which the stern. "A family living on this cove," Trask had said to Joe, "has got to have a rowboat, and a good heavy, beamy one like mine, to be safe with old women and children aboard when a storm blows up." It had greatly pleased Joe that Trask wanted him to have it, but he enjoyed Trask more than he looked forward to the inheritance, and did not wish for Bill and Betty's leaving.

One day in the springtime, Joe spotted a big new pickup truck with a couple of towheaded kids in the back pulling out of Trask's driveway across the street. About three days later, Trask came into Joe's shop for a rare reverse-direction visit. "You know, Joe, I've been thinking," Trask said. "That peapod of mine, that's a lot of boat for you, garaging it, maintenance, the whole deal."

"It's not a problem, Bill," Joe had said. "I won't let the Sugar Snap (that's what Betty called it) deteriorate on my watch."

"Earl Cooper has a boat for sale right now. It's a dandy aluminum job, perfect for you and Maggie. Flip it upside down in the backyard in the winter, indestructible, no maintenance, and he's selling it cheap. I told Cooper you might be interested."

What had happened was that Trask had fallen head over heels for the Schumachers—father, mother and cute kids who were going to buy his house, and had decided that anybody living in his house could not possibly enjoy life on the Connecticut River without a peapod. They got Sugar Snap, thrown into a package deal with the house, Trask's Troy-Bilt rototiller, and 22-caliber rifle. It was Trask and Trask's need to understand

and control what parts of his world he could. He had spent an angry and fearful life and it was natural and sort of sweet that he wanted, albeit from the grave, to look after the new tenants of his and Betty's beloved home. Joe was a little disappointed, but not mad.

So now, when Joe and Maggie and Will want to go for a row, they walk down to the cove carrying their own life jackets and oars, gear they bought when the inheritance of the rowboat was imminent, and take Sugar Snap out without even asking. They have an open invitation. Maggie implored Joe that he never tell Sarah and Pete Schumacher that the peapod had been promised to them. "It's not their problem."

In the years before Bill and Betty Trask started to fail, Joe often went across the street to sit in their kitchen in the late afternoon. After a second glass of sippin' whiskey, the enemy four-flushers oftentimes turned into "bastards" in the conversation, and Joe understood that in the less gentle era of Bill Trask's heyday, a powerful class of men needed to be warred against almost on a daily basis.

So, even if Joe wasn't much of a hardball player, Trask, from his kitchen table in heaven, looking on the present business deal, must be thinking that his Yankee indoctrination had put Joe in a strong position. Maybe it was the emotional high of the big score in selling the table to Pappas, or the busyness of the Christmas season, or just that pleasure of remembering the old friend that he had loved, and who had loved him. Joe found himself crying. To be sure, good crying.

Ari Pappas was going to get something beautiful, my very best art, all for the thirty thousand that he had already bargained for. That was the thought at the front of Joe's mind almost non-stop since the meeting in the law office. This matter was not settled, Joe would repeat to himself, sometimes right out loud. I'm going to give him more, much more, for the same dollars.

It's not about my pride, Joe thought. It's that the mahogany calls out for my sharp chisels and gouges to work out its beautiful, final destiny. Giordano Tiezzi understood that and understood that he couldn't do it. Carini was dead and would never see it, but Giordano found me, and I found him, and he will see the wonderful table.

Ari Pappas only needed to be persuaded that the table would be just as good, not better, because Pappas hadn't the taste or education to know what he'd be getting, so just as good is the best I can expect, Joe thought. That's where I need to move him, gently move him in the next few weeks, with him thinking that it's all his idea. In the meantime, the building of the base of the table and the laborious hand-planing of the huge board can go forward. There were many weeks of work in all of that. By then, I can get back together with Ari Pappas to work out the details.

Chapter 14
A Great New Year

Joe had to force himself to not phone Maggie at work with his big news. It would be too weird on her end, to hear about the thirty thousand, maybe with Ari Pappas standing right there next to her in the office. So, when Joe saw her at the end of her work day on that Monday, right before New Year's, he told her that he had an understanding in principle with Ari. "It's a done deal, Mags, thirty thousand dollars. Unbelievable. Not that it's not worth it, but we've never seen that kind of money."

The understanding in principle phrase would normally have called for elaboration. Maggie knew that Joe always wished for her understanding the details of his thought processes, and even the way they affected his woodworking business. But on this day Maggie was bushed from her work and only obliquely inquired about the design. Joe would tell her about it in the morning—that was his intention—when they weren't both so tired.

"That's terrific, kid. You did it," she said as she put a bag of groceries on the kitchen counter and gave Joe a hug. Maggie was not thinking about the money; she never thought about the money. She was happy for Joe. He deserved some good fortune. For too many years she had watched him size up each customer, one at a time, trying to guess the exact price that they could afford for a business sign or a piece of furniture, the number that would not drive away the sale they needed to pay an overdue bill. Joe had been scared more than once in the years before she went to work for Ari Pappas. Maggie recalled the time (it was probably several times rolled together as a recurring memory) when the electricity was miraculously saved by a one-third deposit that Joe proudly brought into the house, before the customer's car was even out of their driveway, whooping with hallelujahs that God had rescued them again. "He has always given us everything we need." That's what Joe always said.

But Joe was tired of cutting it so close. He knew that on this eve of a new year, when the oil tank was low because they had phoned the oil company last week to delay the automatic delivery until they could catch up with some things, God had rescued them again; but it was getting old.

Maggie was ashamed to be so sick of the poverty. They both were, knowing as they did that they were better off than most people in human history. Joe's art was what he cared about—after his family; he didn't want to be rich. Even so, she knew what this meant to him and tried to see the money thing as he did.

They weren't like most couples of their generation. One time, Annie reminded Maggie of the reading from Kahlil Gibran that both couples had used at their weddings. "You're forgetting what we believed back then about the pillars of the temple standing apart."

"Sing and dance together and be joyous, but let each one of you be alone," Maggie easily recited.

"Are you alone?" Annie had asked.

So very not alone was Maggie, on that day and now, that the question scarcely even made sense. Annie had said, more than once if in different ways, that Maggie and Joe stood too near together, but Maggie had always responded that she and Joe weren't like everyone else, that she was not diminished by her closeness to Joe, that their unity was what she desired, and that it had worked pretty well for a lot of pretty happy years. And today, they stood as one with a terrific furniture commission that God had given them. Life was good, she thought, as she collapsed into her favorite chintz slip-covered chair, surrounded by her flowers and vines, and accepted the glass of red wine that Joe had poured for her.

Most New Year's Eves Joe and Maggie had been with Dave and Annie, but this year their friends were in Florida with Annie's father and stepmother. Annie called Maggie a few days ago to report the emergency trip to Sarasota where her stepmother might be dying. She had been dying at least two other times that Maggie could remember, but Annie had come home with outfits that Naomi had forced her to accept on shopping trips, after the danger had passed. So, Annie had betrayed her annoyance with her father by relating to Maggie this latest Sarasota report, confident that her extremely thin and elegant stepmother, over-the-top elegant really, was going to survive—again.

This New Year's will be different without their pals, but Joe said they should dress up anyway. Joe thought he looked good in the Bill Blass tux that Maggie found for him at the Salvation Army Thrift Store. The pants were a little short and Joe had to hang them low by the suspenders and cover up the uncomfortable ruse with the cummerbund.

It was close to midnight and Joe went into the den to check on Will, whom he had left with Dick Clark at Times Square. Joe found his boy asleep on the floor close to the TV having popped his favorite movie, *Breaking Away*, into the DVD player. The lead character, Dave, was one of the local boys—the cutters. Their fathers didn't work in the stone quarries and they hardly knew anyone who did anymore, but Dave and his teenage buddies live with a vague hurt over how the college kids see them, condemned to dreary futures cutting rock, futures light years different from those of the privileged frat boys at Indiana University.

"Quantos sera," the movie character, Dave, said as he sat in the grass studying a book of Italian phrases so he could better execute his plan of pretending to be an Italian cyclist in order to woo a pretty Indiana coed.

Joe turned the volume down on the TV, but Will had inherited his father's antennae for somebody messing with his TV show. "I'm watching it, Dad." He gathered his sleepy self to persuade his father that he wasn't all the way out. "I don't know why Dave doesn't just tell that girl who he really is. Dave and Mike and Cyril and Moocher are just as good as those college punks."

"You're a good man, Will Carroll, sticking up for us working stiffs. I hope you won't forget us when you get to college yourself." Will has watched this movie twenty times, many of them with his dad right there in the den with him. And he'd been wearing a cycling cap backwards for the last six months while saving up for a new bike. About a year ago Joe and

Maggie decided that he was old enough to baby-sit and he got lots of jobs, mostly for the same family down the street. There was just Lucy to watch and her parents always came home by ten or ten-thirty.

Joe was proud of Will. He explained to Maggie that "pride is not the right way of putting it, that being proud probably makes it more about what great parents you and I are—producing such a fine son. I'm pretty sure, Mags, that's not what I mean. I mean that I'm happy that he is such a good guy, happy for him that he's not a hideous blight on the community. Can you picture Zander Howe baby-sitting—or doing anything useful— as long as he's under Linda Howe's influence? I wonder who they get to watch Zander when they want to go out. Probably an adult professional from some kind of agency who gets paid a bundle."

"Happy New Year, little cutter," Joe said to Will.

"We're wood cutters, right?" Will said, sitting all the way up now.

"And valiantly holding up our end in the struggle against the rich bastards here on the Gold Coast, but you ought to get to bed—big race tomorrow."

"What big race?"

Joe dropped to his knees on the carpeted den floor and wrapped his son in his arms. "The race down to the bike shop. I've got my half of that Specialized if you've still got yours?" and he carried Will toward his bed.

"Tomorrow's a holiday, dad. They're probably not open."

"You're right. Well, I tried anyway, son? I've got the money. We'll go the next day. It's still vacation, right?"

"No, but we could go after school. That's great."

• • •

Joe and Maggie's living room was pretty, but strangely spare. There were brightly varnished wide pine floorboards, and mismatched sofa and chairs covered with pretty fabrics. The only other piece of furniture in the room was a handmade, shallow maple bookcase affair that dominated the whole wall behind the couch. Joe made it. It had cubbies of varied sizes and shapes and was faced all around with an elegant, dovetailed trim. In the cubbies rested beautiful antique woodworking tools: odd molding planes, spokeshaves, measuring devices, rosewood levels, little folding rules, and all manner of calipers.

Joe knew that the prettiest thing in the room was Maggie. They had gotten dressed up, just for one another, and Maggie was perched on one end of the couch, one foot under her, a shoe in one hand and a champagne glass in the other. She was wearing a little sleeveless dress and earrings and lipstick, a simple formula that Joe thinks only works for certain girls.

Joe removed a little block plane from its cubby in the display case and moved it into another spot occupied by a brass thumb plane. In the vacated spot he placed Ari Pappas' check for $10,000. It was on exhibit. Maggie looked up and sideways to honor the theatre her tuxedoed friend was directing on the wall behind her. He said, "This is going to be a great year, Mags."

"They've all been good years." Maggie wasn't just saying that. They had been good, but the big score with Pappas, especially on New Year's Eve, had Joe a little puffed up. All the past New Year's Eves had melded into one. Dave was always there, Dave and Annie, and when the ball came down in Times Square and the four friends kissed one another and clinked wine glasses with toasts and good wishes, it seemed like this American holiday was about money. That was probably not entirely fair to Dave. It was about prosperity: degrees of prosperity experienced or not experienced during the year just past, prosperity wished for, prosperity stated by Dave as an inevitability for all of them in the year ahead, even if Dave didn't really believe it. Joe had said to Maggie on other years while getting into the monkey suit at eight o'clock for a fashionably late dinner (when he would like to be going to bed), "I hate New Year's Eve."

But this night, in these first few minutes of a new January, he was in the spirit of the thing. "I told him we'd get him his bike—finally."

"Was he excited?"

"Too sleepy, we're going down to the bike shop tomorrow—the day after tomorrow. More importantly, what should I get you?"

"More champagne?" was what immediately came to mind. Truth was though, in the days just ahead, unless the washer broke or something, Maggie didn't want anything.

Joe poured her a new glass of bubbly. None for himself. He didn't like it. "Last year we were all together and, do you remember, Annie started in about Dave spilling his coffee in her SUV, which he only drove on the weekends, and that it was stinky and making weird noises and within a couple weeks she had a new car. You're not like other women. I think you should hint around about something. That sort of thing can be very attractive to a man."

Maggie said, "Actually, that was two years ago. Last year it was that Annie's wristwatch was clunky and ridiculous, but fine really, tells perfect time. That's all she had to say, and it got her a new watch." Maggie laughed and sipped her wine. "Drive inexpensive cars, but own the best house you can afford. Remember? *Life's Little Instruction Book.* We agreed that cars are stupid, didn't we?"

"You're wonderful—cars are stupid." He poured himself a tiny bit of champagne into an already nearly full glass. "It's just something about men. You know how truly pathetic we are; you just refuse to play the game. But occasionally it might make me feel better about myself to have a fragile, needy, waif of a girlfriend. Picture us as characters in a movie: Me, the only thing between you, a fragile, needy creature played by Sissy Spacek, and a total psychological meltdown. You'd be clutching at me for dear life. I'd have to work like a demon to take care of us, coming into the house all the time to check that you hadn't wandered down to the cove in your nightgown, or overdosed on barbiturates. It would be very difficult for me, but satisfying to the male ego, my being the only thing between you and destruction."

"Oh, Joe. Take me in your arms. I'm so cold and afraid, afraid of what tomorrow may bring."

"Ooo, I queued up one of our favorites," and Loudon Wainwright III came on their stereo at one touch from Joe.

"Last year was a fiasco, a real disaster, so full of sorrows,

This year will be a great year; I just can't wait, dear, until tomorrow."

Maggie loved to dance and they had the floor to themselves. She danced with her champagne glass in her hand. Joe tried to take it from her so he could hold her more closely. She decided to play the movie part. "You know I need my little helper. Please don't take it from me, Joe—not just now, baby."

"My, you are so vulnerable. I've got you now, baby, and I've got thirty thousand bucks that'll buy whatever you need to make you happy. Let your great big old man take care of you. It's all going to be all right. And if it comes to it, we can send you off to Betty Ford for a while." Maggie put the glass down and they danced close and with a confident style cultivated in their years of dancing with one another. Not bad, really, if Joe could hold off other thoughts and hear the rhythm of the music.

Joe was thinking about making love with his wife. There had been lots of days when he hadn't felt very powerful, but this was not one of them. He had hung onto his dream of self-reliance, to his dream of making art, and now they were paying him good money for it. He had a beautiful wife and a great son, and he looked damn good in his old tuxedo.

Their bisecting of the living room floor had slowed now and the dance had become more of an embrace. Joe's nose was in Maggie's hair near her forehead and the familiar lyric of the Wainwright song went:

"...it's time to kiss me, this year."

It was perfect, everything was.

Chapter 15
Which Leg

Joe's chance to talk to Aristotle Pappas about the design for the table top had not presented itself, but Joe had gone ahead and bought the sixteen-quarter stock for the table's massive turned legs. It was mid-afternoon and he was busy squaring up smooth, thirty-two-inch lengths in preparation for the prototype first leg. Number one of six. The shop was bright and clean, tidy and spacious.

It was Will's routine to go out to his dad's shop after school, mostly to see Joe, but today, especially to park the new Specialized in a dry place. "Do you think the Japanese guys blew his leg off?" Will said.

"Hi, Daddy, I love you. How's your day been?" Joe responded to the unusual and provocative greeting from his son. "Hey, did you hear the story about the Yale guys that went skiing last weekend in Vermont?"

"You know that I love you. I don't need to keep telling you, Daddy. What's that got to do with—"

"Everything, you'll see, true story, I heard this today from a customer. And I just like hearing you say you love me. These four buddies, all good students, just a little spoiled—like an only child with a brand-new expensive bicycle."

"I paid for half the bike," Will said as he parked it on a wall between a drill press and a bench sander. "What customer? Did Mr. Pappas come over to decide about the table?"

"Different customer. These kids went up to Vermont skiing and on Sunday night there was new snow—I heard a foot or more—and they wanted to ski the new powder, so they blew off Monday classes, which included a history test. They skied till they dropped on Monday and headed back to New Haven in the BMW that one of the boys' dads had given him for a high school graduation present. When they got back to college—Yale—they went in to see their history professor to tell him about the flat tire they'd had on the way home from Vermont and how they had to stay in a motel near Brattleboro and how bad they felt about missing the big test. No problem, the professor told them. Come in at 3:00 this afternoon and you can make it up; it's not long.

"So, the four Yale fellas came over to the history building feeling pretty darn grateful that they were being treated mercifully, and a little guilty, too, I suspect. The prof hands out those blue books that they use for exams in college, which I too attended, but nevertheless chose this career in wood carving, and the prof walks to the front of the class.

'One question, boys. It's written out for you on the first page of your blue books, and, by all means, take your time.' All together, they flipped open the blue book to the words the teacher had written on the first lined page. Which tire?'"

"That actually is pretty funny, only thing is, you haven't talked to anybody who knows anyone who went skiing last weekend. You've been out here all by yourself." Joe looked at a scale drawing of a turned table leg and made marks on the clean, new, square turning stock. Will took Joe's big rafter square from its place on the wall and held the long straight edge against the middle two feet of the width of Mr. Tiezzi's board. "It's not cupped at all. How come?"

"Which leg?" Joe said.

"The big board, why do you think it stayed so straight all these years?"

"You've ruined my whole very funny joke. Which of Giordano's brother's legs did the Japs blow off?"

Will laughed, a small controlled laugh, but an authentic one nonetheless. "That was a pretty long setup for that punch line. I need to go back to Saybrook to see Mr. Tiezzi. Can you take me on the weekend?"

"It's not important, except for the weirdly coincidental connection to the Yale story, but I'm pretty sure it was his left leg, that was left, after the Japs shot the right one off, not the correct one, the righthand one, the righthand leg, not his right hand, but his righthand leg. Not the left looking at the picture, rather the left from the point of view of the victim himself, Giordano's brother. I think the board is flat because mahogany is extremely stable and because it was properly kept up on edge and there was no sun shining on either side."

Will looked down the board and saw a pretty good crack running in from the end, right at the middle of its width. "It's checked though, right?" and Will held the ruled face of the big square along the crack. "A seven and a half inch check," he said loud enough for Joe to hear.

"That's nothing, seven and a half inches. You remembered your lumber lesson. I'm impressed."

"For history, we have to do this oral history thing. We can interview anybody we want."

"Fire away. We may as well start at the beginning. I was born in Armonk, New York, in 1958, the son of William and Ann O'Hearn Carroll. You're not writing any of this down."

"I think they want you to do someone old, and like from a different country—like an immigrant. Can we call him up, maybe tonight? You can come if you want—I mean for the interviewing part. Could we go on Saturday?"

Chapter 16
PT 109

For Will, Saturday morning had taken forever to come around. Joe put on his coat and hat that hung on hooks in their little foyer. "Come on, son, let's go," Joe shouted up the stairs.

"I'm looking on your bureau—for the boat pin," Will shouted back to him. He opened a small mother of pearl box that held Joe's few jewelry items. He poked around a little. There it was. "It's here, Dad. I'm coming. I've got it." It was just as he remembered: a little gold boat, PT 109, a campaign badge from John F. Kennedy's 1960 presidential race. He slipped it into his pocket and darted from the room.

When they were in the cold pickup, buckling up, Will said, "He was really nice to us the other time. Do you think it's okay, going back over there again, like we're his friends? Maybe he just thinks we're the people who bought the big board." Giordano Tiezzi had been in Will's imagination since the day the three met a couple months back. "Do you think it might make him sad or, you know, mad, if I ask him about his brother? Like if it's none of my business."

They were up on the high bridge over the Connecticut River now between Old Lyme and Saybrook. It was half the trip really, the big bridge that Joe always said was just like the one over the Mianus River near Greenwich that collapsed some years back.

Joe said, "If it drops into the river, you know, the whole damn bridge, there's no way we'll drown, which is great because I'm scared to death of drowning."

"Why won't we drown?" Will said, going along.

"The impact will kill us."

"I'm not afraid of drowning," Will said. "I'm afraid of heights, and when we're up here, I look straight forward. I didn't think you could be in America almost your whole life and talk with that thick accent. He's right over there in Saybrook, one town away from us. Can you see his neighborhood from here? I can't look around. I hate it up here. He's been there all my life and a long time before that, too. When do you think his brother died, I guess they both lived over here," Will rambled, coping with excitement and anxiety as Joe's Ford truck began the long, slow downgrade of the second half of the bridge. "Over here, in Saybrook, all his life, talking like that, working in that old shop, all his life."

"And not doing anything with the giant board," Joe completed Will's nervous non-sequiturs.

"Are you going to tell him about the job for Mr. Pappas?" Will asked.

"No, there's nothing to tell yet, you know, the details of the carving, I'd rather wait, maybe even wait till it's done. Anyway, I'm not coming in with you. This is your deal. You and Mr. Tiezzi will be fine without me." Will was still looking straight ahead, and smiling, smiling about being with Mr. Tiezzi in his odd world on the Saybrook side of the river. "Probably don't even say that we sold the table to Pappas. We told him we were going to do something fabulous, which we are, but what if he knows Pappas? Almost everybody around here knows something about Pappas, usually the main thing about Pappas, which is that he's a jerk. We should probably wait for it to be finished and show it to him then."

· · ·

Giordano had said that ten o'clock was good and to come right into the shop, that he would be waiting for them, but no liquor this time, because it was before dinner, which Joe explained to Will, was what these old-worldly types say when they mean lunch.

They found Mr. Tiezzi's house and shop easily and pulled past the house into the blacktopped space at the front of the shop, dirt-covered now with dead grass coming everywhere through cracks in the paving. From his high, slippery vinyl seat in the Ford, Will slid to the terra firma of Mr. Tiezzi's world, a little anxious and clutching a spiral notebook. "Good luck, son. Do a good job. I love you," Joe said and he was off.

The old wooden door into Giordano's shop stuck. Will saw that the rails and stiles had pulled apart, that the panels were sagging, but it finally opened with loud rubbing noises. The place was as Will remembered—old and strange. There was soft music playing. It was like opera music; a man was singing in Italian. There was one light on in the whole place, a round one on the ceiling of a little closed off space to the right of the entry door. "Mr. Tiezzi. Mr. Tiezzi, it's Will Carroll." Will was a little scared.

He approached the small space and saw that it was sealed off from the rest of the shop by an accordion folding door. The old man was in there, slumped in a big red leather chair. Will had never seen a dead person. No, he's probably not dead; he's not blue, or gray, or with his eyes wide open staring off into space, Will thought. He's asleep. The old man had just fallen asleep in the red chair. In front of Giordano, on an elaborate console that had an old black telephone receiver built into it and a flat writing surface, there were bottles of pills. Of course, a guy as old as Mr. Tiezzi took pills, maybe took pills for lots of things. Anyway, Will thought, I can't just turn around and leave, whether he's dead or sleeping. Dad won't be back to pick me up for an hour.

Will slowly pulled the handle on the folding door and worked the accordion arrangement to the right. "Ah!" Will exclaimed not too loud, but startled when the overhead light automatically went out at the opening of the door. The whole shop was in half darkness.

A voice said, "Is that you, Will Carroll? You have found the old man asleep in a phone booth. I am sorry. How do you like it? It was a gift to us, many years ago, from my great friend Picia. I must tell you about my friend Picia. He was a big shot at the phone company, and he said that if my brother was to run a big business, he needed to have a quiet place to talk on the telephone. We built this thing from two real phone booths that Picia delivered here. We put the red chair in before we hung the doors. Sometimes I come out here by myself. There is no one else, and I sit in this chair. And fall asleep—waiting for a nice young friend to visit."

"It's so cool. It's a phone booth, but you don't need money to make a call, right? Oh, the lights, when I opened the door, it turned off the only light in the shop." Giordano rose from the red chair, eased himself down the one step from the booth to the shop floor, and walked in darkness to a light switch.

"I move slowly, but I can find my way around in the dark. I am very glad to have a visit from you, Will Carroll, so we will treat ourselves to some electricity. Is your papa here?"

"Dad wanted me to do this with you—just us alone. It's sort of school work, he's going to pick me up in about an hour; if we don't need that long, I can, maybe—"

"How can an old man help a smart boy like you with school work?" Giordano asked.

"In my history class—with Harding—Mr. Harding, my teacher, we're doing oral history, well, some kids are tape recording, most of them are tape recording, but I'm writing stuff down, and we're calling it, The Immigrant Experience, well, that's what Mr. Harding is calling the whole unit, to learn from old people, not because you're old, but that you have seen a lot of history, a lot of life. So, if you are an immigrant, you'll be great for my part of the project, if you are an immigrant. Dad thinks that you are, that you did come to America from some place else?"

"I don't think that I am an immigrant." Will thought that he had hurt Giordano's feelings. He remembered that his dad said that it was a stupid idea, saying that somebody was an immigrant, making an assumption that this is the defining thing about a man, that he's an immigrant. "I have been in America for 74 years and in this shop for 67 years." Giordano saw that he had rattled the nice boy, a bad start. "I'm sorry. I am an immigrant, of course."

"It's dumb, putting that title on the thing, instead of just talking to people about their life, that's what Dad and I think. I'm sorry, Mr. Tiezzi."

"Your father is a good man—an artist. The Tiezzis are from Tuscany. In our town the people say that an artist is the best thing a man can be. *Vissi de arte*. But mostly the Tiezzis make more wine than art. It is excellent wine."

Will got his pad opened to a clean page. "I'm just going to write down what you say, the most important parts, is that okay, Mr. Tiezzi? I'd like to put that part down, about the art—and the wine."

"Please. You may write down whatever the old immigrant says. I will answer all of your questions. Just don't let them send me back." And the old man gave Will a sweet, wry smile.

Will was beginning to understand Giordano's sense of humor. "When did you come to this country?"

"We came to New York City in 1928—Mama and Papa and my brother and me. I was 10 and Carini was 8."

Will put his pencil in his teeth and reached into his pocket. "Did you ever see one of these?"

Giordano took the little gold badge from Will. He was quiet. He smiled the beautiful, gentle smile that Will and Joe had stored in their memories of the day they first came to this place, the day the crazy thing happened, of seeing the six-foot-wide board, of being able to buy it from the old man, of paying money, but of believing that they had received a gift. Will had seen a change in his dad, something that had made his dad happy, as though some part of Giordano's spirit had come into their family—from Giordano's family, the Tiezzis. Will was okay; it was like he thought it would be, being with Mr. Tiezzi, even if he was a little afraid.

"Not for many, many years." Giordano walked over to a rack of lumber scraps and pulled from under a dusty stack a foot and a half long pine carving of a PT boat, identical to the one in the campaign button. "I started to make this in 1960. I was not so good at carving, not like your papa. So, you remembered about Carini and the PT boat?"

"The picture of the guys. Dad and I saw the picture of the guys, and you told us." Will looked in the direction of the framed photograph on the shop wall.

"Do you want to ask me about the leg?"

"Is that one your brother, the one with the leg that's hurt?"

"We didn't think of it as hurt, but gone." Will was thinking that he should have begun the interview a nicer way, not going right to the missing leg of the dead brother, but Giordano was not angry, more like happy sad.

"Carini Tiezzi, my brother whom I loved. Carini, like President Kennedy, was a hero in the war with the Japanese." Will wrote that part down, about President Kennedy and Giordano's brother. Mr. Harding loved that stuff—when you tied the oral history in with other stuff from school books.

"Carini left me and our papa alone in this shop in 1942. Every day for three years we talked about Carini, and we were afraid for him. The Japanese had attacked America at Pearl Harbor in Hawaii and Carini was trained very fast and soon he and many thousands of boys were in the Pacific Ocean fighting the Japanese. It was like that for most of the boys. One day living in a place like this, your life is your friends and your family, maybe you have never been anywhere, and next thing, you are on the other side of the world."

Fighting the Japanese. Will was writing madly. This was the immigrant experience stuff that he was supposed to get. An immigrant that was a hero like John F. Kennedy. He thought that the other kids wouldn't get anything as good as this.

"We knew that Carini was in a terrible place in the Solomon Islands, you can find the Solomon Islands on a map. Many American men were dying at Guadalcanal and Bougainville and such places that sound nice, but were a horrible nightmare. I will slow down so you can write down those long names. I can spell them, too, even though I am an immigrant. Years ago, I trained myself to spell the names of the places where my brother went in the war."

Will got down the main points and looked up at Giordano who went on. "We received some letters from Carini and we could see that he was not afraid. Our papa said it was good that he was unafraid and we were proud of him, but our mama was angry and would wail and scream at Carini's words, words in his letters that we could only barely read because his writing was so poor. Carini hated school and was poor at reading and writing, but that did not matter because he was brilliant with his hands. Our mama said that Carini was a fool; she screamed it out loud as she read his letters, and that he would not be safe if he was not even afraid."

"I would be afraid, over there, so far from America, fighting in a big war."

"Maybe so, maybe not. Those things we cannot know for sure until the thing really happens," Giordano said.

"When we were little boys, living right here, Carini loved the river and the Long Island Sound. He loved the sea so much that for him, the War was a great adventure. The Great War was that way for lots of the men."

"You never see it in the movies, but in those islands, the Navy men were in the water all the time. And when someone from the PT boat had to go into the sea, they would call for Motor Machinist's Mate Carini Tiezzi. Everyone knew that Tiezzi was happy to go in the water."

"The Patrol Torpedo boats, that's what PT stands for, patrol torpedo, would only move at night to do their sneaky work, and they would go very near the islands occupied by the Japanese. They moved around in very shallow water and many times the boats would get stuck in the coral. Do you know what coral is? We don't have it here."

"Like pretty flowery shells that some sea creatures make," Will said, scribbling madly, leaving big blank spots that he could fill in later.

"Early in 1944 the fighting was going okay for the Americans. Carini had survived many horrible battles which he told us all about in his letters, not even thinking about how Mama would be frightened. He just thought it was exciting to be alive, out there in the Pacific with the other young men. Carini's boat was working in a beautiful place called the Green Islands in the Solomon Sea."

"One night the boat broke anchor in a typhoon and ran aground on the coral reef while the men slept. All the time this happened, the propellers and the little rudders getting stuck in the coral. This time, the little boat was stuck good and it was not funny because the sun was coming up now and they would be exposed to the Japanese planes. Sitting ducks."

Will got that down—sitting ducks.

"On the radio, the skipper had called for a Navy tugboat to pull them free. Sometimes, Carini was able to swim under the boat with a hammer and, little by little, break up the coral all around the little propeller fins. But on this morning, big waves were breaking on the reef, right where the boat was stuck. With each wave the boat tossed wildly. The coral was sharp like a razor."

Sharp like a razor. Will was racing to keep up and still get down the really colorful stuff. Coral sharp like a razor.

"All the men on the PT boat were very nervous. They were stuck there in the bright yellow light of the rising sun. They were thinking, this is how you get killed. What is Carini doing down there? All the other times, he has freed the prop from the coral. All the officers and crew were out on the stern of the boat now, looking over the edge into the shallow water—looking for my brother."

"Always when Carini could no longer hold his breath, which was a long time, he would come to the surface. He would be laughing and sometimes he would have a piece of the pink coral in his hand, showing off his progress, and he would toss it onto the PT boat and say something like, 'Hey, Flynn, send that home to your kids. Tell them that Tiezzi saved you again today.'

"On this day, he came to the surface nearly worn out. He was covered with a thousand small cuts from the coral. A wave would come and wash him clean. Carini liked the danger and even the blood and the stinging of the little wounds. He said that the cuts made him feel alive."

Will had kept his coat on in Giordano's chilly shop, but he looked down at his own hands, the only bare part of himself that he could see. I want to be like that, Will thought. It's not crazy for a guy to want to do hard things—maybe not so hard that you lose your leg. Dad is like that, Will thought, and had thought before. Dad would rather try to do hard things and maybe suffer a little. It was something that Will had thought about himself, that he wanted to do something big with his life. Will didn't think that anybody else told him that, that he had to do something big, and he had never said it out loud to anyone. Why would he? It was an idea just taking shape in his mind.

It had been many years since Giordano last told the story of Carini on the PT boat. He wanted to tell it well—for this boy—and out of respect for Carini. And because he knew the story had its own power, he was forced to tell it slowly, leaving nothing out. "When Carini's hammering did not free the prop, Carini's captain asked the tug officers to help them pull the PT boat off the reef. Men in a small launch slowly brought one end of a long cable to the stern of the PT boat. The commander of the PT boat ordered Tiezzi to hook up the cable."

"And the captain could see that Carini was covered with blood?" Will asked, saying the brother's name for the first time.

Giordano nodded. For him, it was as every time before. Telling this story, conjuring up the images of Carini, it brought Giordano Tiezzi to life. So many times, he has had to face that about himself, that he was a man whose being mostly had shown itself in its connection to another, to his brother. His mama knew it from when her sons were little boys. "God has designed this family to love and rely on one another. It is His plan." But to Giordano, it had always seemed that he was doing the relying, that Carini, though loyal, did not truly need any of them. And so, sometimes, Giordano had felt something like shame. It was a paradox, the great paradox of his life, that in his need for relationship with Carini, he found life.

Today, he was alive again, with a new friend, Will Carroll. Giordano picked up a heavy yellow extension cord from the shop floor and handed one end to Will. In a commanding tone he said, "Here, Carroll, take this end of the cable and go down there."

Will looked up at Giordano as if to say, what, it's an extension cord and the old man said to him, "This is what happened next. You will understand," and he gave Will a little push.

"Go ahead, Carroll, go down there. Tie your end to the table saw, to the PT boat, and climb on the deck."

Giordano picked up the other end of the extension cord lying at his feet. "Carini did as he was ordered, and came to the surface. Carini was about to climb up on the little PT boat. But the Captain of the tug did not wait for a signal from Carini's skipper." Will was on his knees now, acting in Giordano's play. "The tug was underway at half throttle and Carini was still in the water. The PT boat was about to be dragged right over my brother.

Everyone was yelling, "Tiezzi, Tiezzi, get out of there, Tiezzi, quick get up on the table saw, please hurry."

Will was uncertain. He thought Giordano meant for him to actually climb up on the old saw, like it was the PT boat. So, he did it, though the sharp edge of the cast steel tabletop hurt his shins as he struggled to climb up.

"Carini jumped at the transom and was pulling himself aboard, when—" Giordano, now fully lost in the story, with a big, violent, sideways whipping action sent a giant sine wave of yellow extension cord flying toward the table saw. "—the cable snapped."

"Ahhhhhhhhhh!" Will screamed. The wire had not hit him at all. It had whacked hard against the end of the saw and dropped harmlessly to the shop floor.

"The broken cable flew toward my brother. In an instant Carini's leg was cut loose from his body. The leg flew through the air, flew through the air in rolled-up white pants, and bounced for a while on the waves." Giordano was transfixed by the story and did not at first see Will sobbing on his awkward perch on the table saw.

Will looked up, and back toward Giordano, and rubbed his face with a shirtsleeve. Will made a small smile, a sign that he was okay. "And he lived, didn't he, Mr. Tiezzi? Your brother was okay."

Giordano came back to the present moment, to this child whom he barely knew, up on the table saw crying. He dropped the yellow cord and hurried to where Will was hunched, hesitated, and put an arm on Will's shoulder. "God, what have I done? Have I hurt you? Have I hurt you like I hurt him?"

"No, Mr. Tiezzi, no, no. You didn't hurt me at all. I startle real easy. That story—I want to write it all down. Is that okay? That was amazing." And Will climbed down.

"I am so sorry. Can you forgive me, please? I think I hurt you."

"No, I just scare easy. I'm so glad you told me about it. I wanted to know what happened to Carini's leg."

Will was able to retrieve his notebook and pencil and there was more time before Joe would come for him, so Will left two pages empty with a note: **cable snapping story**. And Will wrote down more stuff that Giordano told him about the years after Carini came home from the war.

A spurt of joy and relief jumped in his heart at the familiar sound of his dad's truck outside the shop because it had been hard, exciting like the other time, fun, but hard.

Once in the cab with his dad, Joe said to him, "Did you get what you need?"

"Yeah, it was good."

"What's wrong with your eyes? Your face is all red."

"Nothing, I'm okay. Probably sawdust. That old place is dusty."

Chapter 17
I'd Be a Lawyer

It was a Saturday night; the evening of the same day Will had been with Giordano working on the Immigrant Experience project. Joe was over on his side of the double bed. He held a small radio near his ear to listen to a UConn basketball game. Maggie in a flannel bathrobe sat in a painted wicker chair with books on her lap, law books about contracts and estates.

Joe said, "That's stuff that people who know naturally how to treat one another don't need to go to lawyers for."

"Ari said that if I can do all the paralegal stuff, I may as well go to law school."

"Yeah, then he can still underpay you, but because you're an actual attorney he won't even have to double-check your work. He won't even go to the closings, just take half the money. It's brilliant, really."

"No, he'd actually find that he had been an agent in what would be my liberation from him. I'd eventually go off on my own. I'd be a lawyer, Joe."

"Great, just what the world needs. One more lawyer and one less mom."

"They're not exactly mutually exclusive." She put down her book and looked over at her husband curled up small in their bed. "You know that being a lawyer isn't important to me. It's nothing. I'm just thinking that if I'm out working, I may as well make more money."

That stung. Both Joe and Maggie said that money wasn't important to them, but somehow it had always been a hot button with Joe. He was disappointed, a little ashamed, that he wasn't doing better. The big paycheck for the table had not made everything right. Maybe it was because it was money from the same guy, Ari Pappas, keeping them afloat, Joe thought.

"It's me that needs to make more money so you can be here at home. I need you here, Mags. Will needs you here." Maggie tossed her robe on the chair where she had been sitting and climbed in next to Joe. She nuzzled her face between the shoulder blades of her husband and his radio.

"He's at school," Maggie said.

"Who?"

"Will's at school most of the time I'm at work, and you probably don't really need me at home either. You just get bored here all by yourself and you'd like my company; I understand. Hey, he must have had a great time with your Mr. Tiezzi. He's got pages of notes from his interview."

"Do you think he's okay?" Joe asked, rolling over. "His face was all red when I picked him up—like he'd been crying. Really, red and wet, like tears. I'm serious."

"Did he say anything was wrong? He seems okay now."

"Sawdust, that's what he said—like an allergy. I don't think he should go over there anymore. We don't know anything about this guy. Just because he seems old and sweet, that doesn't mean we should leave our kid with him. He's never had an allergy in his life. I don't like it." Joe rolled back toward the low tones of the radio.

"He's teaching him things," Maggie said.

"We're getting advice from all over."

Chapter 18
The Shop Floor Bleeds Red

Joe's big lathe was turning. Chucked into it was a seven-inch-thick length of mahogany that will be a leg for Ari Pappas' table. At this stage, still crude and out of balance, the turning table leg shook Joe's massive bench and everything on it.

There were about eight inches at the top of the leg, and another five inches near the bottom that were going to stay mostly square. Joe had drawn bold lines in pencil on the square stock. Tightly gripping a long-handled skew, he confidently drove it at the marks that will separate the square portions from the round ones. From then on, it was a fun and easy process to turn the rest of the thing round. It was a little violent at first as Joe brought his widest gouge down to meet the spinning square corners. Sometimes big chunks tore away all at once and even Joe, who had performed this operation dozens of times, was startled. Then, the shaking lessened, the whole thing began to be in balance, and lovely red chips systematically peeled away, flew into the air onto Joe's goggles—flew everywhere.

He was just getting it down to round, down to where the four flat sides of the lumber all disappeared at about the same time. Joe feared that he'd gone a little too deep in one spot. He threw the on/off switch that years ago he had rigged to the lathe's old washing machine motor. From the nearby wall he took down a large pair of wooden calipers that spread to measure the outside dimensions of the round turning stock. Turning was fun, but in the course of Joe's career, there hadn't been very much of it.

The radio was right there and Joe hit some buttons and his old faithful country FM station came on. Lost his girl, lost his dog, pickup truck broke down. All good stuff that soothed his soul.

Next to the radio was the black bench brush that was passed down from a dead uncle. This whole space, it was his world. In the dark he could find the middle toggle on his Superadio that switched it between AM to FM. And the big black brush was right behind the radio—always. He'd spent most of his adult waking hours right here; everything was familiar. Sometimes Joe closed his eyes to reach for a Phillips head screwdriver in the boxes suspended under the overhang of the bench, or for an Allen wrench sticking up out of drilled holes in a thick plank on the windowsill that held all kinds of small drills and widgets. This was his little test of his mastery of the place—a proof that nobody else needed to see. Joe looked at Tiezzi's board. It had been sitting there untouched for weeks while he had worked on the table base, but he will put his hands to it soon. Without looking he picked up the brush and he went right over to the big mahogany board that was completely covered with the fresh, red mahogany chips that had flown there from the lathe.

He took a broad sweep at the piles of red chips, then another, but at the third, the lovely rhythm of the thing was broken. "Oh my God," he said, and then made lots of short, frantic sweeps all over one end of the board. He raced to the other end—made the same frenetic short strokes—then back to the other end.

This can't have happened, Joe thought. The main check on this end of the board, right in the center, had traveled another six inches toward the middle. Is my shop that dry, so much drier than Giordano's stupid shed? No way. But it had happened. That crack was only about seven inches long—that's what Will said—and now it's like a foot. "Oh, my God," Joe said. The other end looked okay, but it could pop too.

It was all fixable. Joe knew that, but he was in a panic. His pride was involved here. Giordano took care of the thing for fifty years and now in mere weeks he'd messed it up.

Joe ran to the house for a pail of warm water from the kitchen sink. What had not sloshed out on his sprint from the house he poured on the shop floor. Moisture. He went for more water and this time poured it over the hot wood stove. Loud popping of water went to an instant boil. A big cloud of steam filled half the room. The mahogany chips mingled with the flood and the cement shop floor bled red.

Oil. Grease it up fast. Joe mixed linseed oil and turpentine in a coffee can and grabbed a big paint brush. He was on his back now, lying in the wine-red mess, slopping the oil on the underside of the table all around the crack. Then the same thing on the other end.

He stood over the crack. I don't think I should oil up the top, he considered. It would make an oily layer right where I'm going to be scraping and sanding to get a new, smooth surface. Humidity in the air, oil on one side, that will stabilize it, and I can fix the check later. What a jackass. It will be all right, he thought, probably it will be all right. He took off his wet chambray shirt and wrung the red water onto the shop floor.

Chapter 19
Let's Get a Drink

Never mind that he and Maggie did the same thing when they were young. But Joe over-thought these church weddings of kids who hadn't darkened the door of a church since they left home for college. They'd been to lots of them. Joe and Maggie have had the discussion and Joe said that Maggie was right, that a lot of our response to faith was really age-appropriate. Maggie had reminded him that it was only after Will was born, when they felt at a loss to meet the tasks of being a family, that they started going to church, that they invited God into their lives. These goofy kids, she in a gown that cost more than Joe's truck, and he the recent product of six years of a fancy undergraduate college, all awkward now in rented tails—they'd respect the sacrament differently someday. Maggie was right. The church muckety-mucks and the lady priest knew that these kids just wanted a fancy church wedding, and that, more importantly, their parents wanted it. In ten years, they may remember that the church loved them when they were young and stupid and they'll come into this fold, or some other fold, perhaps feel a twinge of embarrassment, and move on with their lives. Maggie had said that it was all okay.

Lately, Joe had seemed sort of on edge. These days he was preoccupied with the table for Ari Pappas. Maggie understood that Joe didn't much like the customer, but thought it shouldn't make that much of a difference, once the work started in earnest. She had hoped that the wedding of a neighbor's daughter would be fun for both of them, especially since the ceremony was going to be in the chapel at Trinity College in Hartford, one of Joe's favorite places.

They were standing at the end of one of the long oak pews that faced one another across the nave. Maggie was one seat in from the end and reached across Joe at the waist, took his right hand, and placed it quietly on Teddy Roosevelt's head. The top of every oak pew end had a different three dimensionally carved object or animal or human figure. Maggie's eyes passed over many of the great carvings that filled the church. Joe had brought her to this place twice before and had always been captivated by the carvings that a Connecticut man named Greg Wiggins executed over many decades.

As her part in the ceremony, the lady priest said, "Give them grace, when they hurt each other, to recognize and acknowledge their fault, and to seek each other's forgiveness."

Joe was finding no joy in the ceremony or even in being in this place. "Is it almost over?" he whispered to Maggie.

The priest continued, "Bless them in their work and in their companionship; in their sleeping—"

Maggie was trying to look like she was paying attention to the service, but her attention was on Joe. She held his left hand now, and pointed their joined fingers toward Teddy Roosevelt. "You could do this," she whispered.

When the service concluded and the wedding party had recessed back up the aisle, Joe was in haste to leave, but Maggie lingered in the church among the last guests. She paused at a relief carving of a woman tending a garden. To Joe she said, "It was just an oak board. Now it tells somebody's story. Don't you wonder who she was and what her garden meant to her?" She looked to Joe for his reaction. "Is this the kind of thing you're picturing for Ari's table?"

"More or less."

"You've hardly told me anything about it—what it's going to be?"

"I've been thinking I'd like to surprise you. Would that be fun? Let me get it most of the way done and then we'll talk about it?"

She walked to a panel of a fisherman catching a trout, then a finial of three children singing in a choir. "Aren't you inspired by these? What's the man's name who carved them?"

"Some guy with a robber baron patron with a guilty conscience—Greg Wiggins."

Her response came very easily. "Some guy like Ari Pappas, right? What's new? The Medici, this guy's patron, Ari Pappas? And Michelangelo and Leonardo and Wiggins and Joe Carroll get to do something wonderful." This was the girl she had always been for him.

"Come on, Mags, let's get a drink."

Chapter 20
Kick the Sawhorse

It was a weekday afternoon after school and Will had come out to his dad's shop as soon as he got home.

"Oh, good. I'm glad you're here. Give me a minute to get organized and you can help me move the big board. I've got all the pieces for the base done and I'm ready to start gluing up the bottom deal, but the damn thing is taking up the whole shop."

"Where the hell are we going to put the damn thing, Dad?"

"It's so cool when you swear," Joe said.

"I just want to be like you, Dad. No, really. I don't know what you want me to do. Where are you going to put it?"

"Just let me consolidate some stuff—I was going to say shit, but then you'll repeat it, like maybe in the wrong company—tighten up this stuff over here. Then we're going to put the board up on edge close to the wall." Joe got on his knees and began rearranging and stacking wood scraps and parts of old projects against the wall. "Come on Will, hand me all that stuff and I'll stack it up. We can do this quick if you move your rear end. I'm not swearing in front of kids."

Will was tired. He was making the kind of effort at pitching in that made Joe think he'd be better off by himself. Joe fished three short lengths of two by four lumber from among the scraps, grabbed half a dozen long drywall screws and his yellow cordless screwdriver, and, at intervals, screwed the scraps to exposed ceiling joists so they hung down a couple feet.

Joe said, "We're going to lean the board against these guys so it can stand on edge while I work on the base of the table. Get it?" The giant board was resting on two sawhorses—the kind that have two-by-fours as the bearing surface. "Okay, you take that end."

"Huh?" Will said.

"We'll each take an end and let it down easy. Don't act stupid." Joe placed several scraps of blue Styrofoam insulation in a fourteen-foot row on the floor between where they were standing. "We're going to get the edge of the thing on the Styrofoam so we don't dent it up, but if we miss a couple, it's not really important."

Joe lifted his end off the sawhorse to waist level and looked down the length of the board at Will who was straining to lift his end. Joe shifted his body weight slightly and in one swift and continuous action momentarily stood on one foot and used the other to kick the sawhorse off to the side. "You've got to get your horse out of the way so we can let it down."

"I can hardly lift it, Dad."

"Just kick the horse out with your foot—just like I did."

"Sure," Will responded.

"I just did it, come on!" Will's skinny arms trembled under the strain. He made a weak effort at kicking out the sawhorse. "Come on, son! Give it one hard kick with your right leg!" Will had the board off the sawhorse again and gave the horse another kick, and spun it ninety degrees, but not out of the way. Joe's expression betrayed his annoyance.

Will's strength and grip gave out. His end of Mr. Tiezzi's board suddenly dropped. "Ahhhhhhhhhhhhh!" they both gasped. It had dropped right on the narrow long dimension of Will's sawhorse. Joe saw Will's end literally fold over the sawhorse which had acted like a wedge. The violent crash of the board had broken it virtually in half along its entire length. It held together now only by stringy fibers.

"You let go. You idiot. Oh, my God, Will. Oh, my God."

Chapter 21
The Wounded Monster

It was Friday afternoon now and Will arrived home from school on his bicycle. In the middle of January, Will was the only boy still riding to school on the dark, cold days. He wore his cycling cap backwards like the boys in the movie and was carrying his school backpack over a winter jacket. Maggie's small Japanese car was in the garage, home earlier than usual, and Will took care not to bump it with his bike. Joe had screwed plastic coated bike hooks into studs high on the wall and the skinny arms that dropped one end of the big board yesterday, today strained to get the bike up on the hooks.

"Mom, I'm home," Will shouted at the kitchen door.

"Ciao, Will. How was school? I'm so glad you're home. I miss you."

"Why are you home? It's too early."

"Boss's idea of a long weekend, sending us home two hours early on a Friday," but she was fibbing. Maggie knew what happened in the shop the day before and wanted to be with her guys, so had planned to leave early. Ari wasn't in the office after lunch, so Cecile had said to Maggie, "Just go; I'll tell him something."

So often her spirit had been the lubricant that eased their little family through hard days, and this, she knew, was such a day. Maggie examined her son. He really was changing fast these recent months. She had not thought he was this tall and some of the baby fat was gone from his face. You could see more what he was going to look like as a man. And for a moment she thought she understood why Joe thought Will could manage one end of the board. And she could see that he was glum and listless.

"Dad says it's not a big deal. He's going to fix it and it'll be good as new. Really, sweetie. He's really good at stuff like that."

Will didn't even look at her, he was miserable. Maggie said, "Dad told me that he thinks he yelled at you and called you stupid. He feels terrible about that, Will. Why don't you go out and see him? He wants to say he's sorry. And maybe you can help him. I think he's patching it all up this afternoon."

Will gazed at his mom now with a cocked head and questioning look that said, yeah, sure. He put his backpack down near the kitchen table. "Okay, I'll go out there."

Will knew that it really was his fault that he dropped the board and it broke right in half. The only thing worse was if I'm chicken to go out there and face up to it. He slunk the short distance from the kitchen door to the shop. I am an ass, he thought, or, I was an ass yesterday anyway. He felt like suffering over the thing a while longer—not just going out there and hearing his dad's apology. Maybe Dad pushed me to do something I couldn't do, but I could have just told him, no, Dad, I'm not strong enough to hold the weight of the thing and move the sawhorse at the same time. How hard would that have been, just to have said, I can't do it, Will thought.

There were long windows along one wall of the shop and on the outside Will crouched to the side of one of them in dirty leaves and old granular snow. It was nearly dark and Joe had thrown on overhead fluorescent lights. I'm sorry, Daddy. That was all that Will was thinking as he perched there, not even aware of the coming of damp, cold evening.

The wounded monster was lying flat on the shop floor, pretty much where it came to rest the day before. Joe had slipped thick scraps of wood under both ends of the board and had it about six inches off the ground. Narrow pieces of oak had been cut in length to the width of Tiezzi's board, four of them, two positioned at each end. Will watched intently, not sure what this maneuver would look like. He was cramping up, too long in the crouch, and decided to just sit on the cold ground. Joe slipped one oak scrap under the wounded tabletop and lined another up with it on the top. Then with big steel C-clamps at each end he made a sandwich of the whole assembly, the oak boards acting as a splint. The process was repeated at the other end. Joe went to the middle of one side of the board—tested the weight of the assembled disaster. Will was thinking: should I go in there now and help him lift it up on its edge? Oh yeah, he'd be real happy to have big strong me there. Maybe I could lift one end and Dad the other. No, Will decided.

Joe thought nothing of doing this alone, like he should have done yesterday. It would have taken him about five minutes longer by himself—probably not even that—and he would have saved himself a half a day of work and, more importantly, the hurt feelings of his son. My beautiful son. What's wrong with me? What's wrong with a man who could come out with something so angry and mean? Was that the real me—the unfiltered true me that came out in an unguarded moment?

One quick exertion— "Ahhh" —too high a pitch to have risen from his own throat, and he hoisted the mahogany, oak, and steel sandwich up on edge.

That human exclamation was not his; it came from outdoors. Right now, his attention was on making certain the board sat still for a few minutes while he readied the sawhorses for the next move. The board had actually hit the little temporary braces screwed to the ceiling joists he had put in place yesterday. Joe knew whom he had heard, that it was Will in the yard.

Joe went to the shop door, opened it part way, and yelled, "Hey, Will. I need you, are you out there?" Nonchalant, matter of fact, he stepped away from the doorway, so as to not be in Will's face when he first appeared. Joe thought maybe he could take some of the edge off the thing for Will. No big deal; we'll just fix it. That's why God invented glue.

And Will did come through the door, red-faced from crying, cold and tired from crouching in the damp at the end of a long day. "I'm so sorry about what happened," he said. "I could have just told you it was too heavy and you'd have tried something different."

"I know it seems like a big deal, Mr. Tiezzi's fabulous board broken in half. I'm kidding—making it worse. No, really. I was foolish to make you do something that you're not strong enough for yet. Then I was mean to you when you failed. That is so bad. Please let's forget about it. Let's just move on. I think we've both done the same thing; it's like we've given the board too much power—like everything that happens with it and with us—on this whole job, just gets exaggerated, the ante upped somehow. Let's just get it back up on the horses—isn't that what you do after a fall, just get back on the horse?"

"Can you really fix it though?"

"Absolutely, piece of cake—and the whole damn table will be done in just a few weeks."

"Really? That fast?" Will said.

Joe scooted the sawhorses into new positions, threw blankets over them for padding, and went back to the middle of the board. "Okay, this is going to be easy and your father is going to be more patient than yesterday." Joe pulled the weight of the thing onto himself, got it to shoulder level, and said to Will, "Okay, the horses are about right, but I'm going to let this down a little further, like almost to my waist and I'll hold it while you get the horses both hard up against it. So, they're going to run just parallel with the length of the board, in line with one another and as near the middle as you can figure. At first, they'll be running the wrong way, just so we can teeter-totter the board onto them, and then when the weight is on them, we'll swing 'em around."

"I understand; I'm good," Will said.

They did all that, without a hitch. The broken board sandwich was at rest on the sawhorses again. Then Joe told Will, "Come over here where I am, hold the edge of the table with both hands, kind of lean your weight on this side of it—don't worry,

I'm staying with you till we see that it will work, then I'm going underneath to swing the horses around ninety degrees. Will came to his dad's side, Joe hitched over a bit, and watched as Will slowly rested his weight on the edge of the slightly teetering board. Will had all the weight by himself now. He was back on the horse, and Joe leaned over and kissed him firmly on the top of his head. "I love you, kid. You are a fabulous boy and you are going to be a great man. Thank you for your help."

As if he'd almost forgotten the task at hand, he exclaimed, "Oh," and dashed underneath and yanked the horses into their final positions.

During the next few hours Joe fussed with the repair of the tabletop. None of it was rocket science. There was lots of trial clamping with big bar clamps to see where the two pieces could be pulled back perfectly against one another, and discovery of spots where splinters and torn fibers needed to be delicately cut away before gluing. Joe knew that he could take less care with the underside, err on the side of planing off a little extra of the splintery stuff, the top being the part that counted.

It couldn't all be done in one shot. On this first night he would get the two halves of the table trimmed up, glued and clamped, and then, in a couple of days he would belt sand the whole length of the surgery, even drive some skinny, gluey wedges of mahogany into any voids, especially the checks that were already there on both ends. Little bit of filler here and there. Pretty good. Everything important patched up.

Chapter 22
I Have a Leg

Maggie smiles to herself when she finds Joe wide-awake doing absolutely nothing, like now, propped up on the bed, not a book in his hand, not praying, not listening to the radio; and if she were to ask, she knew that he would say he was fine. It was a guy thing that Robert Bly years back reassured Joe was in his genes from countless generations of ancestors sitting silently for hours in duck blinds, waiting for the ducks to come along. Maggie came into their little room from the shower, wet hair, their one decent big towel wound around her.

Joe figured it was a girl thing, the way she so easily distinguished her lovely, womanly nakedness from this nakedness of washing up at the start of a day. She was immodest and unself-conscious as she put on underwear, blue jeans and her favorite sweater—a big, loose, nubby, purple turtleneck. He would like to intrude on the freshness of her day's beginning. His solitary duckless musings had not landed on much purpose for his morning. He resolved to leave her alone, but it was hard, there being no book or newspaper at hand for a prop, there being just fully dressed him on his bed on a Saturday morning.

Maggie said, "Did Will tell you that he wants to go see Mr. Tiezzi? He's already phoned him." It was plain to Joe things were happening around him, without him, and that he was going to be alone today. He scrunched his eyes and the corners of his mouth to speak surprise and disapproval. Maggie said, "I can do some of my errands. I'll just drop him at the shop for an hour. It's okay, I really don't mind."

"He already finished that interview thing for school. Why go over there? Isn't it all a little strange, him hanging out with that old man?" Joe said.

"It is odd. It is. They're not exactly hanging out. But it's sweet, and it's actually what you believe in. You've probably told him that young people should be learning from the old folks—like on the Waltons—and now he's doing it. He'll be fine. He has a great time over there."

"An hour, I guess you're right—just an hour. I was going to take him to the lumberyard with me, but I'll go by myself. Pay attention to his eyes when you pick him up. Remember his eyes last time?"

"It'll be fine," she said.

•   •   •   •

Davis Lumber, the place where Joe shone—or like the Bible said, let his light out from under the bushel. He always had his eye out for friends, some of them tradesmen from the area that he might only see here at Davis's, but it had been a lot of years and truly they were his friends. And he hoped that he was a small blessing to some of them, too. Joe Carroll, a college educated guy who worked with his hands, struggled like them to make a living, and treated everybody with respect. But today Joe had his head kind of down, just grabbing the few boards he needed for a repair.

"Hey, Maestro, how goes the destruction of the rainforest?" Gary, the yard worker shouted, startling Joe.

"I'm sorry. What's that, Gary?"

"The big mahogany—the table job?"

"Good, it's going good, Gary. Looks like we'll have food on the table a while longer," and Joe forced a smile.

Inside Joe was poking around the glues and fillers on the shelves of the little hardware section that adjoined the checkout.

"How goes the artistry on my mahogany?" It was Jimmy Newhouse, the big loveable man who tipped Joe off to Tiezzi's board in the first place. Gosh, everyone's so interested in the table, Joe thought. Maybe Pappas has been talking about it, like bragging that he'd hired Joe Carroll for the biggest job of Joe Carroll's pathetic life and basically owned him, lock, stock and barrel. To Ari Pappas, it was rather inevitable, wasn't it, that he'd get it. Who did these locals think would end up with the big mahogany board but Joe Carroll's wife's rich boss? It wouldn't be unusual even for the details of the deal to be fodder for gossip in Old Lyme.

"How's that?" Joe responded.

"My giant mahogany board. You haven't frigged it up, have you Joe? I shouldn't have told you about it. Probably should have bought it myself and sold it to one of those fancy wood carvers out on Cape Cod," Jimmy said.

"Yeah, Jimmy. I understand your concern. A treasure like that in the hands of a local hack." Joe was smiling now. He couldn't help it; just being in Jimmy Newhouse's presence made everybody smile. "It's actually fine, Jimmy. Going good. Has Ari Pappas been talking about it—telling everybody my business?"

"Just says you stuck him real good for it. And everybody around here's glad you did. The guy's an asshole. Hey, can I get you a cup of coffee? Made only four hours ago." Jimmy tallied up Joe's small purchases on the computer, sent the file to the big printer behind him, and tore off the triplicate paperwork for Joe's signature.

"Can't this morning, but it is very generous of you. Generous of you and your employers, you know, the fresh coffee and the Styrofoam cup and the generic non-dairy creamer and all. I'll take a rain check. You off at noon, Jimmy?" Jimmy nodded. "Good. Have a nice rest of the weekend. And Jimmy, I really am grateful to you about the board." As Joe walked to his truck, the idea came to him to make a gift of some cash to Jimmy Newhouse when the whole thing was done. He wondered why he hadn't thought of it before; it was a fun idea. A couple hundred bucks out of thirty thousand. Maggie would like it too, and Joe knew that it would really happen because when he decided something like this, he always followed through.

"Just make sure he's in there and give me a wave," Maggie said as she and Will came to a stop in Giordano's drive. Will saw that there was a light on and he heard a low machine sound; he waved his mom on her way

105

without turning around. He cannot now come to this door without a small surge of awe and fear. Only good things had ever happened here, but then even the good stuff had left him thrilled—and exhausted. Will had been thinking on the ride here with his mom that he had never had a secret from her and Dad. It's not that I am doing anything wrong, it's that I have this friend who's old and kind of magical and is sort of separate from them. Like today, I don't have any special reason to see him. I just want to be with him. I wonder what Mom thinks. She trusted me all the time and didn't ask me about it, just brought me over here, but she and Dad probably think I'm acting strange, which I am.

Will had been told to just knock and come in, come in and find the old guy, like maybe asleep in the phone booth-office thing, or maybe even dead. But today was less creepy because there was an electric motor humming; it was over at Giordano's lathe. Little chips were flying, just like from his dad's big lathe, and there was a skinny spindle about sixteen inches long chucked in. It could be a piece of a chair or a stool. Giordano threw a switch that stopped the pulleys. "Look at the sad little things the old immigrant is making and your papa is making the great masterpiece from the giant board that sat in Tiezzi's shed for fifty years," the old man said.

"Hi, Mr. Tiezzi. Mom dropped me off. She'll be back probably in forty-five minutes, maybe an hour. Is that okay?" The old man smiled and nodded. "What are you making?" Will asked.

"I will spend about four hours today making a part to replace a broken stretcher from a chair bought at a yard sale that I do not need. There is already too much furniture in my little house and you can barely move from room to room. I don't often throw anything out. We old people get like that. These are the economies of Tiezzi and Sons Woodworking these days. Is your papa making progress?"

"Uh huh, it's going okay. I think turning on the lathe is really cool, but Dad says it can be dangerous, not for the person so much, more for the thing you're making. You can wreck a turning pretty easy if you don't know what you're doing—really mess things up."

"You must invite me to see the finished product. I am anxious to see the table you men make from the great board." Will was quiet. "Or maybe other things will come up and your papa will need to set it aside for a while. I understand how these things go." There was a long silence.

Giordano continued. "Sanding on the lathe is not."

"I'm sorry, Mr. Tiezzi," Will said. "Not what?"

"Dangerous. Sanding a turning while it spins is a lovely thing and is only dangerous if the old man is lazy and has left the tool rest in place and he spins his fingers into this space." He pointed to the gap that was variously an eighth of an inch to three-quarters of an inch wide between the turning spindle and the tool rest. "Yes, I have done that many times. It hurts a lot and makes a black and blue fingernail, but you will not lose the finger. You will get blood on the project, but that is not a big deal. Not like really messing up an important job."

"What about that, Mr. Tiezzi, what you just said, messing up an important job? Did you ever mess up something really important?"

Giordano was quiet for a moment and then said, "Yes, I did one time, many years ago."

Will was straining to ask the question a different way. "You did? That's what I've been thinking about, Mr. Tiezzi, like what do you do if somebody close to you really messes up?"

"Grab that medium grit paper and come over here, I'll show you how to do the fun part that cannot be messed up. Get up here on my stool." Giordano stood beside him and demonstrated a gentle pressure of the sandpaper to the turning wood. He took Will's hand and led it to an urn shaped place in the turning. He pressed gently on Will's fingers. "See the dust fly." Will smiled softly. It was the magic again; it was why he had come.

"Forgive him," Giordano said. "Nice and easy. Fold the sandpaper to make a sharp edge to sneak into the narrow places. You really cannot go wrong."

Will looked away from the work just long enough to see into the old man's eyes. Him...forgive him. Does Mr. Tiezzi know that I am asking about a real person? Does he know who I am asking about? Will wondered.

"Maybe we have time for me to tell you about how very many years ago Giordano Tiezzi, as you say, really messed up."

"I like your stories. There's plenty of time, sure," Will replied.

"When I was your age, and even older than that, I was always better when Carini was around. It was always that way and I knew that about myself from when I was very young."

"I don't think that's a bad thing."

"It was a weakness, my weakness, that I needed him so." Giordano was gazing out through a sawdust-covered little window right behind the lathe. "One day, in 1945, after the war was over and all the boys—all the living ones—had come home, Carini and I were working right here in this shop. I remember it very well because on that day my brother gave me the biggest gift that I ever received from another human being.

"I was standing here at this machine making some small part just like we are today. Carini was singing loudly and his voice was drowned out by the deep, low whirring sound of the thickness planer. My brother did not sing very well and he would often sing while machines were running. He said that in his own head he thought that he sounded very good—like Frank Sinatra. He had a beautiful head of black hair and a thin moustache that made him very dangerous looking.

"On this day I had been trying to get the courage to tell something to Carini that had weighed on my heart for a long time. So, when he had finished pushing a great stack of rough boards through the planer, had turned it off and came hopping around the machine toward me, I turned off this little motor. 'Rest a minute, Carini; I want to tell you something.' There was a big new pile of shavings, right over there, and Carini playfully fell backwards, right into the fluffy pile. I said to my brother, 'I am to blame that you have no leg.' So, what did he do? He stuck his one whole leg up in the air and said, 'What is this? I have a leg.'

I said, 'Listen to me and see if for a minute you can stop making jokes. Around the time of your accident, I was praying every day that you would come home. I missed you like crazy and I was doing lousy work here in our business. So, God gave me what I asked. You were nearly killed and they sent you home.'

So, this is what my brother did. He just lay there in the pile of sawdust and gave me this huge loving smile. He said that having one leg in some ways was fun, and that it was not my fault, that it was the fault of a jackass named Dwyer on the tugboat."

"Do you think it was Dwyer?"

"I think it was Giordano Tiezzi, but my brother had forgiven me. We were together here for fifty more years. He had a lot of pain—arthritis in all his limbs made worse by having one leg—and there were many things he couldn't do. But he never spoke of it again and he never tried to make me feel bad. Not a single time."

Giordano switched the lathe back on. "Go ahead, you do it. You are doing very well, a quick learner," the old man said.

Chapter 23
Still Doing your Art

It was an unusually warm evening in late March and Joe and Maggie were expecting Dave and Annie for supper. Just the four of them, which was the way they all said they liked it best. Joe and Maggie had showered and were most of the way dressed. Maggie fussed with buttons to her blouse that were small and up the back and asked Joe for help, a task she knew he would accept willingly.

"We still have fun with them," Maggie said. Joe was a little slow in approaching the task because he had reached for his bureau drawer and grabbed a small pink package. Joe's hair was wet and he was shirtless as he threw both arms around Maggie at chest height.

"Yeah, we do." He put the package in her hands. "Because you still look like you did when we were in college and it just makes the other three of us feel young and alive to hang out with you."

Joe shifted his grip to waist level to free Maggie's hands to open the package. There was no real unwrapping. She just pushed the stretchy ribbon off the corners, snuck a peak at the little nightgown in the box, and set it down gently on her dresser.

"Oooo. This'll keep your favorite catalogs coming for a few more years." She turned around, smiling, and kissed him on the cheek. "They're going to be here soon and I've got lots to do. Hurry up and get dressed so you can help."

"I'll be right down, but next time couldn't we just pretend that we've invited them, get all pretty and dressed up, and see if we can enjoy a smaller party. It would be my preference."

In the living room Maggie picked up Joe's big, stiff Carhartt barn coat from the sofa, which was centered under Joe's display of small antique tools. She gathered into one pile all the woodworking catalogues and magazines from Brookstone, Minnesota Woodworkers, Fine Woodworking, Woodcraft Supply that lie around the room. In the kitchen bay window Maggie's prize gardenia plant had produced one mature bloom and she cut it and floated it in a glass bowl, which she placed at the center of the dining table. The dining table was made from a barn or shed door of well-weathered gray wood. At one end, centered in the middle, there was a small glass window. It was comical—a table made from a door— and it suited Maggie's spare, arty style.

There was a short horn blast in the yard. Joe pulled on a blue cotton shirt and walked to the bedroom window that overlooked the front driveway. He saw that Dave and Annie had arrived in a highly polished, black Mercedes Benz that he had not seen before. "Oh, man, look at that thing." He walked a few steps from the bedroom to the top of the stairs. In the kitchen Maggie stood on tiptoes on a stool reaching for the good wine glasses. "I'll be right down, Mags. I hope your friends don't arrive in an outrageously expensive German car."

Annie and Dave knocked and came right in. Maggie greeted them and took their coats and hats as Joe shouted from upstairs. "Honey, I think the Goebbelses have arrived."

Dave, in an expensive banded collar shirt, looked up in the direction of the wisecrack. Even if this allusion to the Nazis was unexpected and a little much, especially since Annie was Jewish, Dave was well accustomed to Joe's edgy banter and it was something about Joe that made him interesting, set him apart from the buttoned-down local society. He said loud for Joe's benefit, "I guess to an artist, all PR guys look alike—and by the way, the car's used."

Maggie poured white wine for them both, an ice cube in Annie's, grabbed her own glass of red, and herded them to the living room where some cheese and crackers and raw vegetables and dip had already been put out. Annie was in a chair and Maggie and Dave were practically cuddling on the couch. They were intimates all, comfortable with one another and almost always loved their time together.

"Where's Ole Will?" Dave asked. Annie had remarked very matter-of-factly when Will was about five or six that he was an "old soul." There had been a lot of talk about how humans degraded or perfected their souls over a lifetime and, after they were dead, incarnated as somebody new. Joe had conceded the possibility, partly because the intimation that his son was a highly evolved soul was a compliment, and because his reading of the Bible didn't rule out reincarnation, but he didn't think he believed in it.

"Sleeping over at Jack Brennan's," Maggie answered.

Joe entered the room with more wise guy stuff. "At Dave's office they've just completed a new sales contest. 1st prize was a Mercedes Benz. Anybody want to see 2nd prize? 2nd prize is a set of steak knives."

Annie played along with the *Glengarry, Glenross* parody that they'd all engaged in before. They remembered that the cruel burning out of the Jack Lemmon character, not to mention Joe's own father and other men Joe had known, was part of Joe's motivation to have his own business—be his own boss. "My Dave is a closer. What you need is some new leads. You can't sell your hand-carved, one-of-a-kind furniture without some decent goddamn leads."

"It's a three-year-old car at the end of a lease," Dave added. "Somebody else got the three best years out of it, so cut the crap. Hey, you guys look great."

"We're so glad you're here, guys," Maggie said. "It's sort of a celebration. Tell them about the big job, Joe."

"It's no big thing," Joe said. "I'm making a fancy table from the huge mahogany board I'd told you about—for Ari Pappas. I'll show you later."

"Come on," Maggie said. "It's more than that. It's the best commission he's had in a long time—maybe ever—and he's going to carve something fantastic in a gorgeous table." She looked at each of them, and quieted her voice. "It's a big break, a chance to do something really special."

Dave understood what this meant to them both. The four of them had traveled together for a long time. "You're the only one still doing your art, Joe."

"Yeah, I probably should be euthanized."

Annie said, "Oh, shut up. Really, Joe, we admire you. We all started out twenty some years ago with the same ideals about the creative life and doing our own thing, and you've been faithful to that. You and Maggie, you've made a nice life for yourselves and your kid. You do your wood carving, and we still come over for dinner—even though Dave is hugely successful and we drive a gorgeous fascist car."

"Thanks, kid," Joe said. "Maybe if my pickup truck was just a little newer."

. . .

They had a nice dinner and empty, dirty plates were in front of them all and they'd finished a second bottle of white wine, and most of a bottle of red. By now they had redistributed themselves at the table and Annie sat to Maggie's left at one end. Dave pushed himself back and brought his wine glass to his mouth. "Have I ever told you, Maggie, what we all thought about you when we were in college?"

"Uh, I think so," Maggie said. She looked at Annie and said, "Would you mind awfully if he tells me again?" Joe smiled. The occasions when Maggie allowed herself to be the center of things were rare.

Dave pretended to compose himself to tell an important story and they all knew what was coming. "We all thought that Maggie was a goddess, a model of beauty and grace, put there, probably by the administration of the college, as an idol for the art students to contemplate."

"Oh, I think that you've improved on your recollection," Maggie said.

"Only in the telling has it been altered," Dave said. "You are a princess to be placed upon a pedestal. Joseph, do you keep her on a pedestal?"

"There is an occasional gift, an online order typically. Other than that, I am afraid the gift from the college administration has been under-rewarded," Joe answered.

"All that fantasy was never mine, Dave. My life is pretty good," Maggie said.

Annie had antennae that picked up the emotions of people in her company. And tonight, she thought she was hearing more than what was on the surface. She had found over the years that her sense rarely betrayed her. Annie's nature was to be frank—blunt even—and her personal challenge was usually about discernment, knowing when to stifle the words that jumped into her head. So tonight, Maggie had said life was pretty good. People build safe places for themselves, not just Maggie, most people. They only process the bits of truth that won't impede their ability to keep on. It's not my job tonight, Annie thought, to rock the dinner party with insight, even offered lovingly, but things are not happy here. She was sure of it.

From where the men were seated, they couldn't see through the little window at the end of the dinner table and that Annie had reached out and taken Maggie's hand in hers.

"How about the men taking a look at the masterpiece out in the shop?" Dave said. He was thinking about the after-dinner cigarette that was part of their guy habit on these evenings.

It was only a short walk through the darkness to Joe's woodshop, and even Dave was steady on his feet along the gravel path as they approached the shop door, laughing. Dave said, "Have you really got smokes?"

"Would I let you down?" Joe said as the door opened.

All at once several fluorescent lights came on. In the unheated shop the cool blue lights flickered. The big mahogany table dominated the room; it was right there demanding a response. "Holy shit. It's fantastic—really spectacular."

"Thanks." There was a long, odd silence that the wine and Dave's natural gift of banter ought to have filled. Joe finally broke the silence. "So, it's pretty cool?"

"I was expecting a lot of carving, but I think I like the plainness, too. It's huge."

"It was what the guy wanted. Let's light a fire and have a smoke," and Joe adeptly retrieved a pack of Marlboros from behind some books. Dave was still studying the table, fondling the massive turned legs and the hand-planed bead along the upper and lower edges of the thick pieces that made up the lower stretchers of the trestle base.

"It's terrific. I don't know how you make it look so antique. Pappas is going to flip."

Joe led Dave to his woodstove and pulled a milk crate close to the open door of the stove to make a seat for his friend. Ready at hand were newspaper and wood scraps and Joe, crouching, quickly kindled a fire, a task that he had performed at this spot a thousand times. "A little draft will help draw the cigarette smoke up the chimney. Thirty thousand dollars, can you believe that?"

Of all Joe's friends, Dave valued money the most, so Joe was disappointed and surprised that Dave did not react to the big dollar amount. Silence.

"What?" Joe says.

The stove door was ajar and Joe looked obliquely at his friend and was startled at Dave's eyes staring out of his flickering yellow and orange face.

"Come on, what?"

"It's definitely worth it. The thirty thousand. Don't feel bad about that," Dave said.

"About that?" Joe pressed his friend.

"You must be disappointed?" And Joe felt Dave's expression still quite deliberately cast his way. "What happened with Pappas? You wanted to carve on it. You were kind of committed to it, weren't you? What happened, Joe?

"I don't know. I couldn't talk him into it."

"Are you disappointed? You've seemed kind of bummed out all night. I'm sorry."

"It's all right, don't worry about me. I'm fine. And it's a fair deal."

"And what about Maggie?"

Joe answered, "Yeah, I think she'll understand. She—"

"—doesn't know?"

"No."

Dave shifted on the fly. "He'll never find anything better than that piece of mahogany. And besides, it's perfect free-market capitalism. He wants to own big expensive things and has lots of money. You own the board and have no money. He wants the board. You sell him the goddamn board. Genius. This is what I do all day—make deals. It's not exactly evil." Dave drew on his cigarette and sent a thick plume of smoke into the open stove and not a whiff escaped into the shop. "They catch us smoking and we're screwed."

"Those two knew what we were going to do before we even thought of it—and when we go back inside, we'll smell like ashtrays, but we're entitled to have some fun in life. Don't you think?"

Inside, Annie had not let go of Maggie's hand and Maggie said, "He's so unhappy."

"Maudlin," Annie said.

"I'm aching for him. Everything seems all right to me, you know—our circumstances. You know what I mean? But he's suffering. The joy's gone out of him. It's very real and it's all the time—like his dreams aren't working out," Maggie said.

"I think we're all a little disappointed," Annie said. It's a throwaway line and she cringed inside because she'd made a dishonest remark, just like almost anyone would in the same situation, to soften the bed of the conversation, and out of ordinary kindness. But what Annie really thought was that when someone knew that you truly loved them, it was more helpful to be direct. She was still holding Maggie's hand.

"Maybe because his dreams were so beautiful it's more painful," Maggie said.

"What are you going to do?" Annie asked.

"Just keep loving him," Maggie said.

Annie released Maggie's hand. A feeling came upon her that she disliked. It was when Maggie expressed herself in this way that betrayed the difference in the way they saw things—a gulf that had widened over the years since school, over the years that they had been married and living separate lives.

Love. That was what Maggie really believed in most. And when she used it like she just had now, Annie wanted to tell her she was being stupid.

Okay, Annie thought, Maggie was pained that her love for Joe didn't seem to be able to fix him, so why wasn't that an opening to a different idea?

"Can't you act out of love, but take some concrete action? I know you love him—you've been loving him all along, but that's not doing anything."

"He's excited about his big board," Maggie said. She thought that loving Joe was doing something. At other times when she had shared spiritual ideas with Annie, she had gotten to a point where her words, patiently and carefully expressed, felt preachy and trite. It had at times caused a loneliness that had not been there before—what felt like loss. Tonight, though, Maggie had shared her thoughts about Joe, and Annie had understood that he was in trouble and was saying that there was something Maggie should do.

"I hear what you're saying. I'm paying attention because you love us. Right now, Annie, I know that you love us, and I'm so glad to have you."

The kitchen door banged shut and whispering, joking voices approached from the kitchen.

. . .

Later, upstairs, Joe stood at his bureau in his boxers and put on a tiny bit of cologne. He heard the sink water running and turned to where the Victoria's Secret box still rested on Maggie's bureau. He lifted a corner of the box and saw that the fun present was still there.

"What was all that about the Mercedes Benz?" Maggie shouted from the bathroom.

"Dave loves the verbal sparring, don't you think? And he's still good with words, and making money at it."

"I could have married Dave, if I'd wanted a big car. There's nothing that you could buy me that would make me happier." Joe was lying in the bed waiting for his wife. Their bed sat right on the floor surrounded by bookshelves of cinderblocks and pine boards. It had not changed in all the years they had lived in this house.

In the bathroom Maggie brushed her teeth and washed her face and tried three times to make the faucet stop its steady flow of cold water. There was a green stain on the porcelain which betrayed months or years of slow drip.

Maggie came into the bedroom in boys' pajamas. "I love those guys," she said. She walked around to her side of the crash pad and got under the covers. Her back was at first turned toward Joe, but she rose up a little, turned toward him, kissed him on the head, and said, "Except when Dave forces you to smoke cigarettes. You should be stronger, but I love you anyway, Joe Carroll. I love you to death."

Maggie turned back away and Joe thought that she probably did smell the cigarette, but that it wasn't that; she didn't care that much about the smoking and he probably didn't smell that bad. It was just late and who wouldn't be tired after the day Maggie had put in. He put an arm around her cuddling close. Maggie said, "He must be orally repressed or something. Guys like that are so pathetic." Joe flipped over on his other side and they were back-to-back.

"What wrench will stop that dripping faucet?" Maggie asked.

"The big silver adjustable. I'll do it," Joe said.

"When you get a chance. Will's going to show Mr. Tiezzi his report after soccer. You won't have time tomorrow."

"He came home happy last time, didn't he?"

Maggie curled into what Joe had memorized as a remarkably tiny and beautiful ball of girl. "He's fine. 'Nite, hon," she whispered and purred a soft exhale.

Joe quietly rolled onto his back and lay rigid, staring at the ceiling. He said to himself that he was not at all sleepy.

Chapter 24
I Saw It

Maggie had been at church by herself. Joe and Will could have gone, too, but they would have been cutting it close because Will had a soccer game at noon at the town recreation park. Games on Sunday had become the norm. A couple of years ago Joe had gone to a Recreation Commission meeting at the town hall to express his family's view of the Sabbath. Wasn't Sunday wide open for activities like youth soccer because for years people have been keeping this one day as a family time? People would put aside their other busy activities and either worship or stay home. It was the culture of the place and people respected it. There had been others at the meeting who agreed with him and several folks had thanked him and told him that they were with him and Maggie, but the imperative to provide healthy recreation for the kids had prevailed. So, on this morning in early spring, Joe, having said that he was tired from the night before with Annie and Dave, had weaseled out of church and driven Will to his game.

Maggie was going to join them at the game after church, but entering the house she remembered the dripping faucet. With the Sunday *New York Times* under her arm, and wearing a long camel-colored wool coat from the Salvation Army Thrift Store, she made a hurried dash to the workshop and the box under the back side of Joe's workbench where he keeps his wrenches and screwdrivers. She grabbed the big silver adjustable wrench and turned to dash to the house.

There it was—the big mahogany table that Joe had been working on for a couple months. She knew the order of things in Joe's work, and she stopped. She processed instantly the way his carved furniture projects had

119

always gone before. But the table top looked like it was already fastened to the bottom of the thing. Everything, top and all, was shiny and the smell of the finishing materials hung newly in the air.

She looked more closely and the steps that Joe always followed ran through her head speedily. Mr. Tiezzi's huge board, planed and finely sanded, would have been on the workbench, the artwork would have been transferred to the raw wood with carbon paper and many days of carving would have followed. Then Joe would have stained the whole thing, carving and all, with alcohol-based dyes. Then he would brush on the creamy paste filler, filling the open pores in the wood grain darker than the stained wood.

He'd already done all those steps. There was no mistaking it. Maggie saw the subtle hint of the orange shellac under the finishing coats of varnish—what Joe says was an old trick that gave his furniture a warmth and softness. And the top coats of spar varnish were there, too. Maggie pictured the fine sanding between coats, the care taken not to sand through the shellac and stain and accidentally work back down to the raw wood—an error not easily remedied.

No, there is no mistake. This table is complete; it is done. There was even the scent of carnauba wax in the air, a last step that Joe said protected the finish and unified the whole look of the thing. There was the can of wax over on the bench. Oh, God. It is done. And there is no wood carving at all.

The adjustable wrench hit the hard cement floor first, then the *New York Times*—all the slippery sections of Arts and Leisure, the Week in Review, Real Estate and colored advertising supplements slid over the shop floor.

Her legs weakened beneath her and she fell forward onto Mr. Tiezzi's big board. Her fingers clutched at the red and black surface, but it was smooth and there was nothing to clutch. She didn't know if she was really shaking, but every part of her felt like it was wrecked and convulsing. Wetness was on the table top. She didn't know if it was from her eyes or if fluids had just let loose from her pores. With her coat sleeves she instinctively wiped it around and the liquid just beaded on the waxy, smooth surface.

She backed away now, bracing herself against the workbench from where she took in the whole breadth of the thing. Dave had been out here last night and seen it. They both knew—Annie and Dave—knew what Joe had known for a long time—that he sold the table to Ari Pappas without the beautiful carving. She wanted what Joe said he wanted. He thought he had been given—a chance. Years of rooting for him and sharing his dreams—and this—this vulgar joke. She was in the presence of something awful—not just an accident, or some arbitrary out-of-the-blue sadness, but a horrible death. The putrid taint of the thing was on her. She shook and did not think to resist it. It was on her—the vileness.

"Oh, Joe," she said, alone there in the shop. "What have you done? What has happened to you, Joe?" There was not compassion in this. She had never been angry. But she could not now, by her will, fend off a feeling of humiliation, of stupidity, of nauseating sickness.

Maggie stayed there for a while; time was confused. It might have been only minutes until she gathered herself to see if her legs would move her. She walked toward the house. She knew that Joe Carroll was not there and she was glad.

The town soccer fields were in a big clearing in the woods and there was a long view down to the Connecticut River that, on most days, Maggie took in with gratitude, a thankfulness that she and Joe and their child lived in such a majestic place. But today she saw nothing but the well-worn path to the fields where she knew she would find Joe Carroll. On other such days she would spot moms and dads her age, decked out in upscale, sporty outfits and she would do what she instinctively always could do. She would think loving thoughts about them all and look into their faces, and they would all be happy to be there at a soccer game with Maggie Carroll.

But today the details of the scene were not there for her. She did not see the individual people, Will's friends Jason and Ricky and Timmy, and not Jason's father doing a version of what he always did.

"Take him, Jason," shouted Jason's dad.

Jason was a midfielder on Will's team and with humiliating ease he had just stolen the ball from the other team's stopper. He looked around and paused to give the rest of Parkinson Pharmacy time to get spaced on the field in the fashion that Ricky Santelli's dad had taught them.

"Go all the way, Jay," Jason's dad screamed. Three opposing players were in Jason's path and Will was positioned alone on the left wing, available to accept a pass. But Jason, who was very skilled, beat all three defenders and dribbled toward the goal. Maggie, oblivious to the action, approached Joe who was watching his son. Will glanced quickly to the sidelines and raised his arms in a questioning shrug as if to say, there he goes again, Dad. Joe returned the shrug.

"Did you see that?" Joe said turning to Maggie.

"I saw it, I saw the goddamn thing," Maggie said.

Joe looked back at the field. Maggie doesn't talk like that, he thought to himself. He stiffened and returned his attention to the game as Jason glided toward the net and scored—again.

Jason's father was in full testosterone-fueled excitement now. "Did you see that?" he said in the direction of Joe and Maggie and anyone who might share his pleasure.

"I've seen it, Joe. I've seen what you did and it is horrible," and she turned from him and walked fast toward the unpopulated end of the field. Joe was right behind her; she sensed him following her and said, "What has happened to you?"

"Nothing."

She turned toward him and her face was contorted and unlovely. "What has happened to you?"

"Okay, so you've seen the table."

Maggie was staring right through him.

"What's happened? I've sold the biggest job of my stupid life. What's happened? The bills are all paid and you can go to law school and that kid has the first bike of his life that's not used."

And Maggie added to the catalogue: "And Ari Pappas is getting a table that he could have gotten from goddamn North Carolina."

Joe replied, "Dave liked it."

Maggie who never said anything unkind about anybody emitted a vulgar gagging, "Echhh. Dave liked it. I thought Dave wasn't like you, like us. Dave quit art school. I worked while I waited for you to finish. Do you remember that? I cleaned houses for spoiled ungrateful faculty assholes waiting for you to finish. Do you remember that? Well, I'm still waiting."

"What's that supposed to mean? What was I supposed to do? He wanted it plain. He didn't care about my ideas. I tried to—"

"—and neither do you. He wanted the trophy, and you almost gave it to him," Maggie said.

"I sold it to him. For a lot of money," Joe said.

"Too cheap, Joe, too cheap."

Thirty thousand. It was a fortune to Joe and he had been looking forward to the twenty grand more only a couple of days away. "Well, it's too late and we made—"

Maggie had always given her blessing to Joe's decisions about his woodworking business, but not now, not about the big board that he said was his big chance. "Tomorrow, tomorrow morning. You're going to tell him he can't have it."

Joe cocked his head and made a smirking face to say, you don't really mean that, you know that's not really possible, not now.

But Maggie was serious. "I'll tell him. Would you like that? Would you like your wife to do that for you, Joe? I'll tell him for you." She turned and began to walk away. "And hey, maybe you'd also like me to tell Mr. Tiezzi that the big promise is off, that he sold the board to the wrong man."

That really stung. Joe was supposed to take Will back over to Mr. Tiezzi's shop in Saybrook after lunch, but he had not allowed himself to think about the old man. Maggie had offered Joe an opening to talk about Will, to talk about family logistics, the managing of their schedules and stuff that they just need to get through—a reprieve from the hurt that she had led him into.

"Mags, can you run Will over to Mr. Tiezzi's after the game? I told Tony I'd help him put the soccer gear away and clean up."

"I don't think so, Joe. No, this is a chance for you to explain it all to Mr. Tiezzi, don't you think? I'm going to Annie's. Please ask Will to phone me over there this evening. Will you do that, Joe? I might be staying there for a while."

Chapter 25
If You Knew Him

Joe dropped Will off on the street in Saybrook in front of Giordano's little house with its dated, wide asbestos shingles. He lowered and craned his head toward the open window and said to his son, "Hour and a half, right? When I come back, I think I'll honk and you can just wander out here and save me getting involved with Giordano? It's not a good day for a visit, okay?" On the drive across the river, he had not told Will anything—not about what he had done with Mr. Tiezzi's board, not about the fight with his mother.

He had never looked at Giordano's place this way, never thought disparagingly about the peeled old sign in the front yard, Tiezzi and Sons, Millwork. He thought that this afternoon Maggie had told him that she was leaving him—well, sort of. She was going to Annie and Dave's and that's only six miles from their own home, but it felt like she was going very far away. He was already angry that those two were going to understand her disappointment, say all the right things. It was Maggie they really always loved and they, mostly Annie, she was the leader, will take Maggie's side.

His attention returned to the sign. Giordano had not taken down the stupid plywood sign, even though he, one of the Sons, was eighty-five years old, and the other of the Sons was long dead. And so was their business. He hoped that Will did not turn around and see him still sitting there in the truck, but he had not thought what to do, where to go. He made himself put the truck in gear and it rolled toward the street.

Will walked up the pot-holed asphalt driveway past Giordano's house toward the workshop. Outside the shop was parked a fabulous old black truck. On its driver's side door were hand-painted letters: Tiezzi and Sons, Millwork, just like on the sign at the street. Will had seen the truck before, parked nearer the house, but had not had a chance to really look at it, another piece of Mr. Tiezzi's old world. Will stepped right up onto the running board and pressed his face against the rolled-up window to look at the interior and to imagine himself going through the gears along a quiet road somewhere.

"Ahhh!" he shouted suddenly.

"Pretty nice old truck. Sorry to startle you, young man."

"It's okay, I startle real easy," Will said.

"I'm Giordano's friend, Peach." The tall man had a handsome head of wavy silver hair, carefully parted and combed straight back, neatly trimmed at his ears. He had on a coat and tie covered with a blue-black, long and slinky topcoat. "I think Giordano should have a phone for this rig, don't you? I think I will get him one," Peach said.

Will could not quite picture Giordano driving around, much less driving and talking on the phone. "It's really nice," Will said and extended his hand to Peach. "Is Mr. Tiezzi in the shop?"

"Of course, he is always in the shop. He never goes anywhere these days," Peach replied.

They went through the shop door together and Giordano was right there waiting.

"I caught this young man coveting your truck, Giordano," Mr. Peach said.

"We will forgive him, Picia. After all, what man does not love a shiny old truck?" Giordano answered.

"I will leave you men alone. I think Will is here for important school work." Will was surprised that this man knew who he was, but accepted it as part of the magic of the place.

"We're all done. Oh yeah, Giordano, Mr. Tiezzi, here, I brought my Immigrant Experience report," and he handed the typed pages to Giordano who looked at it briefly, then at Will.

"Let Mr. Peach read what it says. He has younger eyes," Giordano said.

Peach took the paper and read the front cover aloud: The American Tiezzi Brothers of Saybrook, Connecticut.

Giordano was pleased. He looked off straight—not at anyone. "What mark did the teacher give?"

Mr. Peach answered, "A+. And there is a note written in the teacher's hand on the front. Excellent writing, crazy Italians." They all laughed as Mr. Peach handed the paper back to Will who looked down at it for the words that he already knew were not really there.

Will said, "Did you know Carini, Mr. Peach?"

"Oh, yes, Carini and I shared some exciting immigrant experiences. One in particular." Peach raised an eye at Giordano. "I knew him. And if you knew him, Will, you would not forget him. Every inch of him would be stored in your brain, and if you needed to smile, you could call up a picture of Carini Tiezzi. People would look at you and say, ah, look at Will. What is on his mind? He is a happy boy. But right now, I must go or get into big trouble with Mrs. Peach. Giordano, you must tell Will about Carini and the cables. I think he would like that."

Picia was gone. It was very quiet and the old man was looking all around the workshop. Will broke the silence and said, "Mr. Peach didn't know that you already told me about the PT boat and the cable snapping."

"It's something else," Giordano answered. He was quiet for a moment. Picia wanted him to tell Will about the cables and the thought excited him. Carini's power over him was still there; it felt wonderful. I may hurt myself, Giordano thought, but the boy is here and maybe there is a reason the idea has come into Picia's head. I will make this fun for Will Carroll. "Will, over there on the shelf, bring me the gray duct tape."

As Will went for the tape, Giordano took off his shop apron. He took off his shirt and had on the kind of sleeveless undershirt that Will's dad said lots of men used to wear, especially Italians. Giordano's face had the same expression that Will had seen the time Mr. Tiezzi startled him with the flying extension cord.

Will accepted willingly the tinge of fear he felt rising in him.

Giordano took the duct tape from Will and said, "Now get me a small piece of coal from the coal hod over by the woodstove." Will walked to the hot stove. He hadn't said that he didn't know what a hod was, but Will poked around in the bucket thing full of ashes and found a hard piece and brought it to the old man whose mind seemed someplace far away.

With difficulty Giordano lifted his left leg up behind him. "Take the tape and wind it around my thigh."

Will saw the tape on the bench and saw that Giordano had fed off a foot-long length from the big roll. Will obeyed the odd command, but slowly and gently. He thought that he had never touched an old person, except just shaking hands.

Giordano made a pained grimace and said, "Faster." The sticky tape unwound reluctantly as Will walked the spool of tape around the old man several times, while Giordano balanced himself against the workbench. As Will wound the tape around the bent-up leg, Giordano drew a thin moustache on his lip with the charcoal.

It all looked very painful and Will said, "Is it too tight?"

The old man was silent; he was somewhere else. So, Will just tore the duct tape loose from the spool with his teeth like he'd seen his father do. Giordano was wild-eyed, transfixed, and smiling.

All at once Giordano let out a scream, "Ahhhhhhh!" and jumped—jumped for something. Will followed the ridiculous trajectory of his ancient friend and saw that Giordano had grabbed a short, knotted length of heavy manila rope. Will had never before noticed a taut steel cable strung just below the ceiling.

Giordano exploded with energy as he pushed off with his free leg and flew fast across the room. This was, Will realized, a pantomime of a system that the brothers crafted for Carini to navigate the workshop with one leg. At the table saw, Giordano dropped from the pulley and pushed the large red button that fired up a big, loud motor. Then he jumped up to the zip-line again and, one leg driving hard, raced back to where Will stood frozen in amazement. Giordano picked up a length of wood, tucked it under his arm, turned, and flew back to the roaring saw.

Giordano, imitating his wild brother, shouted over the din of the motor, "Giordano, you must finish Mr. Griswold's window sash today. He is coming at five."

Will, laughing out loud, walked a few steps into the middle of the play.

Now Giordano jumped at a different pulley and hurdled himself toward a massive old thickness planer at the other end of the shop. He dropped from the zip-line and threw on a huge three-phase motor that drove the antique machine. He picked up a board from the floor and started it through the planer sending fine shavings into the air on the back side. Over the low drone of the machine he shouted, "Brother, have you finished the cherry panels for the library of Mr. Davis?"

He jumped to yet another pulley, let out another war cry, this one fainter because he was red-faced and out of breath. He traveled the pulley, his one free foot dragging a little now, to the door of the telephone booth that was the office. He hopped through the folding door and picked up the fancy telephone. "Hello, Yale University, no, I am very sorry, you can't buy our big board. It's not for sale. We are saving it for something special."

Will's eyes darted around, guessing where the old man would go next.

Giordano hopped on one leg out of the booth, struggled to jump to another pulley, and rode, one crooked old leg driving, back to the table saw. He let go of the rope and turned off the table saw motor. He jumped back to the zip-line. He was losing steam. He scooted his way back to where Will was watching, and collapsed against the workbench. Breathless, chest heaving, he reached into a pocket and produced a pocket knife, handed it to Will and said, "Cut the tape."

Will looked at the unopened knife hesitantly, and then at the layers of duct tape wound about the old man's leg. Louder this time, Giordano shouted, "Cut the tape." Will was not very adept at handling a knife. His dad had given him a Swiss Army knife for Christmas, but he had used it only to attach some reflectors to his bicycle and once to open a bottle of red wine with the corkscrew when no one else was home. He had taken one gulp of the wine and guiltily put the rest down the drain and carried the empty bottle to the recyclables in the garage. Now, he thought, I am supposed to take the sharp big blade to the leg of this old man. He was uncertain. But Giordano was in pain and was screaming. He cautiously attacked the gray layers. "Please hurry," Giordano said.

Will was working at the duct tape pretty aggressively now. He was excited and doing better than he thought he could. Giordano's old knife was very sharp. He freed up chunks of the tape. How many times had he walked around Giordano to make all this mess? He tugged. Whole chunks were loose and bits of stickiness remained on the old man's green work trousers. Giordano was nearly crying and Will helped ease his old leg back down to its natural position—slowly. This felt weirdly personal, handling the skinny leg of an old person, but he did it and Giordano was okay, even walked in a small circle getting his feet back under him.

Giordano gathered himself and said to Will, "On one day in 1944 the steel cable took Carini's leg, and nearly every day after that, for fifty years, Carini was the master of the cable. By the end, he had completely defeated it."

"Was he like that every day—wild and yelling at you?"

"Every day," Giordano answered.

"What happened when he got stranded away from all the pulleys, when he couldn't get where he wanted to go?"

"Sometimes he would hop or crawl, but mostly he would just yell out, "Crocetta," and I would go to the pulley that he needed and send it flying in his direction."

"What is crocetta?" Will asks.

"It was a nickname that he gave me and it was the only time that he used it—when he needed a pulley. It was our own system."

Will says, "What does it mean?"

"In our village in Italy, half of the people had the family name Tiezzi. All the families would be called something else, usually the trade of the men."

"So, what is a crocetta?"

"It means cross maker. Someone in our family had once carved the markers for the dead."

Will asked, "Did you ever?"

"No, nor did my papa. What about your papa? He is a wood carver."

Will stiffened a little at the mention of his father. "No, I don't think so." Will looked back up at the zip-line—the whole network of wires that he had not even noticed before.

Giordano said, "Do you want to try it?"

"Yeah, can I?"

Giordano, returning now to the play, said, "Go ahead, Carini, go down and turn off the big planer. Press the big red button."

Will said, "Can I do the tape?"

"Yes, but then you must do the undershirt and the mustache." As Will scrambled out of his long-sleeve shirt, Giordano drew on him a narrow black mustache. Will eyed the zip-line, plotting his course as Giordano bound up his left leg. Giordano had found a small block of wood, which he tossed at Will. Will caught it. "You almost forgot your cigarettes, Carini. Your precious Chesterfield Kings."

Will rolled the block of wood into the sleeve of his undershirt like he'd seen guys do in old movies.

Will thought that he knew the route back to the thickness planer. He jumped to a pulley and, not as efficiently as Giordano because his feet scarcely touched the ground, propelled himself to the phone booth. He dropped to the ground and lost his balance. "This isn't so easy with one leg." Giordano laughed and watched affectionately.

Will got back up, braced himself against the booth, and jumped to a second pulley. He rode the zip-line toward the planer, let go, and fell against the still roaring machine. For an instant he thought that it could drag him into its knives and slice him into tiny pieces. No, he realized, I have regained my feet—foot. He turned off the machine and the shop was quiet again. He retraced his route back to the booth, jumped at another pulley, let go with one of his hands, and propelled himself back toward Giordano. When he reached the old man, he pirouetted out of control and Giordano caught him. Will was moaning, puffing, and laughing—all at once.

And right at that moment, Joe walked into the shop.

The first words that Joe heard were Will's. "Cut the tape. Ahhh, cut the tape."

Will spotted his dad. "Oh, Dad, I didn't hear you honk. You should see this thing that they had for Carini to—" but he was cut short by his shocked father.

"What the hell is this?" Joe shouted. "What are you doing to my son?" He grabbed Will by the arm and in the same motion gave Giordano a hard push. Giordano flew against a corner of the workbench and dropped hard to the shop floor.

Will said, "Dad, no."

Giordano was on the floor and his forehead was bleeding. There was no anger in him. He wore the forgiving face that Carini had worn so many years before on the day Giordano confessed that his prayers had caused the loss of Carini's leg. But now, no joke came to Giordano's mind that would dispel the anger and confusion.

Joe looked into the face of the old man. "What have you done?"

Will was still all taped up and Joe dragged him bodily to the shop door. Will said, "We were playing, Daddy. We were just playing." Joe awkwardly maneuvered his son through the doorway. He got Will to the truck, leaned him against the fender and got the passenger side door open. Joe made a vain attempt to tear the duct tape loose.

There was a cry in Joe's voice and he asked, "What is all this?"

"Get the knife from Mr. Tiezzi. You're hurting me, Daddy. He has a good knife. He'll loan it to you."

Joe went back in and found Giordano on his feet. Giordano handed Joe the knife, handle first, and said, "He has done nothing bad. Your son is perfect."

Chapter 26
Good on ya, Joe Carroll

A day had passed after Maggie found out about the table and she had not come home. "Mom's mad at me and is sleeping over at Aunt Annie's. She thinks I've sold my soul to the devil," was what Joe said to Will, but these were words Maggie had never spoken. The idea of phoning her had crossed Joe's mind and each time he had quickly dismissed it because he couldn't think what he could say that would make a difference.

Joe was just putting one foot in front of the other now. He didn't know what he would do tomorrow, or the next day, so it was an ironic blessing that he was supposed to deliver the big table to Ari Pappas. It was something to do, finishing this soul-to-the-devil transaction. Last week he had reserved the Ryder box truck and lined up Chad from the hardware store to make the two-mile delivery to the law offices. On his second night sleeping alone he set the alarm on their clock radio so he'd be up to get Will off to school. In the morning he had made frozen orange juice for the first time in many years and had offered Will an egg, but Will said he'd just have cereal. It was a silent and brief half hour before Will was off to school on his bike.

As soon as Will left the house, Joe emailed Maggie at work to let her know that in just a little while, he would, unavoidably, be at her workplace, in her space, with Chad and the table. He assumed that she did not want to see him. Maybe she will make up an errand and get out of there, Joe thought, or maybe find a little job that she can take to the second floor.

It was past nine o'clock by the time he and Chad moved the table, which was in two pieces, into the box truck, padded its edges and cozied it fast against a forward corner of the truck. No straps or ropes. There were no hills on the short trip and they'd creep slowly to town to keep the thing from shifting.

At the law office there was a big wide parking space in front of the building on the main drag. The plan for getting the table off the truck would work easily, even though the table top and the base were both very heavy. On the way over, Joe had repeated three times to Chad the steps they would follow in the unloading.

The base of the table came off the truck first and was on the sidewalk. When they got the big board out of the truck, they put it in place over the base and it looked like the assembled thing. There were business people around at this hour and a guy shouted from across the street, "Good on ya, Joe Carroll." In moments a small crowd gathered around the big table. A couple of girls from the insurance office next door were there, the realtor who sold Joe and Maggie their house, and some strangers. The realtor set up a brief round of applause for Joe's work and a young man asked if he could touch the table. The insurance company girls had heard about the table already and one said to the other something about its being one single piece of mahogany. It was a spontaneous little celebration and Joe was able to smile.

Joe asked Chad to guard the table while he cleared the way into the building and the table's final resting place in the law library. The old secretary, Cecile, had been expecting him. Everything at Pappas' office ran like clockwork and furniture from the lobby and hallway that could be in the way had been carried off somewhere.

Cecile was on her feet to greet Maggie's husband. "This is very exciting. Mr. Pappas is busy this morning. You understand. Please don't bump it into anything." She handed Joe an envelope with Joseph Carroll written on it and said, "And I didn't give you this until the table was safely installed."

Twenty thousand and no sign of Maggie.

Chapter 27
I Don't Think So

That very same evening there was an intimate party in Ari Pappas' law library to celebrate his taking possession of a great new table. Everyone was dressed up for the event. It was the very spot where Joe and Ari consummated the deal for a table that would be crafted from Tiezzi's board.

It was just Ari's inner circle, his family plus Peter Antonopoulos, a boyhood pal from the neighborhood who had navigated the same route from child of immigrants to the state university and law school to wealth and power in their small town.

If Ari had ever considered his wealth and security an opportunity to study or dwell on other things so that on a night such as this they would talk about a book one of them had read, or about warring in the Middle East, there had been no sign of it. And no one in this inner circle had ever challenged him. He was their demigod and meal ticket and they were all willing props in his theatre. There have been lots of other nights like this one: the first Mercedes Benz, the fancy antique house on Main Street converted into the law offices, various big malpractice suit paydays, the election of one of Ari's toadies as First Selectman or state rep—the same cast and the same single malt scotch and the same words of homage to the great man.

At the back of the room Ari's mother sat in a leather armchair and was holding a half-finished glass of sherry. With difficulty, she rose and took the arm of Ari's wife, Georgia. Georgia was flashy and attractive. Everyone said that she had some help looking so sharp and young. Georgia took her mother-in-law's drink and handed it to their nephew, Teddy.

"It's a beautiful table, Ari," his mother said. "The biggest I have ever seen." Ari approached his mother and leaned in to receive the kiss that he knew she would offer.

"I'll take Mother home," Georgia said. "Good night, Teddy, Pete. I'll see you at the house, Ari."

The men rearranged in the most comfortable chairs and Ari took a spot by himself at the back end of the room against shelves of bound leather volumes. He carried a large crystal glass of golden liquid and a handsome and healthy expression of mature satisfaction.

Pete broke the silence. "We've come a long way from the old neighborhood. We are all pleased, Ari, that you have bought yourself a wonderful present."

"Only about a mile and a half, actually." There was a pause followed by Teddy clapping his hands at Uncle's jest, and then Ari said, "Too damn big for this room. I'm going to knock out this wall," as he touched the bookcases behind himself with his hairy knuckles.

With his free hand Ari reached into his coat pocket for a small block of maple with a hole in it, one of the many buttons Joe had told him were sliding in slots in the rails, then fastened with screws up into the table top, working in unison to pull it down onto the trestle base.

"How'd they get the damn thing in here?" Pete asked.

"Two pieces," Ari said. "The top's held down with these guys. I looked in this morning when he put it together. Here's one the damn fool missed," and he slid the little block speedily down the fourteen-foot length of the table—right at Pete who snatched it out of the air with one hand.

"Still with the quick reflexes, old friend. Teddy, did you know that Uncle Pete was the shortstop on our high school baseball team and the second-best player?"

"All leather, no stick," Pete answered, not disputing the historical assessment.

Teddy had by now crawled under the table to examine the construction detail that he had not quite understood. From under the table he shouted, "I can't remember who was the best player, Uncle."

"It's one hell of a piece of wood, that is for goddamn sure. Pappas, centerfield and pitcher," Ari said.

Invisible now, Teddy offered, "I think it's actually two pieces."

"One solid piece. The damn thing was fifty years in a shed across the river."

The others could see Teddy's legs and rear end moving around beneath the table. "I don't know. It looks like there's a long glue joint the whole length of it, Uncle. I don't know."

Chapter 28
Fetal Position

The next day Joe woke up at 9:30 and found himself alone in his and Maggie's bed for another morning. This time he had forgotten to set the alarm to get Will off to school, but Will was not in his bed and there was a milky bowl in the sink. It was a cold, drizzly spring morning and unlike the day before, not only had Maggie left to stay with Annie and Dave—for how long he did not know—but with the table all delivered, Joe hadn't a single thing to do.

Joe put some coffee on, made the same amount he always had for himself and Maggie, and turned some music on the radio so as not to be quite so alone. He put on the same shirt he wore yesterday, and after a brief, startled moment, he reached into the breast pocket and was relieved to find the twenty thousand dollar check still there. He walked to the living room and placed it in the same cubbyhole where he had placed the deposit check on New Year's Eve.

So many years spent alone in the shop, he had learned to feel every vibration on the street and in the driveway and now he felt a low, steady rumbling under the radio music. The vibration was definitely close by. Joe looked out into the gray morning from the kitchen window, and saw his yard and his shop.

An orange and white U-Haul box truck was in his yard and its backup bells were ringing as it slowed to a stop near the shop doors. What the hell, he thought, as Ari Pappas' man Nick got out of the driver's seat and was joined from around the other side by a young guy named Frankie whom Joe had met once or twice. Nick and his helper conferred at the back of the truck and Nick looked toward the house, shook his head at dark windows, looked away, and opened the back of the truck. Joe saw them pulling the aluminum loading ramp from its track under the truck. He made no movement. Now they were walking the big mahogany table in one piece down the ramp. They'd gotten it halfway down the wet ramp and the kid, Frankie, who had the heavy lower end and was walking backwards, shouted something to Nick. His left foot went out from under him; he was down hard on his right knee and just barely saved his end of the table from tipping onto the ground. The ramp was not wide enough for the table's six feet to rest all at once, so Nick held up his end and let the kid scuff his end the rest of the way down the ramp on just one corner leg. When both men were on the ground, they set the table down in the mud and the drizzle just outside the shop doors. Joe had not moved. He saw the two of them get back in the cab and leave without a word.

. . .

At the kitchen door of Ari Pappas' law office, Maggie awkwardly shook the rain out of her hat, slapped what water she could from her shoulders and arms, all the while trying to keep the rainwater off the new packages, she had brought from the stationery store. As she reached for the storm door handle, Ari's nephew Teddy opened the back door and added to the difficulty of her maneuver by not getting fully out of her way.

"Don't go out there, Teddy," she said. "It's awful."

Teddy took Maggie and the stationery packages and all of her wet self into his arms, even gave her a peck on the cheek, and held her for a few beats too long. He looked soulfully into her eyes and said, "Maggie, I need to tell you something."

"Tell me anything you want, Teddy, but don't ever do that again," and she pushed past him to where she could get out of her wet stuff and put her bags down.

"Maggie, I don't know how to say this. The big table, Maggie, Ari's angry about the big table, I don't know—something about it being two pieces," and Maggie tossed her coat and hat on a hook and moved right back into the carpeted hallway. Ari's secretary, Cecile, had been waiting for Maggie and, grim-faced, looked up from her desk just off the foyer. Maggie made brief eye contact with her and quickly turned up the hall and into the law library.

"Ahhhhh," was all that Cecile heard. Cecile was the only person at Maggie's work she knew really cared for her, so she did not resist when her friend came close, put a gentle hand on her shoulder, and whispered brief words. From a safe distance Teddy watched the exciting drama.

. . .

For a long time, Joe stood frozen at the kitchen window. Why had Ari's goons brought the table back? He didn't know. But he knew that he was in terrible trouble. If Ari had sent it back, back with these guys who felt no compunction about setting it down in the rain, not even knocking on the door, Joe knew in his gut that he was in trouble. It could be as small a thing as the stain being the wrong color. It didn't matter. Ari was always right and Ari had his way with the likes of Joe Carroll. Ari Pappas, Joe knew, had squashed bigger bugs than him.

Joe went out the back door, no hat, no coat, and walked cautiously toward the table that he had lived intimately with for months. There was a single sheet of yellow legal pad on the tabletop and the rain had already floated the tape free from the smooth table surface. Inked words were running. *One solid piece?*

Joe grabbed his hair and cocked his head over to one side. He put both hands on his head and threw his head back and began a wailing cry that his ears and brain had never heard before—a range of pain that was new and horrible. He bent over and supported himself with his hands on his knees. By their shaking and straining, his movements bespoke agony.

It had only been a few minutes, but Joe did not know how long he had stood there in the rain staring at Mr. Tiezzi's wonderful board, built now into a huge table and bringing him such grief. He looked down at the water standing on the hairs on the back of his hands, and at his shirt, already soaked through, and he thought about the water puddling on the tabletop.

He half-ran to the shop doors and slipped and fell in the wet lawn before he reached them. He got up, and this time made it to the doors and opened them wide. He went to the end of the table farthest from the shop, got his weight low and pushed with all his strength, but it barely moved. He went to the other end now, determined to pull the table toward the shop, but almost right away he slipped and crashed again to the ground.

Joe got back to his feet and now was staring at the table that Ari Pappas had dropped in his yard, the table that was not at all the piece of furniture that he told Giordano he would make from the giant board, the table that was without the amazing relief carving that Maggie had looked forward to, which she had envisioned as his great opportunity, his miraculous big break. His muddy shirt clinging tight on his back, he stared down at the thing and it became in his mind, not the inanimate object that he had crafted by his own hand, but a hated enemy.

Joe grabbed a spade leaning against the shop near the doorway. Holding it very near the handle's end, he swung it hard against the side of the table, and a second and third time hard against the very top of the beautiful piece of furniture. More swings sent splintered chunks of the big turned mahogany legs flying into the wet grass.

Exhausted, Joe dropped the spade, leaned on the long side of the table and looked to the sky. No one was there to hear the pathetic, begging cry of Maggie's name.

• • •

At the law offices of Aristotle Pappas, Maggie Carroll, who had only once left work early, who most nights stayed several minutes late, was standing in her coat at the big front door looking through its sidelights for Annie's car that she knew would come any minute to take her away. Maggie's own car was parked there behind the office, but she knew she was too upset to drive and she just wanted to get out of this place, so she had called Annie. Maggie had gone to Annie and Dave's Sunday afternoon, angry at Joe for deceiving her about the table, and for selling out on his commitment to make something wonderful from the big mahogany board. In all their married life, she had never been mad at Joe for more than a few minutes and even these past couple days, she'd been forcing herself to stay mad at him, forcing herself to maintain this exile, when truly she missed him and could not stop herself from relating to his pain. It was her nature, and now, with their quiet lives unexpectedly convulsing with a series of hurts, her heart was unchanged.

Dave's new black Mercedes arrived in front of the office and double parked. Maggie was quickly out the door through the driving rain. Annie had gotten out to help her into the car. "We'll get you warm and dry, sweetie," was all Annie said.

·　·　·

Joe had rolled under the table and was motionless in a fetal position. The rain was falling steadily and dripped hard and evenly along one of the long edges of the table. It was early afternoon and he had been in that spot now for hours. At first, he had gone to his knees in agony, responding to the body blow of the table being dumped in his yard.

The horrible note: One solid piece? Pappas had discovered the secret of the repair caused by Joe and Will accidentally breaking it in half. After that first jolt, he had felt a horrible confluence of loneliness, disappointment, rejection, and anger that shook him head to toe, that caused muscles everywhere to spasm, that released floods of tears from his eyes, and that dropped him crippled and weak to the ground. And he was just plain tired; he'd pushed for several days to finish and deliver the big job—to get the money.

There was no one there who could say that Joe had gone into shock, or that he had gone to sleep, or who could explain in a medical way what was, mercifully for Joe Carroll, escape.

·　·　·

On a lush, velvety sofa in Annie and Dave's den, Maggie held a cup of tea. Annie had propped her safely in a corner, wedged her in with pillows. Her feet were under her, hidden by a luxurious, borrowed silk robe. Annie saw that Maggie couldn't pay attention to the tea mug and took it from her and put it on the glass coffee table.

"I've got to go home. They're going to need me. Will will be home from school and—"

Annie got to her feet and got the phone. "Just stay here for a while longer, Maggie. Call Will and tell him you're with me. They'll be okay."

In the Carroll's house a phone rang and should have been audible outside, but Joe did not hear it, and did not even move.

. . .

It was around three-thirty and Will, wearing his bike racing cap, pulled into the garage on his bicycle. He took off his backpack and lifted the bike up on the hooks on the garage wall. That maneuver had been a struggle only weeks before and Will knew that he was getting stronger all the time. To his left there was a windowed door to outside, and nearer, to his right, three steps up to the kitchen. He was about to go inside when he glanced left into the gray of the afternoon and an unfamiliar dark shape in front of his dad's workshop. In a flash he was standing over his father who was still huddled under the table. Quickly he crawled under and was right on top of his dad.

"Daddy, Daddy."

Joe came to half-consciousness and stared at his son. The boy grabbed at his father's chest, then rubbed his wet hands on his father's gray, cold face. Joe did not speak. The note from Pappas was still legible, but was on the ground now next to Joe. One solid piece?

Will ran into the house yelling, "Mo-o-m! Are you here? Mooooom!"

He went to the phone in the kitchen and dialed Maggie's work number. "This is Will Carroll, is my mom there?"

"No, she's not." She was not there. Cecile wanted to keep him on the line to see if he was okay, if there was something that she could do, but Will hung up.

Will grabbed quilts from the TV room and dashed into the backyard to his father. He covered Joe with two quilts and frantically tucked them in tight around him. "Dad, say something, Dad. Are you okay? I'm the one that broke it anyway. It's okay, Daddy, we've just got to get you up and get you warm inside." Will put an arm under one of Joe's shoulders to help him sit up, but Joe had closed his eyes. "I'll tell him that it was me that did it. I will. I'll tell him, Dad."

Will was off to the garage now. The phone rang in the house, but there was no one to hear it.

Chapter 29
You're Going to Get Killed

Who can help us? That was all Will could think right now. Me, Mom? Mom's gone. Uncle Dave? What could he do? No, not Uncle Dave. Before Will can even remember, he must have been told to call them Aunt Annie and Uncle Dave, like they were family, but he had never felt that way about them. In these last couple days since his mother had gone to stay with them, Will decided that he did not like them. Right now, right now with his dad lying wet under Mr. Tiezzi's board, relationships looked entirely different. He just knew that right now he and his father needed a different kind of care.

The decision by Will Carroll, now almost thirteen, to go and get Giordano Tiezzi, age about eighty-five, happened in a flash. Will took his bike down from the garage wall, by habit grabbed his cycling cap from a nearby nail, and was off into the gray drizzle.

Perhaps the exertion of the hard pedaling over the first half mile from his neighborhood streets out to the River Road that led to the highway, cleared his head. He realized now that this ride was pretty far and that it was getting dark. Dad would say that it was stupid, but Dad wasn't saying anything right now and Will decided that it was up to him to do something. Dad was curled up practically unconscious under that stupid table. I'm the one who's able to do something, Will thought, and riding to Saybrook was what he decided to do.

If Mr. Tiezzi is home and will help, Will thought, I'll only have to ride one way. He was not tired yet; anyway, his legs weren't hurting. He'd run ten times around the town track at soccer practice and always finished near the front and always felt like he could go farther. I'll be all right. I'm getting help for Dad, Will thought.

• • •

It was near closing time at the law office and Cecile had tidied her desk and bid a terse goodnight to the boss. Returning the big table to Maggie's husband, she thought, was more cruel, even more heavy-handed than what she was accustomed to seeing from Ari, and she was heartsick.

Ari looked in on Teddy, who frequently tried to stay later than his uncle, even if he had nothing real to do, just to project a reputation for long hours and devotion to the family practice. No one was fooled. Teddy hardly had any cases and certainly no difficult ones. "Has he called, yet?" Ari asked Teddy.

"No, Uncle, but Nick came in looking for you while you were at your meeting. He was nervous about leaving the table out in the rain."

"What'd you tell him?"

"I told him that you knew it was raining when you told him what to do, and that it was pretty waxed up anyway and a little water probably wouldn't hurt it. I hope that's right."

Everyone in town knew Ari Pappas was a hardball player and a ruthless negotiator, but this time, even Ari, never accused of sensitivity or honest self-appraisal, considered that he'd played his hand too hard. He'd thought that he'd get Joe Carroll to knock off a few thousand dollars, or make some other furniture for free, or, at the very least, kiss his ass and apologize for the lie, admit that he'd made the table from two pieces of wood. But now, his Maggie is all upset. Of course, she is, he thought. And Ari knew that when he got around to telling his own wife what he had done, as inevitably he must, she would tell him that he'd been a fool.

"Wrap up what you're doing and call it a night, Teddy," Ari said, speaking more kindly to his nephew than was his custom.

• • •

The traffic on the River Road had gotten busier as several roads converged ready to take the big sweeping turn up onto I-95. This was where Will knew he would need to steel his courage for the dash across the big highway bridge over the Connecticut River. I'll be up there for just a few minutes, he said to himself. There was a big wide breakdown lane. That's where I'll ride—just for a few minutes, Will told himself.

As Will began the uphill peddle onto the highway ramp there immediately rose several loud honks. He didn't notice that this afternoon he was not startled. He just wondered, did they almost hit me, have I already been in an accident? He needed to control the bike and not look around too much, so he looked down to see that his tires were still on the pavement. Somebody held a horn down steadily making a long angry blast. Several cars swerved to avoid him, but another car slowed right next to him, a window rolled down on the passenger side, and a man inside said, "What are you doing, kid? This ramp takes you up on the highway and the bridge. Don't go up there." Will just hopped off the bike and nodded at the guy, waiting for him to go on by. Maybe he'll think he's saved me and I'm turning back, Will thought. As soon as he was on his bike again, other slow-moving cars honked at him. A young man in a pick-up yelled, "Get off the fucking on-ramp, kid, you're going to get killed," and sounded several short blasts.

Will thought about Carini Tiezzi and the day the PT boat got caught on the coral reef and the officers on the boat went to get Carini to go into the water. Giordano said that his brother was crazy, but Will was thinking now that Giordano and Carini were just different and that Giordano's gentler mind just couldn't understand his brother's natural way of facing the world. The dozens of small stinging cuts from the coral—they made Carini feel alive. I feel alive right now, Will realized, ascending the gentle rise of the big bridge. I'm cold and wet and these cars and trucks are whizzing past me, but I am alive and I'm not going to get killed up here tonight. I'm doing the hard thing that I have to do. I'm alive.

And he was not afraid. Giordano had told him that a person couldn't know for sure what would frighten him until you were right there in the situation. This was really funny, Will thought. I was up here with Dad in the pickup a few months ago and I looked down at the river and my legs got all wobbly, but now on my bike riding over the bridge practically in the dark, I am not scared at all. Those wobbly legs weren't about courage or bravery, just something about how my body works. Will was not afraid; he knew that there were dangers all around him. He looked at the big trucks, the wet pavement, and at the pedals to check that his pants weren't going to get caught in the bike chain, but he was not scared. And the most exciting thing was, this was the first time that he'd known for sure that he was a person designed for hard things.

Suddenly Will was aware of his arms. My legs are plenty strong for this, he thought, but my arms feel like they are working too hard. He'd been steering slightly one way, then correcting, almost with a yank, veering the other way. My arms are still kind of wimpy, Will thought. He was hunched over more than usual straining his arms. He sat straighter to relax his body, to let his arms work in a different way. I can't worry about that right now, he thought. It's getting dark and I need to stare at the road.

Dad said to pay attention to the people who have chosen to do hard things. His Dad was one of them, Will thought. You can choose what you want to do with the life that God gave you—with your gifts—but then don't feel sorry for yourself when life is tough because you're one of the ones getting the fun of doing what you want. I understand all that—and I'm like my father that way.

Will was at the highest part of the bridge now. There were lots of honks and one loud yell, "Asshole." Just a couple minutes more on the bridge and the highway and the real asshole part of the ride would be done. I'm pretty sure, Will thought, that I'm not going to die up here tonight.

Dad always did the hard things, Will thought. Sometimes it was that he didn't have the money for the best modern tools for a job and had to do things the old-fashioned way, but it was usually more than that. Dad wanted to make something unusual or beautiful that the world—that's the word he used when he meant the general desire of most of the people— didn't want, or at least didn't know yet that they wanted. Sometimes, Dad said, you have to create a demand that's not there. Then you get to do some neat stuff. But now Dad's in trouble, Will thought. It really can't just be about the glue joint in the big board. Dad could explain that. It really was one solid piece, but his stupid kid dropped it and it broke nearly in half and we had to glue it back together. So what. Nobody would care very much about that. It must be that Mom was right, and Dad knew that she was right. Will had heard her say he'd sold his soul to the devil. She was probably mad that he didn't carve anything beautiful on the big board—didn't carve anything on it at all. I was surprised too, Will thought. And now it looks like he is paying for his mistake.

This rapid-fire conversation with himself distracted him for moments and he returned to his physical state. There's wetness tickling my cheeks and running onto my neck. I don't think I am crying, but my eyes aren't clear; they're a little stingy, maybe from dampness in the air, or maybe from fumes from all the cars and trucks, Will thought.

Will's mind churned again. Mom and Dad believe in God. Mostly only Mom goes to church, but we talk a lot about big ideas and for Mom and Dad those ideas suppose that God is in control of things and is even involved in what we're doing. I've never thought about whether I believe that, but right now, on my bike riding on the edge of I-95 in rush hour I think that God might send a cop out here to arrest me and take me out of the rain—maybe to the police barracks. Dad said that God probably knows what we are doing and thinking, but made us so we have to make our own choices, that our actions have consequences, but that God doesn't just jump in and reward us, or punish us, every step along the way.

It sure seems like God, not Mr. Pappas, dropped that table back in our yard and put Dad under it, all wet and sad, Will thought.

Will saw the off ramp for Saybrook just ahead. He looked behind him at the bridge traffic coming up on him and looked at the local traffic in town, which he saw through the gray drizzle of early evening. He was flying down the off ramp, right in the middle of the empty road. Almost there, he thought. He could safely swivel his neck around now, looking for blue lights, cop cars, not thinking that he was going to get killed—maybe just arrested.

Will was on the local street now. It was only seven or eight long blocks from here, he recalled. There was a big blue and yellow sign for the brake shop and then the old Tiezzi and Sons sign. I'm almost there, Will realized. What if Giordano was not even at home? I've never seen him anywhere but in his shop. He'll be there. He's so old; he's so old and he's so perfect in that place that he and his brother rigged up over years and years to do their work. He's got that old truck, he can probably still drive, but it doesn't seem like he'd go very far, like out of town to visit someone or sleep at somebody else's house. But I'm going to ask him to drive on the highway over the bridge to my town, to Lyme. I hope he's there; I need help. How long has it been since I covered Dad up and headed over here? Is he okay? Will wondered. Probably just half an hour, but it seems like longer.

There it was, the donut shop, and just beyond it the Meineke sign. Was it brakes or mufflers? Dad said they practically give the muffler away and charge you hundreds of dollars for all kinds of pipes that they say have rotted and rusted out, whether they really have or not. Find a mechanic that you like and trust, and stick with him—that's gold. That's what Dad said. Will's mind was in free fall. We got a glazed donut at the drive-up window in that place once, right before lunch, and I wasn't supposed to mention it to Mom, the donut or that Dad sometimes has a cigarette when we're away from home.

Just after the brake shop, Will turned into the driveway that led past Giordano's white house to the shop. A light from the house illuminated a wet, shiny patch of the pavement. There in the cool evening, Will was now on solid ground and it felt somehow warm.

He leaned his bike against the building and worked the wobbly door handle and pushed the creaky door open, not even knocking. The place was dark like he had found it other times, but the bare bulb was lit in Giordano's little phone booth office. There he was, in his dark gray, scratchy wool jacket and his plaid hunting cap with the flaps pulled down. Will thought that he was just asleep; old people dozed off a lot. God wouldn't make him die today when we need him so bad—he's just asleep right now—but he probably will die right in that spot—probably someday pretty soon.

Will folded open the accordion door, light flooded the space and Will said, "Mr. Tiezzi, Giordano," louder than necessary.

Giordano awakened with his usual, sweet smile. "Will Carroll. You've come to see me. What a nice surprise."

"Mr. Tiezzi, will you help my dad?"

"I will do anything for you that I can. What is the trouble? You are all wet."

"I rode my bike over here to get you. My dad's in trouble. We really need you."

"Is it about the board?"

"Yes, and other things, and Mom's not home, and everyone's all mad. Can you come, right away, can you come to our house?"

There was a small wooden drawer there in the phone booth and Giordano deftly opened it a crack, took a stack of paper money, and slipped it into his pants pocket.

Mr. Tiezzi didn't say anything and there was suddenly in his carriage the vigor and purpose of a man who had a job to do. From a nail over the shop door, he effortlessly took keys that Will had not noticed before.

"Hop in, Will. We'll go right now." It was a good step up into the passenger's seat and Will pulled the stiff door shut. To Will, Mr. Tiezzi didn't look like the right driver for this trip and he thought that he had made a wrong decision and had made things worse, but Mr. Tiezzi put in the clutch and the old Ford started right up. His gnarled hand caressed the gearshift knob familiarly. They were on the local street and on their way toward the highway. Will thought to look for his seatbelt, but there wasn't one. And it didn't seem important.

"We live in Lyme. We get off at the first exit after the bridge, then head up the river a little. It's not far. I'll show you the way. Dad finished the big table he made for Mom's boss, but something went wrong with it and it's back in our yard, just today, and he's not talking, Dad's all upset, not even talking, just lying under the table in the backyard. The table's all busted up. It looks like he whacked at it with a shovel." With the ending of the frightened stream of words a breathy stammer tumbled from his head. He saw the ease of Giordano's downshift to second gear as the bridge traffic slowed in front of them, and the way the old man's crooked fingers found the buttons and toggles that sent a blast of heat into the cab.

"We will help your papa."

They were at the apex of the main bridge span. Will said, "I rode this way on my bike," and smiled a little.

"Crazy," Giordano said.

Chapter 30
We Stole it

"He's back by the shop, I'll show you," Will said, and ran on ahead.

It was like an accident scene: the shovel, the damaged table and wooden fragments strewn in the grass, the quilts in different spots—not under the table any more, but tossed all soggy on the lawn. And no Dad, just a round, matted-down spot in the grass under the big table. "Dad," Will yelled and turned back toward the house where he met Giordano's slow approach. Crying now, Will said, "He's not there. I don't know where he is and Mom's not home. Where is he?"

When they came through the back door of the house, Joe was sitting in the dark at the kitchen table with a full tea mug in front of him. At the sound of their entrance his head did not turn and he didn't speak. Will rushed to him and hugged him really hard. "You okay, Dad? You got inside. By yourself?" It was still scary; his dad was stiff and unfamiliar. "Giordano came. He came from Saybrook and he's going to help us."

"We'll be all right," Joe said.

"You were out there a long time. I couldn't get you inside."

"It was dark when I woke up. I came in and took a shower—even made a cup of tea." Joe could barely look at Giordano. "Thanks for coming over, Mr. Tiezzi. Will called you up? I'll be okay."

"He rode his bicycle to my shop and we came here together," Giordano answered.

Every part of Joe Carroll was profoundly weary. There had never been a time when the mere company of his son would not stir him to his animated best. Today he was just about empty. What was the old man saying? Will rode his bike over the river on I-95? There's no other way to get to Saybrook. Frightening. I would have forbidden it, Joe thought, so he only looked at his son in wordless admiration that this boy had done such a thing. Picturing Will up on the highway bridge, even dimly, began to pull him out of his own grief. Not a very good decision—horrible, really—and amazing, Joe considered. Maggie must be very upset about Will riding his bike across the river. Maggie? She's at Annie's, he remembered. She left me. Will is here, though. And this old man, Giordano. Is it winter? Joe wondered. Giordano is wearing a red and black checked wool hat with earflaps. Will has gone after him and he's here to help me.

"You wished me buona fortuna and entrusted me with your mahogany, but I screwed it up—and a lot of other things." Joe wanted to cry, but Will being here now made him resist the easy impulse. "I was going to make something beautiful from your board. I think I promised you that. Have you seen it, out in the yard? It's still huge, Mr. Tiezzi, but far worse than I found it in your shed."

"That's why we took it, because it was gigantic."

"You should have used it yourself."

"I couldn't. And now I will tell you the truth. We stole it. Carini and I. My brother thought it would be fun, and I agreed to go with him, and there were some other boys from our neighborhood, and we climbed the fence at the boatyard where Carini was working and we stole the giant board."

Will said, "Mr. Tiezzi, that's okay. That was a long time ago."

"Please listen to me. Now I am too old and have lost my strength and can't do very much of anything. But there were many years when I had all my skills and strength and the board was right there in the shed. But the board would not let me do a thing with it. It had power over of us. We coveted it because it was so grand, and we stole it from the government of the United States, the country that had given our family a home. We stole it from the boatyard when our country was at war and they were supposed to build it into a boat to fight the Japanese."

For Will, even this sad confession from Giordano was a relief, a relief from the helplessness of his dad's agony. To Joe it sounded like old world superstition and Joe knew that his own choices were at the root of all the immediate trouble. Joe was still dwelling mostly on his own pain.

Giordano said, "So I thought that if somebody else had it, you Mr. Carroll, the curse of our stealing it might be broken, but the trouble didn't end, it passed to you, and I made it even worse by taking your money—selling a good man something that I stole."

"I don't know what I can say to persuade you, but I think it's just a piece of mahogany lumber, Giordano—a fabulous one, one that may have stirred us all up to big ideas, but really just a piece of lumber that you sold to the wrong man. I screwed it up, but you couldn't have predicted that, so it's not your fault."

"And what will you do with it now? Strike it with some other garden tools?"

"I haven't thought about that, Mr. Tiezzi. Would you like it back? You can give it to somebody else. That might be the best idea," Joe said.

In all of their past dealings with the old man, Giordano had been quiet and had merely responded to the excitement and desires of the father and son: Mr. Tiezzi, do you have a big board that is for sale, will you show it to us now, will you take our thousand dollars, will you help me with my social studies project, will you tell me about your brother with the missing leg, will you ride with me to my house to help my dad? His power had always been in his expression. He seemed to understand their hearts. He was rooting for them, caring for them from deep in his irresistible heart. But now, Giordano had his own idea.

"First thing is to bring the table out of the rain. Put on your coat, Mr. Carroll."

"Joe, I'm just Joe," Joe said.

"Will, get Joe's coat, we're going outside," Giordano said.

The three guys were standing next to the table in the dark and the rain had stopped. "Will it be easier to carry it in separate pieces, Joe?" Giordano asked.

"That's easy enough," and Joe went for a screwdriver and a dry drop cloth from the shop. He spread the cloth on the ground under the table and efficiently worked his way around the underside, unfastening twelve or fifteen of the little maple buttons that had held the top down. Will gathered them and their wood screws into a plastic grocery bag.

"I think that if it is not so big anymore, if it is just two boards about three feet wide, this thing will not make so much trouble any more. Not as much trouble anyway. How about that, Joe, Joe and Will? Can we saw it in two, at least put an end to the bigness of it? I want us to saw it in two—right now with your table saw, Joe. Just set your rip fence at 36 inches and move everything out of the way and we will do it. Maybe it will do something to stop all your trouble. Please can we do that?"

. . .

There was some moving around of stuff in the shop, setting up sawhorses and rollers and such, but in about twenty minutes it was done. One piece hung off the back end of the table saw bed; its twin having already crashed to the shop floor. And the saw blade had traveled exactly the length of the glue joint Teddy Pappas had so cleverly spotted.

Chapter 31
I Live Here

Maggie phoned home several times through that early evening and no one heard the rings. The boys were in the shop slicing the table in half.

"Stay one more night, Maggie," Annie said. "Dave's going to go over and just check in on Will and make sure everybody's okay. I'm going to make you a hot toddy and put on some music. Tomorrow you'll go talk to him when you've had a night to sleep on it. It'll be okay, Mags. It'll be okay, but right now you need rest."

Every stainless steel and glass surface was polished and perfect. The wheaty cotton of the sofas and chairs seemed too nice for Maggie's tired and unhappy body. Not since she was a child in her parents' home had anyone taken such a strong hand with her. And it was making her feel not very good about herself. She had an instinct to be with Joe, but she could not imagine how their conversation could begin, or what she would say to him. Just loving him and encouraging him—eighteen years of that—that was what she had always thought was the way you treat the people close to you—the way you treat everybody. Then at the soccer game on Sunday, she had forced herself to try outrage, anger, indignation. For sure she was hurt—that was real—hurt and disappointed, and even betrayed in the way Joe had deceived her about the table, but she knew it is not in her to sustain that way. I should just go home, she thought, but I am so tired. She succumbed to Annie's gentle ministrations. After all, whatever she had been doing in her relationship with Joe had come to disaster by any reckoning. And someone wants to care for me, Maggie thought, somebody strong is on my side.

Almost with a start, she propped herself up on the huge stuffed couch pillows. "But what about Will? Can Dave go over there? Please, can Dave just go over and talk to Will? Just make sure that he's okay. Tell him I'm coming home tomorrow, and ask him to phone me here. Tell him I've been calling and no one has answered. Could Dave just go over and see if they're okay?"

. . .

There were lots of wet tracks on the cement floor and on the wooden steps when Dave walked through the Carrolls' garage to their kitchen door. This was the way he and Annie always came when they visited Maggie and Joe. After a few knocks, the door opened part way and Will looked out from the yellow light of the kitchen.

"Hi, Will, are you okay?"

"Do you know where my mom is?"

"Your mom's at our house."

"When's she coming home?"

"Will, would you like to sleep at our house tonight?"

"No," with a touch of defiance. "I live here. Mom lives here."

"I'll tell her you're okay. Maybe you should call her. Do you need anything?"

"No, we're fine," and Will closed the door.

Chapter 32
A Pedestal of Sorts

The next morning was a school day and Will overslept. His world had changed. Somehow the inevitable scowl of the secretary at the front desk at school didn't seem so fierce. Last night he rode his bike over the Connecticut River on I-95. It hadn't occurred to him yet that he could tell his friends or that they wouldn't believe him. And that didn't matter either. All alone in the kitchen he made a peanut butter and jelly sandwich, tossed it and an apple into a bag, and the bag into his backpack. There was homework. Science and math, he thought. What can happen to a kid that hasn't done his homework? Nothing much.

It must have been at least ten o'clock when Joe Carroll woke up in the empty house. He went into Will's bedroom, even shook out the quilt and pillows to be sure that the kid was really not still in bed, worn-out like himself. Did all of that really happen? All yesterday, Joe wondered.

God, how I love those two—my wife and my son, Joe thought. It's all on me, on me to fix what I can of the mess I've made for Maggie and Will. He rode his bike to Saybrook yesterday in the rain. My son rode his bike over the Connecticut River on Interstate 95 yesterday and this morning he got himself up and off to middle school. My son. I have said that to myself always, but I think that I will stop. It's kind of silly to think of such a person, twelve, but in many ways already a man, as my son—as though my being his father is the essential thing about him. What about now? It's a good thing for Will, Joe thought, that Will Carroll has just taken a big step into autonomy on the same day that his dad had showed himself a fool and a coward. It's really the same thing with Maggie—the idea that her identity should in any way be wrapped up in her marriage to me, Joe thought. I don't know how I will repair what has happened, but I am not a fit leader of our family right now. I have so little to give them. Best thing now is for me to get out of everybody's way. I'm pretty sure of that, Joe decided.

Get out of everybody's way. The idea felt good to Joe, as though it was almost like doing something. He wondered if there was a 12-step program where that was one of the steps: get out of everybody's way. Maggie told Will that she's coming home tonight. How long has it been?

Joe began the recount in his head. Today is Wednesday. She saw the finished table in the shop on Sunday, confronted me about it at the soccer game, and went to Annie's all mad. Monday, I delivered the table. Tuesday, Pappas dumped it in my yard. Tuesday night, Will went to get old Tiezzi, now it is Wednesday and she is coming home tonight. Amazing that so quickly it should feel right that she is not here. And she is coming back here to our little house to be confined under this roof with Will and me. That's not right, Joe thought. Does she think that the big furniture-maker husband will just wander around the house like nothing has happened? I think that she ought to dread coming back here, and I don't wish it for her.

Joe was dressed now and remembered an old single mattress in their small attic; he carried it and his pillow and some linens out to the shop. He fumbled for the door knob, his arms full, and the door harp bounced. When he had put all the bedding down, he went back outside with a screwdriver and easily took down the harp which seemed to him inappropriately happy and welcoming to suit his new living quarters. Once inside again, he looked at the wood stove, built a crude nest next to it, and thought, this is a good place for my exile.

Joe found some cinderblocks in a corner of the garage and in several trips got half a dozen up to his and Maggie's bedroom. It had stuck in Joe's mind what Dave had said to him, that Maggie was a princess who should be placed upon a pedestal. She was coming home this afternoon. I can make it a little nicer up here for Maggie, out of respect for her, Joe thought. Get the bed up off the floor on these blocks and make the bed up clean and pretty. Get some flowers from town. She'll know pretty quickly that I've moved outside, that the flowers were just a gift, not a stupid romantic suggestion. Do I have any money? Joe wondered. He reached for his wallet in his back pocket—not there. Then he reached into the front pockets and found ten one hundred-dollar bills. He was wearing the same pants he wore yesterday afternoon when he got himself dry. Giordano gave me this cash last night, but I am sure I do not remember when, or what it was for, or why I took it. A thousand dollars. Giordano gave me back all that I paid him for the board—the whole thing.

When Will got home from school he went right out to the workshop. It was a funny sight, Joe sound asleep on a mattress next to the woodstove, a kettle quietly steaming on the stove and a box of crackers there on the floor. He slipped out quietly so that his dad could sleep.

Maggie came home around five-thirty, a little earlier than usual and found Will bundled up on the front stoop awaiting her return, anxious for a first step toward domestic normalcy. At the driveway she got out of her little car and he was there with a great hug.

Maggie said, "I've missed you a lot. I thought I needed time to think. I didn't even go to work," and she made a little self-mocking laugh. "I'm sorry for leaving you guys alone."

"We're not mad." Will had rehearsed the line. Maggie started for her big tapestry bag in the back seat, but Will jumped in front of her and said, "I've got your stuff. Come on inside."

"Where's Daddy?"

"Out in the shop. He's sort of living out there."

"I'm home now, Will. We'll be okay."

"I don't think he's coming inside. He's got a lot of stuff out there."

Maggie had been home only about an hour and had started supper. This not seeing Joe was too weird and she determined to see him and break the ice. Even with what happened, it will be better than this, she thought. Maggie made a pot of tea and got a tray organized with the lemon and sugar that Joe liked and headed out the kitchen door toward the shop. She knocked softly on the shop door; she'd never done that before, and she let herself in.

Joe was on his feet, leaning against the workbench, and right away he looked up at her. His face was impassive and he didn't speak. A little smile came too effortlessly to Maggie, seeing him there, all mussed up in his stocking feet—camping. When you love somebody, Maggie had learned, you just love them, on good days and bad. She had never thought about their wedding vows, whether they said that part about richer or poorer, sickness and health, better or worse. We probably did, she thought, but she hadn't ever considered the vow a stricture to be governed by. It was just something she had spoken when she was young and she hadn't thought about since. Today, to smile at Joe, to love him, she was responding to him and to their life as the person she had become. She just plain loved Joe Carroll. And in a sense, though she would not say it to him, this broken Joe Carroll felt somehow easy to love.

Maggie walked right up to him, set the tray on the workbench, and put her arms around his waist. It was a careful embrace.

Joe stiffened. It was a mild rejection that she surely noticed, and he pushed her gently away.

"You alright?" she asked.

"Yeah."

"We'll be okay. Come on in later, Joe? I saw my pretty room."

"Not quite a pedestal," he said. Maggie remembered the reference.

Joe looked over at the mattress on the floor by the woodstove and Maggie started to say, "You know—" but he interrupted her. He couldn't let her do this work of making up. Maggie had done nothing wrong and things were not so easily fixed.

"I can't be with you, not now." He had anticipated this moment. It had always been their way, to talk about things. But this was different, Joe had thought. He didn't know where they were going or if some kind of healing was ahead for them, but he was sure that when this moment came, words would feel very cheap. And besides, he was so very weary, so he only said, "I'm really glad you're home."

It was on toward eight o'clock now. Maggie was in the kitchen and had reread several times the same page of her book with no comprehension. Will came in the room. There was a noise outside and Will said, "That's Dad running water from the outside faucet."

"Why don't you take him a cookie?"

Will couldn't see into the workshop when approaching it on the path from the house; he had to climb a gentle earthen bank and go around to big side windows to look in. And on this night, Will felt sneaky because he could look inside knowing that his father could not see him perched in the darkness. Will had been out there at night to visit his father dozens of times, mostly in weeks leading up to Christmas when Joe was swamped with jobs for handmade things that people had ordered as gifts. He'd needed lots of visits and treats and encouragement to get it all done. But this was different. This was where he lived now, his kitchen, bathroom, den, and bedroom. This might not be a good time, Will thought, but there he was, stoking the wood fire, so Will decided to go in.

Joe looked up from where he was squatting by the stove. "You still up? I don't know what time it is. I got my watch a little wet the other day. Is it a school night?"

Will nodded slightly. "It's Wednesday, and it's eight something. Mom said I can stay home tomorrow if I feel like it. She says I look tired."

"Does she know why you look tired?" and Joe smiled, beginning to store away the heroic bike ride as an iconic Carroll family story.

"No, I don't think so."

Joe said, "I guess she might have heard about it on the television news when she was staying over at Annie and Dave's. They've got a huge flat screen."

This was great, Will thought, Dad wisecracking, and he looked down at the full package of Oreos in his hands. "Hey, I've got cookies."

"And I was just making tea. I've got two mugs and I just rinsed them outside.

"This is an excellent setup you've got here. What happens when you need to go number two?"

"Oh, I drive to town. That's why they call them convenience stores." This would ordinarily be fun—the silly, imaginative banter that their family enjoyed and was good at, but tonight it was an effort for Joe.

"I'll make tea." Joe poured water from the steaming kettle into separate mugs, dropped in separate tea bags from a little box on the shop floor, and set the mugs down near the mattress. Joe unfastened his khaki trousers and dropped them to the floor and got under the covers. "Take off your shoes and you can get under," and Will did. They sipped their tea, maneuvering around the tea bags and separately feigning sighs of comfort and satisfaction with the camp arrangements. "God, I dislike herb tea." Then they were quiet for a while.

"I guess I wasn't paying attention while you were getting to know Mr. Tiezzi so well. It's fine. He's the person you thought of."

"He told me awesome stories about him and his brother, about them working together, what it was all like back then." Will looked at his father for a clue that he should go on.

"Nice," Joe said.

"It was like he was telling me all the important things in his life, not because he just tells the same old stories over and over, but like he wanted to tell that stuff to someone in particular. I don't know why, and I was the one."

"He was happy that you were interested."

"It seemed like more than that, which is why I rode after him when you were passed out under the table. Were you, you know, unconscious? I talked to you and you didn't answer."

"I remember you being there. I can't describe it, Will. I wasn't unconscious, but I was in terrible mental pain and I wanted to be unconscious—was sort of urging myself to somewhere else. I'm sorry I scared you. Anyway, you went for help. That was good."

"When I was there, in Mr. Tiezzi's shop, it always felt like something big was happening, even if it was just him and me talking and fooling around. It always felt important."

With what strength of mind Joe could conjure, he tried to take this in, to comprehend the significance, mostly out of respect for his son, no, not his son, for Will, for Will Carroll, who had a friend named Giordano Tiezzi.

"Well, for better or worse, our lives intersected when we bought that damn board," and Joe pointed to the two big pieces leaning over near the table saw. "Looks like somebody whacked at it with a blunt object. Did I really do that?" And they laughed.

Will said, "Carini was working in this little boatyard that some local men got up quick during the war to make money. It was north of the bridge in Saybrook on the edge of the river. There's a marina there now. It's the place with the big smokestack. They were making PT boats for the Navy. I knew that part before, but only yesterday he told us the part about them stealing the board."

"I think the old man made too much of the stealing. Sounds like the dead brother was just full of vinegar and they got carried away. People haven't changed."

"He loved excitement—Carini—that's for sure. And he couldn't wait to get into the war."

"Great idea."

They laughed. "No, he liked it. Giordano said that there were some who thought it was fun, and his brother was one of them."

"Crazy, some boys are crazy."

There was more talk, another mug of tea, and Will told more of Giordano's tales. Joe was getting very sleepy, but fought to stay awake for Will's story. It ended with Will rising up out of the bed covers and with his right arm, imitating a broad, high, whipping action that ended with a loud, "Ahhhhhhhhh!"

Chapter 33
Something for My Wife

Joe never had a chance to deposit Pappas' second check. On this morning he was in the living room standing at the shiny, curly maple wall-hung shelf that he built to house the best of his antique tools. The check was still there in one of the cubbies. He took it from its special place and was putting it in his wallet when there was a knock at the door.

Stan Heckenberg, the guy that answered his Craigslist ad, was there on the front stoop. He was a little older and fatter than what Joe expected from the high-pitched voice on the telephone this morning. "Come on in," Joe said.

Joe knew that his antique planes, chisels, rules, calipers and gauges are the Holy Grail to thousands of American men. Not only were they lovely in their simplicity and craftsmanship, but they were icons of a simpler time and a slower way of life about which only the very young are not nostalgic.

"Wow, these are beautiful, Joe."

Joe had not invited him to call him by his first name and was in no spirit to be pals with this man who was most surely going to walk off with these gems that he had loved and prized. There was only a terse reply. "There are a lot more."

From a bureau drawer nearby, he produced a hand-written catalogue of his entire collection: the proper name for each tool, the price paid for the piece, where it was bought, and on what date. From other drawers he lifted shallow boxes containing scores of other little gadgets.

"Wow," said Mr. Heckenberg.

Joe Carroll lifted them quickly, but carefully out of their boxes and covered the sofa and chairs with them. "I've collected them for—" and he looked down at the catalogue, "—well, it says here I bought that Stanley multi-plane in '83—twenty some years."

"So, why sell them now?" Joe turned and looked right in the man's eyes and with his silence made it plain that he didn't wish to engage the question. "I'm sorry, none of my business," Mr. Heckenberg apologized.

Joe answered in words that had meaning only to himself. "I'm buying something for my wife," and Joe looked back again at the list. "The total of what I paid for all one hundred and eighteen pieces is two thousand, three hundred, and forty-eight dollars." There was a twinge of shame in his putting it like that and he corrected himself in a way that the stranger would not notice. "What my wife and I spent at auctions and tag sales over twenty years. Another half a dozen were gifts from friends and relatives. I'm sure the collection is worth nearer five thousand today."

"Do you want to keep the ones that were gifts?"

"I don't mean to be rude, Mr. Hecken—" and Joe stalled.

"—berg, Stan Heckenberg."

"But you are correct that it's none of your business." There was a pause while they regained common ground for what Joe expected would be a simple negotiation. "Do you want to pay what we paid for them, or the current values?" Joe had thought out this dark joke earlier when he was alone and could not resist using it.

"I can only offer you $1,800, Joe, Mr. Carroll. It's all I've got on me."

"Fine, cash, right?"

"Yeah, cash," and Stan reached for his wallet and paid Joe in hundred-dollar bills. "Hey, I've got some boxes and some newspaper in my van. I'll just run out and get a few boxes, wouldn't that be good?"

The packing was quickly accomplished and Joe looked up at the naked shelf left hanging there on the living room wall. Pretty pathetic. "You know, you ought to have this showcase to put the nice ones in."

Stan said, "Would you take two hundred for it?" There was no verbal answer and Joe was already lifting it from the wall. The stranger went back to his wallet and pulled out two more one hundred-dollar bills. Joe didn't want to meet his eyes, didn't care that the stranger was a liar, and Stan Heckenberg put the cash down on the coffee table.

Chapter 34
If It's What You Really Want

Joe didn't quite know how many days it had been that he'd lived by himself in the shop. It was not a complete segregation, really. When Maggie and Will were gone during the day, he had made a habit of bathing and using the bathroom, but his forays indoors were brief.

It had been more than a week since he moved out there. Maggie was glad that Will visited his dad every evening and always came back happy. She had a sense that Joe was okay and their lives, though mostly separate, were on an even keel. She had never thought that the self-help movements and books that friends had spoken of had much to do with their lives. It had always sounded self-indulgent. But these days she had come around to hoping that out there under the blue fluorescent lights, Joe might be doing the work, as they say, of healing the parts of himself that he thought were broken.

On this April evening Maggie performed what had become their ritual. She carried a tray with Joe's supper through the yard to the shop door. She was lonely for him and wanted to go inside, but she fought off what she decided was a selfish temptation and did what they'd agreed to, and set the tray on the stone threshold and knocked on the door—their signal.

And acting his part, Joe waited long enough for Mags to have returned indoors before he went for his food. There was a lot of stuff to clear on the workbench to make room for his solitary meal. His big newsprint roll covered most of it and in several places big oblong rectangles, vertically oriented, in the shape of the two halves of Pappas' table top were drawn with wax pencil. But they were empty—blank. There were books and magazines about the South Pacific theatre of World War II, pictures of men in naval uniform.

He looked down at the meal: broiled white fish, spinach, boiled potato with butter, salt and pepper and chives, a little salad of Boston lettuce and cucumbers. Lovingly prepared. Those were the words that he had sometimes used out loud in a table grace, whether with company or just with Will and Maggie. Sometimes it had felt like more than he could bear, to be so loved and to see Maggie pouring herself out for him. It was not just because of the present order of things; it had always felt like the last straw in an over-blessed life. Of them to whom much is given, much is required. It was in the Bible, Joe knew—he wasn't sure where, but he knew that the principle was firmly embedded in his unconscious mind. I'm educated, smart, free, and able-bodied, he thought. I've got a wonderful, healthy child, a cute house in a cute town in the richest state in the richest country in the world in the era of mankind's greatest prosperity. My wife has a job and the mortgage gets paid every month. Much is required. How am I doing?

And to raise the bar even higher for me, he had thought, that beautiful girl believes in me. I think she prays for me every day though she does not say so, and she makes me good meals—meals that aren't just good, but are properly balanced and nutritious. Oh shit, he had thought sometimes, why don't you make yourself an egg or something, Maggie, and leave me on my own? Give yourself a break. But when he had thought very hard about it, he had concluded that he wasn't trying to give Maggie a night off, but that he was asking for a break for himself, a break from the gratitude.

It was me that had said right out loud to Maggie, "I thought I'd do something important," he remembered. But it wasn't a challenge that she presented to me and I just accepted as mine. I thought it before I knew her. I fell in love with those orange and turquoise hardbound biographies of great men when I was only in fourth or fifth grade and I thought that I would be great, too. And then I was given all the freedom and the means to achieve the high and vague goal. And I haven't done very well.

Joe recalled one time when he was sure he'd said it out loud. It was right after he walked off that job for Linda Howe when Linda wanted him to redo the carved herbs. Alone now in his shop, he picked up a damask linen napkin from his dinner tray. He wound it around his face, stood at the workbench and straightened his back. He remembered standing in the prow of the rowboat out in the cove. Maggie's words spoken as though they were truth, truth that must be an encouragement, rang in his brain: "If it's what you really want, you just will."

Encouraging words that so many times have cut like a knife, a knife filleting away the outer skin of me, Joe Carroll, leaving the tender, bleeding essence of me designed to be good, but lots of times just wanting to be covered back up so that neither I nor the world shall have to consider me.

I remember, Joe thought, a radio call-in program I heard one late night years ago. Through the ether the words had pressed along the amplitude-modulated waves into a shop in Lyme, Connecticut. A fellow was full of vinegar about a small business he was starting from his home some place like upstate New York or Parma, Ohio. It didn't matter. The program host, expert on all things business, law, finance, and entrepreneurship pre-empted the fellow's question with a preliminary, but extremely important edict. "First of all, friend, you've got to get that business out of your house. Go into town. Is there some kind of a downtown near East Butthole, or wherever you say you live? You've got to rent a storefront of some kind and hang a sign. I don't care if you even use the space, but establish a presence outside your home. Trust me on this," he told the guy, "No one takes seriously anything anybody runs out of their house."

How many times had Joe wished that he had been working some place else all day? He could just hop in the truck and drive home, hug the wife and kid, pour a drink, and they would just assume he'd worked hard all day. After all, hadn't he been down at the store from eight till five-thirty?

It was all wrapped up in the same horrible thing of our free will, he thought. I have been living with it all these years. If it's what I really want, I just will. All the freedom and prosperity had just upped the ante of the free will game God has permitted me. It is wonderful and it is horrible and it is a destiny that I cannot now escape. Not wanting this to be my paradigm is not a choice. I have believed these things for too long and I cannot erase the template now, even if I'd like to. I have worked at home all these years and for many of the days I have been free to work as little or as hard as I wished. I have taken naps that I really needed and lots that were merely an escape. All in all, I have probably been more disciplined than the average guy would be in my place. There'd been nobody here watching me. Most people have a boss around somewhere, or at least colleagues subtly holding one another accountable. I've been alone, and I've produced a lot of good work. But I have not become the man that I thought I would be.

. . .

Later that same evening Will came out to visit his dad. He brought him a few gingersnaps and the ubiquitous herb tea.

With a violet blue Prismacolor pencil Joe had sketched a few things in some of the rectangles that are the halves of Tiezzi's board. "Do you know what it's going to be yet?" Will asked.

"No."

"These are about Carini in the war," Will said, tentatively handling a big sheet of newsprint with his father's crude drawings on it.

"All my ideas come back to them. I can't think of anything else." He said this not as a complaint or a problem—just as a matter of fact.

Will reached into his pants pocket for something. It was money, and he handed it to his father. "Here."

Slowly and respectfully, looking up to meet his son's eyes, then back at the little wad, he examined the bills. "Is this what I think it is?"

"Yeah. It's fine. I've got my eye on a used one that's really nice, a little bigger. After all, I'm growing."

"One-fifty's not much for the only Specialized that ever crossed the River on the I-95."

"And I threw in the cap."

Joe reached across the bench and held Will's hand. All this free will stuff was tricky and powerful. And God had dragged the kid in on it too. Wonderful and terrible—this life.

Chapter 35
I Hope You Take Yours Black

A black Lincoln town car pulled into the parking lot behind Ari Pappas' law offices. It was still practically dark out and it could fairly be said that Joe Carroll was lurking in the shadows, even hiding in the bushes. Joe hadn't told Maggie what he was going to do today. They weren't talking to one another much anyway, but Joe hadn't needed to ask her what time Ari Pappas got to work. Joe had heard plenty about Ari's fastidious routine. In fact, most of the town of Old Lyme had gagged at one time or another on the mythology of how Ari and his generation had built what they have, and how indebted everyone should be to them.

Ari parked in his usual spot, turned off the car, the lights dimmed on their own, got out of the Lincoln, and headed toward the office back door. There was never anybody else around at 6:10 in the morning. Teddy tried coming that early a couple of times to make an impression, but he hadn't kept it up.

Ari heard a loud, clear voice say, "I've never been up this early before. It's really not so bad." Joe Carroll stepped out from behind the end of a row of arborvitae and he was carrying a Dunkin' Donuts bag.

Ari was tough and cool. "I've been right here every morning for forty years. That discipline has allowed me to buy nice things." It was not out of the question, Ari thought, that Maggie's husband, what's his name, Joe Carroll, had a gun and intended to shoot him even if he'd never get away with it. "I think you had better get the hell out of here." Staying strong and on the offensive was the smart thing, Ari knew.

Joe walked slowly and unthreateningly toward Ari Pappas and reached into his pocket. Ari stiffened, but did not run. "Get the hell away from me, Joe. I can have the cops here in two minutes." How can I do that? Ari thought. Shit, there's no one around at this hour.

"I'm not here to make any more trouble for you. Please, just listen a minute."

Joe held out cash and a check. "I never deposited the second check you gave me. I'm returning that and $7,000 cash."

Pappas just stared at Joe. I stopped payment, you fool, Ari thought, but did not speak. He put out his left hand and took the money.

"I am sorry that I deceived you—that you didn't get the table you bargained for. And Ari, please don't blame Maggie for what I've done. None of this is her fault."

"We're good to our Maggie."

"I'll repay the other three thousand as soon as I can, but it may take me a few months. I don't have any work." Joe extended the donut bag in Ari's direction. "I hope you take yours black."

Ari's hands were all occupied with his wallet, car keys, and Joe's money, so Joe just set the bag on the ground between them.

Ari said, "Cops and people who owe other people money should stay the hell out of donut shops."

Chapter 36
It's From the Top

Joe went back to bed after the drama in Ari Pappas' parking lot. He wasn't kidding when he said that he was not often out and about town at 6:10 a.m. It was almost lunchtime now and he was at Davis Lumber—one of his first forays from home since the crisis. Will and Joe, when they speak of Tiezzi's board coming back to Joe in the form of a table sitting in the mud in the backyard, call it the crisis, not to be melodramatic, but what else would you call something like that if you were trying to get it down to one or two words. Most people, Joe said, have simply not had anything happen to them that deserves that word.

The old routine felt good. Joe was inside the big steel barn and pulled a 4 x 8 sheet of 1/8 inch luan plywood off a stack and tossed it into the bed of his pickup. Outside against the end of the building were the 2 x 4 and 2 x 6 studs, and an assortment of them was tossed in back to weigh down the plywood.

His old buddy, Gary, was behind the counter in the office. He must be preoccupied with something, Joe thought. Gary was not himself.

"Hi, Gary."

"What have you got, Joe?"

"One sheet of 1/8 inch luan. I took a nicked-up one that was on top. Just making some templates from it. And, uh, 2 x 4 spruce, two 8's, two 10's; 2 x 6 spruce, four 8's."

Gary hit some keys. The computer printer behind him kicked in to produce his slip in triplicate.

"I'm going to need cash for this, Joe." Gary can't look at Joe, but Joe looked right at him, and then at Jimmy Newhouse who had been circling in the background waiting for this moment.

"Really, cash? After twenty years." Joe liked these men so much. "Hey, forget it, Gary," and Gary managed to get the slip in front of Joe on the counter.

"It's from the top, buddy. Sorry. Someone told the boss you were in trouble."

"I can guess. But it's funny, isn't it? I don't even have a balance here, do I?" Joe knew he hadn't been late in several months. Not that he'd never been late over the years, but he was all square at the moment. Joe managed a wry smile, wanting to make this easier for the guys. "I guess the grownups have to stick together and enforce some discipline or the country will go to hell."

"Assholes," Gary said.

Joe pushed the slip gently back toward him. "Forget it, Gary. It's all right, we'll be all right. I'll put the stuff back, no problem."

Chapter 37
Legs Wobbly

It had been a warm and dry day at the very beginning of May. Any other year Joe Carroll would have fired up the rototiller on such a day, cultivating up close to a row of lettuce he had seeded at the end of March. But Joe had stuck out his self-exile to the workshop for several weeks, to the exclusion of all other routines.

He sat at his usual spot at the workbench, surrounded by drawings, and by dirty plates and mugs, stacks of papers and books. Sometimes he was drawing, sometimes he was cutting up images from photocopies of book and magazine articles and rearranging them in his own collage, but mostly he stared into space.

He had thought about God's view of all of this and he guessed that he did believe that God knew what was going on with him—with him and Maggie and Will. God knew about the crisis. Was God laughing? Some crisis: rich white guy in Connecticut had business setback, failed to properly self-actualize as artist. It was not quite as bad as a guy praying for himself just before he rolled a bowling ball, Joe had considered, but praying for His intervention in this, well, Joe wouldn't want to crowd out a prayer for the millions of people starving in North Korea. So as much as he believed that God loves him, he hadn't exactly prayed for help in the present mess.

Joe wanted help; he needed it. It was inherent in his sitting out there for three weeks among the pieces of busted up table that, in his broken state, there remained a strand of faith that something positive might still happen.

As he leaned over the rolled-out newsprint, and zoomed in with a wax pencil on a section of his crude drawing, his hair fell into his eyes. He flipped it away. The hair was not that long, just annoying, and it fell right back to the place that was tickling him at the edge of his eye socket. He shuffled through the mess on the bench with both hands and spotted the orange-handled scissors. In a flash he lopped off a big chunk of his hair which he dropped remorselessly behind him to the floor.

Daylight savings time had started and the days were getting longer anyway. It was past supper time and was still light out when Maggie pulled on her jacket to carry coffee and a piece of pie out to Joe in the backyard.

Maggie respected what she had come to call their jail cell routine. She set the tray down on the stone threshold to the shop door and knocked. Two loud knocks. The other part of the drill was that Joe waited half a minute before opening the door so that Maggie could make her escape. But on this night, Maggie put the tray down, knocked twice, and walked up around the side of the shop and sat right on the ground at the shop window. Joe had one sliding window a little open. She looked inside and saw Joe bring the tray to the bench. Then she tapped twice firmly on the window— an echo of the jail cell knock on the door.

"I'm sorry," she said. "I know how easily you startle. It's wonderfully warm out here."

"I've let the fire go out. I don't think I'll relight it tonight."

"What happened to your beautiful hair?"

At first, he didn't know what she was talking about, but then he brought his hand to his head and remembered. He turned away from the window.

Maggie felt like she was spying on him, invading his privacy, and she turned away, too. She hitched her bottom over a couple feet so that now turning her back to Joe, she was leaning not on the window, but on the concrete foundation wall. Neither could see the other.

"Will you come in the house now, Joe? I miss you a lot."

There was a long pause. "I miss you, too, Mags. Don't think that part's not awful." Another pause. "We chopped the board in half—Giordano and I. But I can't leave it like that. I still have to make something from it—

176

by myself." There was another long pause and Joe looked to see if Maggie was at the window.

"You will."

"I haven't even got a design. And it doesn't feel like I'm any closer."

"Squash pie. Squash pie and a clean bed indoors."

"Mags, remember when we were starting out, how I'd work till bedtime every night?"

"You had to. It's different now—we're older."

"I've been posing. I've been an artist only in my own imagination, and you've been too kind to tell me." Maggie still leaned against the building and had not looked back into the light. "You've known for a long time, haven't you?" It was a rhetorical question and Maggie was glad that she did not need to respond. Joe went on, "I've wasted a lot of time."

"There's probably lots left."

Joe said, "I've let us all down. I know that I've—"

Maggie rushed to soften his self-debasement. "I think you've been—"

"—a fool," Joe finished her sentence. "I've been a fool. I need you to forgive me, if you can."

There were several seconds of silence and Joe for a moment thought that Maggie had not heard him, or had missed a word or two. Then at the door, there was a click. Joe did not turn, but stayed facing the bench and the window. His head was bowed, not quite in his hands.

He knew that she was in the room. His brain did not process it in full sentences, but the thoughts quickly washed over him: how many thousands of times had this beautiful person walked silently into a room where I sat, and I did not marvel at the enormity of the blessing. She is walking toward me right now, wretched turd that I am, and she loves me. Oh my God—terrible and amazing. Joe began to cry, big convulsive cries, the noise of which could not be squashed. He was actually heaving uncontrollably when one arm reached around his left shoulder and a hand rested on his chest. I am loved by this woman, he thought. It is amazing. Maggie's other hand was on his head now, exploring the spot where the shock of hair had gone missing. Joe cried even harder, was shaking, and let his throat give vent to what felt not like pity, but like a primal expiation. Both of Maggie's arms were around him now, holding him tight.

She said, "I forgive you." Joe was silent and she sensed that this was not enough, so she said, "You've been a fool and a fraud, and I forgive you."

She put her head near to his now. "The whole thing. You have been foolish some of the time, and a fraud some of the time, and you have disappointed me badly. And I forgive you."

She let him loose and walked the three steps to his nest by the woodstove and picked up his bed pillow. She turned him around toward her and put the pillow in his arms. Small laughs mixed now with the crying and tears. So many ordinary days we pass together, and then there are ones like this. He was amazed.

Joe slid off the stool onto his feet and, slowly at first, legs wobbly, allowed himself to be led toward the door.

Chapter 38
Warm Bare

Joe and Maggie came in the house and went upstairs right away. Maggie's idea to defuse the drama of Joe's return was to yell through Will's closed bedroom door, "How's the homework coming, Will? Daddy's come home. We're tired and we're going to sleep."

"Hi, Dad," Will said through the closed door. He smiled at what he understood about their grownup business. No way I'm leaving my room right now, he decided without hesitation. "See you in the morning, Daddy."

It was almost dark and there were no lights on in the room. Joe had forgotten about having put the bed up on blocks and there was a pretty spread on it now that on all sides nearly reached the ground. They undressed in the dark; there was no washing up or tooth brushing. In its way, this was scarier than the first time he and Maggie slept together. His bare skin had touched hers thousands of times, and yet, this night was clean and new and Maggie, under the covers as she was, glowed golden and perfect in Joe's mind.

Maggie lay on her side facing the wall, but she hitched near the center.

Joe said, "This bed—I think I've got agoraphobia."

"I don't think you've got that, Joe. You're not afraid of leaving home. You made that long trip into the backyard, and, anyway, you're safely home now."

"No, the other one, acrophobia. Your bed is so high. I'm scared to death up here. We've always slept on the ground."

"Then hang on to me, Joe. Come on, come over close and just hang on."

Spoons, spoon fashion. That's what they used to call it, an eternity ago in their lives together, this perfect ergonomic fit for lovers that they agreed was a sure sign of the existence of God. Anyway, it always felt divine. His right arm was under her pillow extended straight, and his left wound around her so that his hand found rest on the mattress. Maggie took his hand and cupped it firmly over her breast. "Hang on, just hang on, Joe, it's going to be okay." Everywhere, warm bare flesh joined warm bare flesh. In moments, he was asleep, and Maggie right after him.

• • •

The digital clock said three something. Three in the morning, Joe realized it must be. I'm wide awake. Maggie is here next to me. I came up here last night and we went to bed very early and I think that now I'm up for the day. I should call Ari Pappas and tell him I'm up. We could go out for coffee somewhere. Joe wonders if he can slip off of the tower without waking her. It's so early. Out to the shop is where I need to go, he thinks.

Standing naked in the moonlit room, he tiptoed toward his pants and socks.

In the workshop he grabbed shavings and wooden kitchen matches and kindled a fire in the woodstove. Scraps went in on top, a small log, the door left open a crack—the same smooth dance.

He sat at the bench now. He had come out here without a shirt, not easily having spotted one in the darkness, and so for warmth he wound a bed sheet, remnant of his exile, around his bare shoulders. He was looking at his pictures and drawings again, reliving all the fragments of a story about the Tiezzi brothers and the theft of the mahogany and the war and Will dropping the board on the sawhorse and its breaking in two and coming back to him like a bad nickel. He had combed over all this same stuff for weeks.

The two pieces were on sawhorses now, side by side. Joe, draped in the bed sheet, walked to one end of the arrangement. He leaned forward, the end of both pieces cut across the top of his thighs. He spread his arms apart and placed the palms of both hands down flat on the two pieces of mahogany. His forehead was square and hard against the wood. The white sheet fell to the floor.

"If it's what you really want, you just will. Nothing will stop you." Maggie's words rang in his brain. The first time he had heard them as Pollyanna encouragement, but now they sounded like a promise—a gift.

I will? Nothing will stop me. Now we're getting somewhere, he thought.

"Okay, big board. It's you and me; our destinies are intertwined. Doesn't it seem so?" He pushed his torso up off the board and still leaning on the end, he was able now to see the whole thing and found himself silently speaking to an inanimate object. This was not in Joe's carefully built theology—attributing power to a piece of wood, but it occurred to him now that from the day he brought it from Saybrook, he had danced around at its edges, liking the owning of it, but not loving it very well. In this spring dawn the room was brightening and he said, "I am here with you, Big Board. This is the time for me to know you, and you to know me. I commit, invest, whatever it takes."

Joe sprang right up onto the boards, just barely using a knee. Face down, he spread his arms to their full span so that his fingertips just reached the edges of the two pieces. Palms were down, a cheek hard against the shiny, cold surface.

There was an animal undulation of his legs and torso; he had an impulse that he must force his whole self into Tiezzi's board, to become one with it. He turned the other cheek to the wood and continued with extraordinary energy to writhe and press and flex, first the white flesh of the underside of his upper arms, and alternately the ankles, the chest, and the thighs, and ten spread, tensed fingers. Nowhere did any part of his body lose contact with the board by more than an inch, and never for more than a few seconds. And in this improbable act, Joe Carroll believed that he was making progress.

"It is what I want," he shouted out loud. "Let me make something beautiful, God. It is what I want." This was no pathetic lament. He was insistent, loud and aggressive—all in.

The air close around him was suddenly thicker. He lifted himself up a little and looked at a steamy, damp shadow of his chest and belly on the shiny board, but even beyond and below his waist, there was condensation in the faint shape of a Joe. He let himself back down and he was sure that he felt heat from the wood warming his bare flesh.

Alternately, he pressed hard his arms and legs, then his cheek, then his belly and pelvis—forcing himself against the board. There was no yelling or crying out, just small involuntary sounds that were part of great exertion.

Joe lifted his head enough to turn it so that his nose and forehead were right on the crack where the two pieces met. His eyes were shut. He was conscious that he was taking pains to just be there, straining and alone and in a forced darkness. Parts of him should hurt— hurt in this ridiculous posture—but nothing did.

There were little sparkles of light floating just behind his eye sockets; they flashed quietly on and off and some of them were light blue and lavender and pink, but mostly they were white, especially the brightest ones. This is nice, Joe thought, and wondered if it was a show that had always been there and that he had been missing. More pinpoint flashes of light swirled and organized themselves into thick constellations. "It's what I really want," he heard himself saying out loud.

"Comprendo," he heard clearly in a child's voice. Still with his nose pressed to the board, Joe opened his eyes and he was looking at a tan-skinned, black-haired boy. The figure should not have come into focus, nose to nose as they were, but Joe could see him vividly. Curls of dark hair fell over the boy's brow and around his ears. He was smooth-skinned, beardless, and his broad, long nose was right there hard up against Joe's. Limb for limb, his body mirrored Joe's sprawl upon the board.

Joe lifted his head and torso up from the close view. He wasn't afraid. He just moved slowly, not wanting to frighten off the vision. And it remained. The boy was slender and dark. He was moving now, moving seamlessly across the crack between the halves of Tiezzi's board like a digital image dragged across matching computer monitors. White sparkles of light had coalesced into a gown and huge pure white wings. Billows of white cloth rose and fell up the lengths of the boy's arms and legs as he moved around just below the surface of Tiezzi's board. Weightlessly he dipped down and forward as though reaching for something with an outstretched hand. And then, just when he was nearly upside down and about to tumble over, with an audible laugh he saved himself with a pirouette that sent the white drapery swishing and twisting up. Joe thought that he had heard himself laugh too, and the boy repeated the fall and spin a few more times as to put on a show.

Joe closed his eyes and dropped back down hard upon the surface. When he opened them again white flashing sparkles persisted, but they had rearranged and the boy was gone.

He slid carefully off the mahogany, conscious that his belt buckle and zipper not scratch the surface that he was thinking of more as a mirror now. He reached for a cotton rag and wiped from the mahogany his dampness and brought up a soft sheen. He came alongside the righthand piece, dragged the rag around in an area where the boy's face had appeared and looked for some residue of the visitation.

It was light now and he threw the big shop doors open wide. He tossed pieces of Styrofoam and assorted blankets and drop cloths on the shop floor for padding and protection and dragged first one half, then the other half of Tiezzi's board out into the light. He strained to stand them on end by a slow, hand-over-hand method, their tops eventually leaning on rain gutters at the roof eaves.

At first, he got close, right at his eye level, which was at about the center of each piece. A little higher up was where the boy's face had met his—nose to nose. He ran into the shop for a sawhorse so that he could stand on it and examine the board's upper reaches. Close on the right-hand piece he thought he saw something in the wood. He stepped back to take it in from four or five feet, then hopped back on the horse to examine it again up close. He traced his index finger over something, hopped down, ran back into the shop, and returned to his perch teetering on the narrow top edge of the sawhorse. With a piece of chalk, he traced the line that he had found in the grain of the mahogany. Then another white line traced another right next to it. There were several curving concentric lines and soon they were all traced over with chalk. Joe stepped back to look at the finely layered arch that stood four or five feet high and reached up into the upper right-hand corner of the board. It was right in the place where the skinny boy had hovered, moments before, and for all the world, Joe thought, it looked like a wing.

Chapter 39
Don't Die Right Now

Joe had quietly slipped back into the house before dawn and into bed next to Maggie. When he next awakened, he was alone in the house. He washed some dishes and generally puttered around all day waiting for school to get out so he could tell Will what he'd seen.

At the back door of the school, kids began to pour out and, in a few minutes, he saw Will at the bike rack. No bike lock guarded the clunky old red wheels that Will backed out of the galvanized pipes. Joe yelled, "Will Carroll."

Will wheeled the bicycle toward his dad's pickup and said, "Are we going to the orthodontist?"

Joe quickly tossed the bike in the truck and took his son in his arms and kissed him on the top of the head. "It came to me last night—well, it was probably really this morning—out in the shop."

"What came to you?"

"What the board is going to be. It came to me like a vision. I haven't even told Mom yet. I slept right through her getting up for work. I'm telling you first because you might be the only one who'll believe it. Last night, out in the shop, I was up on the board—"

"You were up on the board?"

"Yeah, I crawled right up on it and was lying face down. I was desperate. Anyway, it was the right thing because an angel appeared to me." Joe laughed. "An angel appeared to me—sounds kind of Old Testament that way. Maybe the angel wasn't appearing to me, but there was an angel in the board, inhabiting the mahogany. Are you believing me so far?"

"Yes. I have to believe it because whatever made me ride my bike over the bridge to Saybrook could send an angel to you. Did you fly around with it, with the angel? Did you fly over the river?" Will asked smiling.

"I'm not crazy. But still, I don't think we'll tell a lot of people about the angel. No, we didn't fly over the river, but I want to go over there now. Can you go with me, right now? I want to tell Giordano what I saw."

"So, what's it going to be?"

"The story of Carini on the PT boat, and Giordano praying all the time in the shop, all the stuff you told me, but there's something else, something important for Giordano to hear."

When they pulled up and came to a stop at the backdoor of Giordano's old house there was a tall handsome man coming out of the back door. He was beautifully dressed and moved with a quiet and graceful demeanor. He was noiselessly latching the aluminum storm door to leave when he turned and saw Will and Joe.

Will said to his father, "That's Mr. Tiezzi's friend, Mr. Peach."

"No kidding. Peach was president of the phone company before it was bought up. He's a big deal. Have you met him?"

"Yeah, he's real nice."

The three met at the doorway and Will said, "Hi, Mr. Peach, this is my father."

"I'm pleased to meet you, Mr. Carroll. Giordano has spoken of you many times." Peach turned his head toward the door. "Our old friend is very tired. It's best for us to not visit too long. He'll be glad to see you."

Joe said, "Is he alright?"

"He is very weak. He had a small heart attack a couple of weeks ago. You didn't know? He's been in convalescent care. They wanted to keep him longer, but he hated the place and was making a big fuss, so they let me bring him home a few days ago. A woman comes in the morning and makes him meals and cleans a little, but he doesn't like her and he says terrible things to her, poor soul. I think she will quit soon."

"Maybe you should tell him we're here—you know, go in ahead of us; we don't want to startle him."

"Of course, come on in, it's not as bad as all that, but he's pretty miserable. He wants to die. He's saying that, and I don't think we will change his mind."

Peach opened the doors and let them all in. "Giordano, look who's here. It's your pal, Will, and he's brought his papa."

Peach just winked at them, barely raised his hand in a wave that felt to Joe like a little blessing, and slipped out quietly. The old man was very small, sitting in pajamas and a robe in a velvety maroon chair. A ratty patchwork quilt was draped over his lap and legs.

"Mr. Tiezzi, it's Joe Carroll and Will. We've come to see you, and to tell you something wonderful about your big board," Joe said.

"You are good to come see me, but I am not much of a friend. I haven't been good for you boys." Joe saw that the old man didn't have much strength and he remembered Mr. Peach's caution.

"You gave me a gift, Giordano, and I need to tell you what I have learned about it. It'll only take a moment. It's something that I'm sure you never have known. It's a happy thing."

"I've lived a long time, too long maybe, and now I'm dying. Mr. Carroll," and Giordano pointed to a place behind him, "I didn't know if I would see you again. Please pull that smallest drawer all the way out and hand it to me."

Joe turned toward the only wooden piece in the room, a dark old Victorian desk with a crazed varnish skin. Joe saw that there was one drawer smaller than the others and with some jiggling slid it from its carcass and set it gently in Giordano's lap.

"I want you to be quiet, for a minute, Mr. Tiezzi. Don't die right now, please? Can you not die right now in front of Will and me and be quiet while I tell you something good?" Will thought his dad was talking kind of rough to the sick old man.

"I saw an angel this morning. Do you believe in angels, Giordano? I can't say that I really considered it before, but I know I saw one this morning and I do believe in angels now. I was all alone with your big board—I was right on top of the damn thing actually—and just as sure as I am looking at you right now, an Indian-looking boy angel was moving around right inside of the board."

"It was the angel of death; I am not surprised."

"Shut up. No, if we're going to call it anything, I'd say it was your brother's angel. What was his name—your brother?"

Will said, "Carini."

"It was Carini's angel. Think this through with me. You told Will that you were praying for your brother all the time while he was out there in the Pacific. Right? Well, I think you were praying on that day that they were pulling the PT boat off the coral reef. You were fiercely praying to God for the life of your brother whom you loved. Right?"

Giordano knew that he was praying—praying all the time—awake and in his dreams.

"And you know what? God heard your prayers, and he sent this skinny, hook-nosed boy-angel that I saw this morning. He was there with the PT boat, hovering over the Pacific Ocean and Carini was there in the sea bleeding from a hundred cuts, and that cable snapped and was flying toward him, and this kid reached down with his angel hand and pulled your brother onto the stern of the boat, and saved his life. Your prayer that day called out to God, and this angel that I saw this morning in the board must have been sent by God to rescue your brother from death."

Joe spontaneously started laughing. "He lost a leg, but he didn't die. You told Will he didn't even mind losing the leg. That's pretty funny, isn't it? And you had lots more years together, to love him, and for him to love you."

Giordano looked down at the quilt in his lap and slowly pulled it up and sort of folded it and dropped it to the ground next to his chair, all the time taking pains to keep the little drawer balanced on his skinny lap. He looked up at Joe and saw that he had a big smile on his face. "And seeing this angel has made you so happy?"

"I think it's pretty obvious, don't you? Getting the big board was a big, big thing for me. It's put me through some hard stuff, but it has all been good. I had to decide if it was a curse or a blessing—choose one or the other. I choose blessing. And now, yes, I am happy—it's still all hard, but I'm happy because I am a fool who has been forgiven, and given a second chance."

"Thank you for telling me all of this, Mr. Carroll," Giordano said in a small voice. "I am very tired. I am sorry."

Joe got up and looked at Will, tilted his head toward the door signaling Will that they should leave. He'd said his piece.

Joe reached for Will's arm to lead him out, but Will pulled away. He was crying.

Giordano said, "Why is he crying? I hope he is not crying for an old man who is dying. I'm old and it is just my time to go. It's all right, Will, and, don't leave yet, I have something—"

Will went right up to Giordano's chair and buried his face in his chest. "Don't you hear what Dad said? It's not just about Dad getting another chance to make something from your board. It's about you. Dad saw an angel. It's amazing, what Dad figured out—and it's a gift to both of you, to all of us." He pulled back and looked up into Giordano's face. "You taught me all about forgiving. Remember how you told Carini you were sorry for missing him so much when he was at the war and that you'd prayed for him to come home. Then when he came home without his leg you thought it was your fault, but then he stuck his good leg up in the air and laughed out loud. He told you it was all fine, that you were forgiven. Isn't that what happened?"

Giordano was silent, but was thinking about it, at least. Will went on, talking and crying at the same time. "And remember the time that Dad busted into your shop when I was all taped up for the game on the zip-line, and he didn't know we were just fooling around, and he pushed you and you hurt your head. You were bleeding, weren't you, but you understood and you forgave him right away. It was easy for you. Heck, you put a knife right in his hand so he could cut the tape off and you just smiled at him. You just love everybody, Mr. Tiezzi. I was crying that day. I cry when I'm with you because you are so good and loving. So how about loving yourself, Mr. Tiezzi? Dad's angel must have come for a reason. In the Bible they came to people at important times with important messages for the humans, and the humans wrote it all down so we'd remember the lessons. You believe that; I know you do."

Now Giordano was paying attention.

"I came over here one time and you figured out that it was my father I was talking about when I told you that somebody I know had done something bad. It was Dad patching up the broken board and selling it without doing anything special with it. You knew who it was, that it was Joe Carroll, and right away you blurted it right out—forgive him. So, God answered your prayers and brought Carini home safe, so don't you think that you must have been forgiven for being lonely—for missing your brother? Don't you think God must have forgiven you a long time ago for being, I'm sorry, maybe just a little weak like everybody else? Don't you think God forgives you for going along with the stupid board-stealing stunt with your friends? So what! That's what God must think. So what! You were a kid and full of life and you acted like a human being. I think God cares about people; He cares about you. You are forgiven. I'm sure of it, Mr. Tiezzi. You are forgiven!"

Will had been paying so much attention to his words. He'd impressed himself even, getting all that out, and he stopped seeing Giordano's eyes, seeing his face at all, but now there was silence in the dark room and he focused again on the old man and he saw that it now was Giordano who was crying.

"I am forgiven?"

Joe said, "Giordano Tiezzi of Saybrook, Connecticut, USA; you are forgiven."

"I am forgiven." Giordano was quiet for a moment and looked back and forth at the two of them. "I believe that I am."

Joe started to clap his hands together softly, rhythmically. Will understood that this was applause and he joined in. Giordano put his palms up and together as in prayer—patted them together twice, and just looked into his lap. The little drawer was still there.

"That was a very fine argument, Will Carroll," Giordano said. "I think that you are only twelve, but you sound like a grown man. I think that you should be a lawyer when you are older. You would do very well arguing like that in a courtroom. You have a long time to decide. How old does a man need to be to have a driver's license, thirteen?"

"You can get a learner's permit when you're sixteen," Will said.

Giordano was fiddling in the little drawer and pulled out a small, light blue-gray piece of paper. "Mr. Carroll," he asked, "would it be all right with you and your nice wife if Will has my old truck? It runs well still, and my friend, Picia, says that it's even worth a lot of money. Will and I have ridden in it together, but I didn't let him drive. He's afraid of heights."

Will said, "No, Mr. Tiezzi, that's great, but you need your truck."

"Truly, I am not going to need it any more. It's a good old truck and it has been good to us, but I won't need it any more. I really am dying, you know. I'm quite certain of it. But I am not afraid. I am trusting God and I am very much not afraid."

Joe said, "I'll get you a pen. Where shall I look for a pen, Giordano? I think you have to sign something on the back." He looked at his son and said, "Just thank him, Will. When someone makes you a gift that they have thought about, you just accept the gift. That's right, isn't it, Giordano?"

Will was crying heartily now. He kissed the old man on the head and Joe and Will walked toward the door. Will was making his way through the storm door when his father stopped and turned back toward Giordano, a frail profile in the darkness. "I need you to think about a place that could use a big door—a very tall double door."

Chapter 40
The Fun Part

Joe thought he must have explained it to dozens of admirers of his work. Someone who does office work will say that the wood must smell great and Joe tells them that most of the time, it really doesn't smell very much—not unless you're making cedar boxes or lining rich people's sweater closets. Or they say how pleasing it must be to watch the fine curlicue shaving fall away from the block plane. "No," he has told them, "you don't notice that stuff after a while, it's just work, physical work, pleasant enough, but not so different from knitting or weaving, or, for that matter, xeroxing."

Maggie had corrected him. "You know, you could just go along with them. They're saying that what you do is nicer than what they do, which it is, and they're expressing a generous kind of envy. They're happy for you. You could just let them think that the artist's life is nice. Instead, you demystify it for them. Nothing's gained by that." Then Maggie had laughed to let him off the hook. She is not a scold.

And people think that being a wood carver or furniture maker is rich in creativity. "It is creative," Joe had explained, "but less than you probably think. If I get a job making a sign for a restaurant, most of the real creativity goes into the drawing for the proposal and the meeting with the customer, figuring out their tastes and objectives. All of that might take two days, and then there might be two weeks of labor that isn't much different from the labor on every other sign carving job I've done. To be fair, there is variety to it: sawing and jointing of lumber, gluing, sanding, drawing, carving, painting, gold leafing; but it's not very creative after a while."

For Joe the woodworker, this was the fun part—designing something beautiful that hadn't been seen before. Only with what he could already picture in his head, Joe was excited because he was certain that his design for doors from Mr. Tiezzi's board was unique.

He remembered having told a friend one time that he figured God had already made everything, but that the artist's job was to take the things that already exist and arrange them in new and interesting ways. This was more of what Maggie says is selling himself short—taking the fun out of it for people. I should just shut up, Joe thought. So what, if some wood carver in Connecticut thinks he has discovered some truths of the mundaneness of the artist life? Shut up and enjoy the work.

• • •

When Joe pulled into the driveway at Giordano's shop, Mr. Peach was already there. In a camel sweater and narrow gray trousers, he was standing next to his Cadillac. They greeted one another quietly and approached the shop door. Peach had the old skeleton key and opened the creaky door. Joe said, "I think Giordano knows that I want to—that I am going to make his board into two very large doors."

"He told me that," Mr. Peach replied.

"I hope he'll get an idea about a place for them. Maybe you've talked about it."

"We have. I am following up on that, Joe."

"Thanks so much, Mr. Peach. I hope I can ask you to be my intermediary. Giordano doesn't need me pestering him with my needs and, well, there's no one else. Oh, and by the way, the doors will be a gift, you know, free." Once inside, Peach flipped on some lights and Joe said, "Right now, I'm just thinking about where Giordano might have sat to pray—back during the war."

Peach pointed right away, like he knew, to the far west-facing wall where Giordano's lathe had always been, and still sat. "Over there. Often, I found him looking out the window. I'll wait for you outside. Please take your time."

Yes, this was the place, Joe thought. The little lathe faced the outside wall and a six-paned window. An old leather belt was tacked horizontally to the wooden wall in such a way as to make six or seven loops in which nestled the tools that Giordano would have used at the lathe: skews, gouges, and a parting tool. On big common nails hung the wrench for loosening and tightening the tailstock and the tool rest. On another nail hung some worn old V-belts.

Joe picked up a long-bristled bench brush and swept sawdust and shavings from the corners of the window panes and rattled the window. It was loose and crudely trimmed into its opening, but it was not meant to open. Through the wavy antique glass Joe saw a rickety grape arbor and an ancient, thick, gnarled, grapevine that Giordano had long since stopped pruning. Joe stepped back several steps from the lathe and took a little camera from his coat pocket. It didn't feel right—the way the anachronistic flash and he intruded on sacred space. With a twinge of not belonging, he turned and left. This is surely the place.

Chapter 41
We All Got Over It

The sweater was argyle, off-white with blues and greens. Cashmere. A sweater made precisely for lovely gentlemen like this, and out of place in a neighborhood of modest, two-story, turn-of-the-century houses. Mr. Peach said, "It's not a fancy place, Mr. Carroll."

At other times in his life, Joe knew that he had been snobby about such places. Today his eyes travelled up the street and back down the other side, and he smiled at the funny colors the owners and tenants had painted their little homes—none very recently. And he was thinking kind thoughts about the people that lived in them.

"Please call me Joe, Mr. Peach," Joe said.

"Then you should call me Picia. That was my given name and it's what Giordano and all our gang called me. I changed it. I regret it now, but I wanted to be a big shot in America and I thought I should have an American name."

"So, you chose fruit."

"A delicious one." They laughed. "It's been a VFW hall for several years now. The archdiocese closed the little neighborhood church to save money; the parish had shrunk to a handful of old people—mostly Italians like me and Mrs. Peach and Giordano. Everybody understood. Back then people didn't organize to protest such things."

"It will be perfect. The doors will need to be nearer twelve feet than the fourteen that we have now, and the rough opening will be new—new and bigger than what's there for the present doorway. I'm grateful for your help, Picia, finding the place and talking to those guys for me. It's perfect. Tell them I think it's perfect."

. . .

The two of them were together in Joe's shop days later. Picia had laid lots of things on Joe's bench: old yellowed photographs of himself and his friends, pictures copied from files at the historical society of the boatyard where Carini worked, Carini's Purple Heart and his discharge from the Navy.

"Tell me about the boys in this picture, Picia."

"Today we would probably be called the usual suspects. A couple of the boys you might say were hell raisers, but they were good guys—just full of life." Pointing to the picture he said, "That's Giordano, I think you recognize him, and his brother over here, and Mazzarelli and Domezio, and me in the coat and tie. All dead except Giordano and me."

"I know about stealing the board, Picia. It's not a big deal to me. Giordano told us all about it. He's suffered over it."

"Yes, he has. He's the only one, really. I've always been a little ashamed, I guess, but it has not haunted me, partly I think because I never feared being arrested. From the beginning, the other boys agreed that if anything happened, they were going to say that I went along to try and stop them. It wasn't true. I was just more chicken than they were—chicken to not go along with the gang—and scared of getting caught. The others—they dealt with it in their own ways.

"These two, Domezio and Mazz, they were the other thieves. This chubby one is Domezio. He was a good churchgoing Catholic—a very religious family. Domezio went to confession with the priest, actually at the church where your doors are going. He went right away, within a matter of days. He told us that he had been forgiven after doing the penance the priest gave him, and everything was fine.

"This one's Mazz. Mazz's father heard from some of his friends that there had been a theft at the boatyard and just figured that it must have been us. It was a lucky guess and Mazz confessed to his father right away. I think somebody saw the truck leaving the scene and pretty soon the whole town knew. Stupid kids. What did we think? Mazz's papa told him that he wanted to beat him, but that Mazz was too big for a beating, and that Mazz had better get down to that boatyard office and straighten things out with the boss man. Mazz told his father, 'If I confess, they'll throw us all in jail.' His papa told him, admit nothing. Don't be an idiot, even if you are one. Just tell them you think you owe them fifty bucks.

"So, Mazz went down there, probably on the Tuesday after the Saturday, and met up with the big bosses. He was scared to death. They asked him where he thought he was going to come up with that kind of money and when he had no answer, they offered him Carini's job. Mazz idolized Carini Tiezzi and was between jobs anyway, so this was perfect. I heard later that the bosses at the boatyard had liked Carini very much, always figured he'd stolen the board, and had chalked up their loss to a going-away present for a good employee off for the war."

"What happened to Mazz and Domezio—I mean, later in life?"

"Domezio apprenticed under an older Italian man in town who laid tile—you know, bathrooms and kitchens. Domezio was very good at it and had a prosperous life and a nice family. He had a bad heart always, and in his sixties, it gave out, years ago now.

"After the war when the boatyard closed down, Mazz got a job as custodian in the high school. He was a fierce little worker and the school kids loved him. He married a local girl; she was unusual. They were childless. He worked his whole life there, in the high school." A smile came to Picia's face. "There was a flap at the school many years ago about a drum of detergent that went missing. Nothing came of it. Mazz died about ten years ago from lung cancer."

"I may not be a good enough artist, Picia, to tell the story of Giordano and Carini as well as they deserve. I've never really thought about the meaning of a man's whole life before, much less tried to tell about it in art."

"Few men your age have. We become interested in such things when we get old."

"Knowing about these men, and knowing you, it demands respect for the subject matter of the art, of all aspects of the design and execution. If I

197

know about you guys as real people, I can hold you all in my imagination while I'm carving, and maybe it will show up in the finished product." For an instant, the impulse rose in Joe to make a promise to Picia, and just after it, the horrible thought that maybe nothing at all had changed, that stupid old habits were too deeply ingrained. He checked himself. "I guess we'll just have to see how I do?"

"Can I look in on your progress from time to time?"

"Oh please, you're always welcome." Joe looked down at the stuff on the bench. "The pictures are great, a huge help. I'll take good—" There it was again, the making of a promise; and he stifled it again.

"Will's finding me pictures of PT boats on the computer at school. They've got one at the Battleship Cove Museum in Fall River, Massachusetts. And we've got a lead on some vintage Navy uniforms. There's a kid who works for me sometimes that's Carini's size, small and really muscular. He's going to model as Carini. I think I've got just about everything we need. This is really fun, Picia. Thanks for everything."

Chapter 42
They Will Sparkle Like Gems

Joe had purchased 8/4 mahogany for the rails and stiles of the doors. These pieces which will frame the two giant panels were four-and-one half inches wide. Some of the pieces were curved because he had designed the two doors to form a gothic arch, echoing the shape of stained-glass windows in the old church which had become a veterans clubhouse. He was at his band saw for a long time today. No safety glasses. He needed all of his eyesight to hold the moving blade just outside the fine curved pencil line, to watch the speed of the blade as it passed through its kerf, to maintain the exact speed which would not burn the wood, would not push the narrow blade off the big wheels around which it turned, and would not tax the old motor and trip the circuit breaker.

Joe's shop was light on the heavy bench tools. No big bench sander, for instance, that today would speed the shaping of the long curves. He had told people that this was because he was biased toward handwork, but it had been more about finances. The sweeping curves of the door arches were achieved by a slow planing away of wood with a spokeshave, a tool similar to a plane which Joe hung onto with both hands and pulled toward himself, stopping all the time to remove stuck shavings from the blade with a sharp stick. Only the last fine cleaning up was accomplished with 80 grit sandpaper on a rubber block, then 100, 150, 220.

The drawing of the humans in the big panels had taken several days to get just right. It was the part with which Joe had the most difficulty. It helped this time that the most prominent figure in the scene, Motor Machinist Mate Carini Tiezzi, one foot still in the sea, his head and torso almost up and over the transom of the PT boat, had been modeled by Chad, Joe's young friend who helped him deliver the table to Pappas. Joe mocked up the transom of the PT boat from 2 x 6's and plywood for Chad to pull himself up on. Joe took photographs that he scaled up, not confident in his ability to draw the figure from life.

. . . .

There were weeks of carving. The rails and stiles were decorated with a twisting grapevine that undulated rhythmically for nearly sixty running feet. Joe found a stylized motif in a book and made paper dolls with which to transfer the grapes and leaves to the wood.

He tackled the grapevine first. He was rusty and figured there was no chance for a catastrophic mistake on varied leaves and bunches of little ovals, and so he charged into the carving. The relief of three-eighths of an inch must be achieved all at once as a first step. The grape motif and its background took up three and one-half inches at the center of all the rails and stiles, leaving just a half inch of flat at the edges. Joe scored the outside margins of the area that would be relief-carved with a sharp utility knife, bearing down freehand and pulling the blade toward himself along the lines. It was okay to meander off the line in places if the line was smooth and continuous. It was supposed to look like handwork.

His bright parting tool was of thin stainless steel forged into the letter V, the wings of which met at a right angle. The place where they met at the bottom of the V was a little beefier and had been ground slightly round so as to enter the wood without much resistance and to send the carved mahogany waste up in a continuous curling worm. The parting tool tapped, tapped, tapped just outside the grapes and leaves and vines, coaxed by a big round mallet that looked like a potato masher. Joe had enjoyed showing people the speedy work of surrounding with V-shaped lines those parts of a design that would stand in relief, and how the speed came from the design of the mallet. "The reason we use a round mallet instead of a carpenter's mallet with a square face is so we don't have to look at how we're holding it," Joe had explained to Will. "A round mallet will hit the handle of the carving tool the same way with every strike. That way the carver can keep his eye on the work."

When every vine, bunch and leaf of the grapevine motif had been surrounded by the V-grooves, Joe got out an assortment of shallow gouges. Gouges are defined by how gentle or drastic their curve, determined by the length of the radius of a circle that their edge could stand on, and by their width. These were narrow ones—1/4 inch, 3/8 inch, and 5/8 inch—and they had shallow sweeps to which the mahogany would yield most easily. Most of this roughing out was done with a gouge and mallet, each tap moving the tool forward only a measured distance and lifting clean chips of near uniform size. Hours and hours of this.

When the first roughing out was done, Joe began chopping straight down with small chisels and with gouges exactly at the edges of the forms which would stand in relief. He used tangential straight chops around convex curves, and gouge-chops with sweeps at least as tight as the curves of the drawn concave lines. Joe was fast. He rapidly picked up and set down old friends without looking at them. It was pleasant work. He played sports talk radio to accompany this rudimentary stuff. He'd talked with Maggie about the figure of Carini in the righthand panel, covered with the small bleeding cuts, the snapped steel cable flying toward his leg, and the men pulling him over the stern of the PT boat. And they had talked about the carving of Giordano, his hands held over a spinning chair spindle in his lathe, gazing out the little shop window, looking to God, thinking of his beloved brother in the Pacific, praying fervently for him to come home. On the days of carving the two brothers, there was only music. Maggie said Mozart was best.

The carving of the grapevines took Joe about ten days. There were hours and hours of shaping half round bunches of grapes with quick, clean slices that must meet one another perfectly in the dark, low places, leaving no ratty splinters or fuzz. As he modelled the areas of relief, he held in his mind the dictum that he had read many years ago: sandpaper never touches fine wordcarving. It is the way light catches and shows the multitude of clean tool marks that gives life to the work and reveals the artisan's skill. Or something like that. During hundreds of solitary moments when, in his hands, a grape leaf rolled over, and then turned back toward him, or a careful undercutting of the angel's naked foot gave it depth and truth, Joe could picture the finished carved forms. He knew that soon he would flood the huge carved panels with stain, that when they were dry again and wiped shiny, he would rub a dark paste filler into every flat and carved surface, filling every pore of open grain to contrast with the wood's redder hue. He knew enough to dread the hours of working the excess filler back out of deep nooks and crannies with scraps of burlap and tooth brushes, and that by not skipping the paste filling stage, which he easily could have done, he was making many hours of extra work for himself. But there will be that payoff on the day when most of the filler on the surface is gone, and it is dry enough to buff with lint free rags and his shoe brush. He will look down at a bunch of grapes worked round without rasps or abrasives, and they will sparkle like gems in the sunlight flooding through his shop windows.

Finally, there came that moment which comes always as a ridiculous miracle. He looked down on a skinny, big-nosed angel on the door panel. He had found the face he wanted in an old National Geographic. That he himself, one at a time, had applied thousands of conscious cuts, stopped hundreds of times to sweep away chips in the way of progress, gone into the house fifty times for coffee—all of that was blessedly forgotten. He only knew that now he was looking at an angel. This angel, like the one who visited him on that day six weeks ago when he stretched prostrate on the board praying for an idea, appeared able at once to occupy both halves of Tiezzi's board. He looked down and saw things that he did not have a sense of having made by his own hands. This angel who transcended time and place, who with one hand lifted Carini Tiezzi from the South Pacific reef, and with the other reached through a closed window and touched the crown of the head of the first man's praying brother—this angel had taken on a life quite apart from Joe Carroll.

There were another two full days of forcing clear carnauba paste wax into the low places and the high places of the carving. It came up and off less easily than it went down. With elbow grease and persistence, toothbrushes and scraps of burlap and bed sheet, he was able to bring up all the excess that, left behind, would dry white, opaque, and ugly.

Brisk passes with the old shoe brush, more with old damask table napkins, and the wood revealed its final patina.

These layers of feathers on the giant angel wings, they are not mine, Joe thought. They belong to this Indian child who had found a wonderful purpose in what we call heaven. These feathers kept him aloft, at once in a grape arbor in Saybrook, Connecticut, and three feet over breaking waves in the Pacific.

Right now, Joe was not remembering the day he sat in his shop and untwisted the end of a length of steel cable to learn the anatomy of wire rope that he would replicate as the violent flying cable that severed Carini Tiezzi's leg.

. . .

It was done. The big panels would be assembled within the rails and stiles and there would be arduous, touch-and-go gluing and wiping and clamping. But it was done. No one else was there with him. There was no customer coming this afternoon to give a final okay, to ooh and ah, and give Joe a big fat check. There was only Joe Carroll, and a brown and red field of shapes and curved lines, of small busy forms and large smooth ones. He remembered that the wood had been in his hands, that he had lived with it for weeks now, but he looked on it now and was moved to be glad for what he had done. His hands had touched it, but he hadn't made it. Not like he'd made hundreds of things over the years.

This must be what they mean by co-creation, Joe thought. I have worked ten or twelve hours most days for several weeks and I am tired and alone out here. I will try to describe this moment to Maggie—to tell her that I think I have had a day of peace—peace and joy. She will understand.

Chapter 43
Come with Me Now

It was lunchtime on a Thursday in June, sunny and cool. Joe Carroll walked into the foyer of the Aristotle Pappas law offices and Cecile looked up from her desk, a little nervous. Joe was dressed for business, she thought. He had what looked like a new haircut and was wearing a sport coat and striped necktie. She surmised he was there to see the boss.

"Mr. Carroll. Good afternoon, is Mr. Pappas expecting you? He's here, but he's heading out in just a few minutes."

"Oh no, don't trouble him. I'm here for Maggie. Would you point me in the right direction?"

Cecile stood up and pivoted toward the hall and said, "She may be in the file room. I'll buzz her back there."

"No, no, I'll find her. I hope you have a wonderful day, Cecile," and he dashed toward the back of the place.

• • • • •

Will had brought a note to school that said Mr. Peach had permission to pick him up and take him on an important appointment for about an hour. They were together now in Giordano's living room.

"Look who's come to see you, Giordano," Peach said.

He was smaller, and weaker, Will thought. Before he had happily surrendered to Mr. Tiezzi's spirit, but now Giordano's vitality seemed mostly gone and Will resolved to contribute his own energy. "Dad and I took your truck to the school parking lot on a Sunday when no one was around. He showed me how to let the clutch out in first gear, but I was lousy at it. I couldn't really reach the pedals very good."

Giordano smiled. "So, did you wreck it? It is yours to wreck, you know."

"No, I was scared I was going to mess up the gears or something. I got it going in first gear pretty good once and we just drove around in circles. It was fun. I'll keep practicing."

"When you are older you can use that truck to steal things."

Picia said, "I hope he won't ask for my help. But right now, we're getting you dressed and taking you for a ride in a Cadillac."

"Dad's all done with the doors, Mr. Tiezzi. He finished putting them up today. We're taking you over to see."

"That's wonderful. How do they look?"

Will said, "I don't know, I haven't seen them either. We're going together—the three of us."

"How about we just get me in my robe. No one will arrest a dying old man on the arm of the president of the phone company."

. . .

In the file room, Maggie was on her knees next to a pulled-out drawer. Teddy was standing close by. Maggie looked up, surprised. Joe had never come to her work to see her—not once.

"Joe!" she exclaimed in a happy voice.

Joe didn't even look at Teddy. "They're up, Mags. Can you come with me right now?" He leaned over and helped her from the carpeted floor.

"Am I kidnapped?"

Teddy backed up hard against the file cabinets and did not speak.

"Yes, I guess you are. Is there anyone you need to tell?"

"I'll just tell Cecile."

Maggie was fetching her jacket and bag from the hall coat closet when Ari Pappas appeared from his office.

Joe said, "I'm taking Maggie to see something I've been working on. She'll be back in an hour and a half."

Ari said, "I think I have been hearing about it. Is it something made from mahogany?"

"Yes, sir, it is. Two big wide pieces."

"I hope to see it myself sometime," and he smiled. "Don't come back, Maggie. Take the rest of the day off; we'll manage."

"I'll see you in the morning, thanks."

• • •

It was an interesting ensemble, these three, Will, Giordano and Picia, struggling slowly down the flight of twelve steps that led from the entrance of a veterans hall that had been a Catholic church. Neighbors had peeked out to watch their progress, first up to the new doors, then back down. Some of them recognized Giordano Tiezzi from when he was around town more; some thought he died a while back.

"I guess not. I wonder who the boy is," one onlooker said, "I think they were childless, so it can't be a grandson." A police cruiser had driven by slowly, just making sure everyone was okay.

Joe and Maggie met the moving tableau at the sidewalk. Maggie said, "Mr. Tiezzi, it is wonderful to see you. It's a lovely sunny afternoon to be out."

Joe was there, too, but Giordano was looking only at Maggie. "Your husband said that he would make something special from my board, Mrs. Carroll."

"What do you think?"

"Tell Mr. Carroll that I have seen what has been made. Tell him that I am amazed; tell him that I have seen the image of my brother, his beautiful mustachioed face and the sinew of his arms and shoulders, just like I remember. Tell Joe Carroll that I have seen an angel and I do believe the angel is real, and that everything that he has told me is true. I do believe it all."

Joe was silent. He stood back from the exchange. Maggie took Giordano's hands and squeezed them and said, "I will tell him all of that,

Giordano, I will tell him all of that over and over to make certain that he understands it."

"God bless your beautiful family, Mrs. Carroll. I am glad to have known all of you."

Will heard all of this and small, happy tears rushed to his eyes. He and Picia led Mr. Tiezzi toward the parked Cadillac.

Joe said to Maggie, "Go on up and take a look."

A little group of pedestrians was gathered down on the sidewalk next to Joe. There was a middle-aged lady wearing a bright green smock and a name tag, an elderly lady pulling a shiny wire grocery cart loaded down with bags of cat litter, and a young man in a Red Sox jersey and sweatpants. The fellow in the sweatpants said to Joe, "You the guy made those doors?"

"I'm the wood carver."

"You must have got a lot of money for them. Was it from the government?"

"Thanks. It was a big job—a very good job for a guy like me. The government did supply the materials, actually." Joe left the onlookers and ascended the steps slowly and stopped half way.

Maggie was up there in front of the doors, all alone, small and vulnerable. She had wrapped her arms around herself and held her head cocked to one side to study the scene. Joe watched her. He thought that he could see that she was shaking a little and that she was crying. He climbed the last several steps and was right behind her now. He gently spread his right hand against Maggie's back.

"Oh, Joe." She turned toward him and put her wet face against his wooly shoulder.

"Here," and Joe took off his jacket, "Take this, you're shaking. I'm not cold at all." He put his sport coat around her and pulled Maggie close. "I'll steal some warmth from you."

She returned her face to a place on Joe's chest.

His hands were at her shoulders. Slowly and tenderly, at no place losing contact with the blue fabric of his jacket, believing that the slightest crude recapture would jar the moment, Joe enfolded her in his arms. He began to sway slightly and even lifted his feet a little off the ground. Maggie quietly moved with him. Joe took her right hand as to slow dance, but they did not move from the spot. They were together in front of the doors in this close dance for several minutes and finally Maggie spoke. "I've always been attracted to you, Joe Carroll. How old are you now, anyway, twenty-six?" "Yeah, I'm twenty-six, somewhere around there. What about you, twenty-two?"

"Yup, today I think that I am about twenty-two and, and dancing with an artist—the best thing a man can be."

And they danced close in one another's arms. From the sidewalk they heard a woman's voice shout. It was the old gal with the little grocery trolley. "It's a church. Do you know that, that it's a church?"

Joe pulled back enough to meet Maggie's eyes and she said, "Mr. Peach took Will back to school, didn't he? Let's go home."

"Lucky us, yes, let's go home."

Acknowledgements

I am indebted to my brother, Jeff Martin, for his early encouragement for *Tiezzi's Board*, the motion picture; to Hope Mahoney for a lifetime of help and kindness; Sam Lyman for early reading; and the late Giordano Tiezzi whose essence keeps everything happening to the big board sweet and happy in my imagination.

Afterword
Tiezzi's Board and the Gerry Table

The story of *Tiezzi's Board* began when the author, himself a wood carver, purchased an enormous mahogany board from the real-life Giordano Tiezzi. That there are parts of Joe Carroll's habits and personality also found in the author was unavoidable. Despite my protestations, my children find the story "embarrassing." They're sure it's about their mother and me. Why? Just because Maggie is gracious and beautiful and Joe is vain. Write what you know; that's what they told me in all those writing workshops. Here's how it all started.

For all but one or two years out of about thirty-five, my family travelled from our house in Woodstock, Connecticut to Monticello, Rock Hill, or Liberty, New York for a traditional New Years' Eve gathering of friends. At first, it was Mary and me and four small boys; and in 1995 when this story began, it had become Mary and me, two young men newly in college, and two in high school. We always knew that we were on our way to a place of wonderful hospitality and a lavish catered dinner for twenty to thirty adults and children. Most years, we were the guests of Kathy and Michael, other years of Sandra and Alan.

Some of those thirty-five New Year's Eves we set out on the three-and-a-half-hour drive in ice or snow—always in a Dodge Caravan. The van could be just purchased, or eleven-years-old, or anywhere in between. We bought them new and ran them into the ground. Our sons were always great about keeping up the tradition and knew how to pack pressed shirts, and coats and ties to make a nice impression. It was the dad who was the wild card.

There had developed a tradition that following the New Year's Eve meal, the dressed-up company would push back a little from the great linen covered, candle-lit table, and Ham would do a reading of some kind, or tell a story. The stories usually had embedded in them a gentle moral lesson or inspiration. The talks were often corny by modern standards, but nobody seemed to mind.

On December 31st of 1995, I must have been busy right up to the time of our departure from Connecticut. If I was tired, or broke, or dreading the long drive—it was not unusual. And I hadn't prepared anything for the after-dinner performance. I brought books along in the car, probably Robert Fulghum from whom I had previously lifted amusing material. In the car, Mary must have said, "Why don't you just tell the story of getting the big board."

I recall that on that afternoon in '95, after unpacking and visiting for a bit with the dear old friends, I went for a run in their neighborhood. There was only a brief window in my adulthood when I ran. I would always have hated running, even if I wasn't slow and with legs that my long-limbed sons say look like sausages. I thought that getting the blood flowing might perk me up for telling "the board story."

Around eleven o'clock, clinking glasses announced the time for Ham's contribution. It went like this:

A few years ago, I was working on a woodworking project with two friends when a lumber salesman made a call on one of the other fellows. I had for years purchased mahogany lumber from his company for big plaques I carved for a local prep school. I teased the salesman that they had cut me off from culling through stacks of one-inch mahogany for boards that were fifteen and sixteen inches wide.

"Hey, if you ever want a really huge piece of mahogany, there's an old guy on North Main Street in Meriden who has a giant piece. Fifty-four inches by fourteen feet." He wrote the man's name and address and the size of the board on a Post-it note.

On a recent Saturday morning, I was doing the bi-annual cleaning of the top of my bureau, and I found the note. "Oh," I said to Mary. "Here's a note about a huge mahogany board. A salesman from McIlvain told me about it." Mary asked how big it was and I told her, and she said, matter-of-factly, "Let's buy it." I said, "It would be a lot of money and I don't have a job for it, anyway. And it's been a couple years; I'm sure it's gone." Mary coaxed me into phoning Dominic Tiezzi.

Directory assistance had no such listing, but they had one Tiezzi in Meriden; it was a woman's name, on East Main Street. You know how these wild goose chases go; I took down the number.

"Hello, yes, my name is Isham Martin and I am calling from Woodstock, Connecticut and I'm trying to reach Dominic Tiezzi."

A small, frail, heavily accented woman's voice passed me on to another person. "Hello," the heavily accented male voice said.

"Yes, my name is Isham Martin and I am looking for Dominic Tiezzi."

"Is it about the board?" the man asked.

"Yes," I said, startled "Are you Dominic?"

"No, I am Giordano. Are you going to buy our big board?"

"Yes, well, I am very interested in the big board; are you Dominic?"

"Dominic is dead. He was my brother. Are you going to make something wonderful from our big board?"

I got instructions to Giordano's shop. I took our son Will with me to Meriden and we bought the board. It was just as the Post-it note said, four and one half feet wide, fourteen feet long, and an inch and a quarter thick. Up on edge in a rickety shack behind Giordano's shop, flat as could be, still in the rough, perfect condition. Giordano and his dead brother had had it since World War II. It's in my shop now. It's incredible and I hope to do something great with it. It just dropped in my lap like a gift from God. You should have seen it lashed to my truck on the drive home. It felt like a sail that might lift us into the sky. Perhaps it was only my excitement.

Everyone seemed to like the story—one of the guests in particular.

On the morning of New Year's Day of 1996, Alan Gerry and I sat alone in the living room of the family who had hosted the party the night before. We doodled ideas for a table on the back on an envelope. In August of that year, another son, Quinn, and I delivered the completed, still sticky, table to Liberty, New York.

Alan Gerry of Liberty, New York, and Ham Martin, the author of Tiezzi's Board, collaborated on the design of a table made from one solid piece of mahogany purchased from Giordano Tiezzi who, with his brother Dominic, had bought it during World War II from a cousin working at a boatyard in Saybrook, Connecticut. The slightly boat-shaped table top uses all but one-square-foot of Tiezzi's board. A five-inch-wide border trims all thirty-seven running feet of the table's edge, and is decorated with carved Christmas fern and red oak from Mr. Gerry's native Sullivan County. The plant forms are interspersed with an excerpt from a speech Theodore Roosevelt gave at the Sorbonne in Paris in 1910.

It is not the critic who counts; not the man who points out how the strong man stumbles, or where the doer of deeds could have done them better. The credit belongs to the man who is actually in the arena, whose face is marred by dust and sweat and blood; who strives valiantly; who errs, who comes short again and again, because there is no effort without error and shortcoming; but who does actually strive to do the deeds; who knows great enthusiasms, the great devotions; who spends himself in a worthy cause; who at the best knows in the end the triumph of high achievement, and who at the worst, if he fails, at least fails while daring greatly, so that his place shall never be with those cold and timid souls who neither know victory nor defeat.

The text is relief-carved in Caxton Italic Light. The sturdy base is adapted from a trestle table (c. 1680-1710) restored by the American furniture maker and historian, Wallace Nutting. The table was built and carved by the author in his workshop in Woodstock, Connecticut.

The author is grateful that in Alan Gerry he found a patron for Tiezzi's big board who was wiser and more generous than Ari Pappas, Maggie's employer in the fictional story. Mr. Gerry allowed me to build from one, solid mahogany board, a piece of furniture of which we are both very proud—and he paid me handsomely, too.

Isham (Ham) Martin Round Pond, Maine December 2021

About the Author

Ham Martin, himself a woodcarver by profession, writes about real, complicated, flawed humans who discover in themselves courage, kindness and love. Ham is the author of the critically praised *Talk Radio*, the debut of a *Maine* trilogy.

Ham has been a staffer in the U.S. House of Representatives, a lifeguard in Tokyo and Singapore, galleyman on an oil tanker, 1st Selectman of his town, sign maker and cabinetmaker.

Ham and Mary live in a small fishing village on the coast of Maine.

Note from the Author

Word-of-mouth is crucial for any author to succeed. If you enjoyed *Tiezzi's Board*, please leave a review online—anywhere you are able. Even if it's just a sentence or two. It would make all the difference and would be very much appreciated.

Thanks!
Ham Martin

We hope you enjoyed reading this title from:

BLACK ❦ ROSE
writing™

www.blackrosewriting.com

Subscribe to our mailing list – *The Rosevine* – and receive **FREE** books, daily deals, and stay current with news about upcoming releases and our hottest authors.
Scan the QR code below to sign up.

Already a subscriber? Please accept a sincere thank you for being a fan of Black Rose Writing authors.

View other Black Rose Writing titles at
www.blackrosewriting.com/books and use promo code
PRINT to receive a **20% discount** when purchasing.

CPSIA information can be obtained
at www.ICGtesting.com
Printed in the USA
BVHW072230030922
646181BV00006B/21